Strong

Terrence Damon Spencer

Dreams To Paper Publishing

INTRODUCTION

Would you believe that superhuman strength is real—and that science classifies it as a disease? Imagine being born with a rare, extreme form of this condition, a mutation so unique it grants extraordinary strength, stamina, and an imposing physical presence. But such power comes at a cost.

For William Strong, growing up with Myostatin Deficiency was anything but a gift. He endured relentless bullying, was ostracized for his differences, and later, falsely accused of murder, he became a fugitive hunted by the law. Forced into the shadows of Milwaukee's grim back alleys, William found refuge in isolation—until fate thrust him into the role of an unlikely hero. His brutal acts of vigilante justice, driven by bitterness and a thirst for revenge, struck terror into the hearts of criminals.

Yet, for all his immense strength, William's greatest struggle lies within. His inability to forgive and his hardened heart weigh heavier than any physical burden, threatening to destroy the humanity he still clings to. His story is not one of power but of its price.

CHAPTER 1

Fast Food

Monday, June 12, 2000

"Alright, alright...I *know*!" Victoria snaps with one arm crossed as she shifts her weight anxiously from foot to foot. With a frustrated groan, she jabs the "hang-up" button and flings the cordless phone like a football, watching it bounce off the couch in the living room. Spinning on her heel, she wrenches open the sticky cabinet doors, her movements sharp and impatient. Cans of corn and pork & beans clatter aside, each one falling short of the ingredients she desperately needs to pull together his evening meal.

Her husband had made it clear earlier that morning—he wanted his favorite dish, spaghetti and chicken, waiting for him when he got home. But by the time Victoria returned from her doctor's appointment late in the afternoon, the promise had slipped her mind. Her thoughts had been preoccupied with the growing list of chores she needed to tackle before his arrival, desperate to ensure the apartment was spotless. It was a careless oversight, one that mirrored the mistake she had made months ago—a mistake that had cost her dearly.

He had arrived home from work with his appetite sharp and his expectations high, settling at the table and licking his lips like a ravenous predator preparing to pounce. But instead of the savory meal he craved, he was met with the unwelcome sight of leftover liver and limp mashed potatoes, reheated and slapped onto a plate from the microwave.

She vividly recalled the weeks spent hiding behind oversized, bumblebee sunglasses, shielding the world from the evidence of his rage—the black eye that took far too long to fade. That night had left a mark deeper than bruises, a memory she was desperate never to relive. But with the clock ticking and the ingredients for his favorite meal still missing, a gnawing fear crept in, whispering that tonight might unfold just like that dreaded evening.

"Shit... shit, shhhit," she muttered through gritted teeth, her frustration mounting as she shoved cans aside, desperate to find the elusive spaghetti noodles she was certain had been there. Her bony, dark fingers gripped the handle of the lower cabinet with a sharp tug, but as the door swung open, a cascade of battered pots and dented pans tumbled out, clanging loudly as they spilled across the floor, surrounding her feet in a chaotic mess.

"Oh my God—I can't deal with this shit!" she yells, furiously cramming the battered, dented pots and pans back into the cabinet before slamming the door with a resounding thud. "His trifling ass is always stressing somebody out, can't never put shit back the way I had it! He needs to focus on keeping his damn job and stop acting like it's his business to micromanage my every move!"

Profanity flowed effortlessly from Victoria's petite, 5-foot 3-inch frame, a 28-year-old Black woman whose sharp tongue was as much a part of her as her dark, almond-shaped eyes. Whether she was angry or in good spirits, her words were always colorful, and anyone who knew her understood that a conversation with Victoria was rarely dull and never quiet. Some acquaintances had even started to steer clear of public outings with her, particularly after the infamous burger joint debacle. It had all started with a tray of cold fries—a culinary sin in her eyes. The limp, lifeless "L"-shaped potatoes sparked an eruption of expletives so explosive it left wide-eyed onlookers in stunned silence and parents scrambling to cover their children's ears. The outburst had been so intense that the manager not only escorted her and her friends out but banned them for life from what she once described as the home of "the best damn burgers in Milwaukee."

"Okay, if I hurry, I can do this," she muttered to herself, her voice strained with urgency as her eyes darted to the glowing numbers on the microwave clock. With a quick glance out the grimy kitchen window, she scanned the sky, hoping the weather wouldn't throw another obstacle in her path. Deciding it was clear enough, she grabbed a clean glass from the dishrack and filled it with tap water. The cool liquid trembled in the glass as she brought it to her lips, swallowing one of the pain pills the doctor had prescribed earlier that week—a small reprieve to dull the ache she carried both inside and out.

Victoria stood at her third-story window, her lips pressed into a thin line of displeasure, her expression mirroring the frustration of a mother confronting the chaos of her child's disaster of a bedroom. The scene below was nothing short of dismal. Overflowing trash bins lined the alley like a series of monuments of neglect, the cracked pavement between them riddled with potholes deep enough to swallow a shoe. The garages, if they could even be called that, looked more like decaying shacks. Some had doors so battered and broken they hung crookedly like loose teeth, while others had no doors at all, leaving their insides exposed to the elements and wandering eyes.

The buildings surrounding her were no better, their facades just as tired and worn as her own apartment complex. Faded and weather-beaten, they were patched together with cheap repairs that seemed to beg for a storm to put them out of their misery. Boarded-up windows punctuated the walls, glaring down like hollowed-out eyes in a skeletal face. Between these voids, scattered signs of life clung on—a line of mismatched laundry, a flicker of movement behind a curtain. The balconies, warped and splintered, leaned precariously like they were one strong gust away from collapse, more a hazard than a haven.

The only grace in the grim panorama was the occasional blessing of a clear blue sky and the warm rays of sunlight that sometimes kissed the battered landscape. It wasn't much, but for Victoria, it was enough to remind her that even in this neglected corner of the world, something untainted still existed.

Despite the decayed, crumbling reality outside her walls, Victoria maintained her apartment with an obsessive precision that bordered on ritual. Every corner was scrubbed, every surface disinfected daily, as though she could ward off the chaos of the world beyond her door through sheer cleanliness. Everything had its exact place—the TV remote sat perfectly aligned on the corner of the coffee table, and *Jet* magazines were meticulously fanned out in the center like a display in a showroom. The furniture, though expensive-looking, was rented, a temporary façade that gave the illusion of affluence, masking the financial strain that loomed over their lives.

Victoria often envisioned the day she'd live in a home she could truly call her own—a modest house with a private backyard where she could breathe freely, surrounded by neighbors who smiled instead of scowled. Just imagining the simplicity of walking to her mailbox without the nagging fear of a strung-out dopehead lurking nearby, or the landlord skulking by the entrance like a predator ready to corner tenants about late rent, was enough to bring a rare smile to her face.

Heading to the closet by the front door, Victoria snatched the phone from the couch, snapping it back into its cradle with an annoyed flick of her wrist. Her gaze swept over the coffee table, and she instinctively straightened the TV remote, ensuring it was in its designated spot beside the neatly fanned-out magazines. With a quick, practiced motion, she gathered her hair into a ponytail, then paused to scrutinize her reflection in the small mirror hanging nearby. Her sharp eyes searched for imperfections, as if finding one might compound the weight of the day's mounting tension. Satisfied—or perhaps too pressed for time to care—she grabbed her keys and darted out the door, her cell phone clenched in her hand like a lifeline, its glowing screen holding the promise—or threat—of what lay ahead.

(3:05 PM)

"Damn, how the hell did ten minutes fly by that fast?" she muttered, shoving her cell phone into her pocket with a frustrated huff. Without wasting another second, she broke into a light jog, cutting through the back alley. The uneven pavement and lingering stink of overflowing trash bins didn't slow her pace—she knew the shortcuts all too well, her feet instinctively navigating the cracked ground and dodging discarded debris.

As she stepped out of the alley onto the side street, a young man's gaze locked onto her. From the window of his car, his eyes followed the sway of her hips, fixated on the way her curves moved in the snug, pocketless jeans she wore. Each step caused her shirt to lift slightly, exposing a sliver of smooth, chocolate-toned skin at the small of her back, a fleeting detail that held his attention like a moth drawn to a flame.

Matching her stride with the creeping roll of his car, he leaned out of the window, his eyes fixed on her like a predator sizing up prey. A slow, deliberate lick of his lips followed, his gaze lingering far too long on the sway of her hips as she quickened her pace. "Where you headed in such a hurry, little lady?" he called out, his voice oozing with unwelcome familiarity.

Victoria shot the driver a withering glare, her pace slowing just enough to convey her disdain. Her eyes burned with a clear message: she wasn't interested, and he needed to move on. She hoped the silent warning would be enough to send the boy in the car on his way, but she kept her guard up, fully aware that persistence often thrived where it wasn't welcome.

Ignoring the honking cars piling up behind him, the boy tapped his brakes, slowing his car to a crawl as he matched her pace. Leaning further out of the window, his voice dripped with persistence. "Aye, I'm talking to you. Where you heading in such a rush? Need a ride or what?"

"Hell no—I'm good, thank you very much. What the hell do I look like? Some kind of fool hopping into your damn car?"

"Damn! You ain't gotta come at me like that!" he said, his tone laced with feigned innocence as he leaned further out the car window. "I'm just tryin' to be friendly, you know, lend a hand." Shifting his posture slightly, he softened his voice in a poor attempt to seem sincere. "Aight, for real though—can I at least ask where you going?"

"Beans, just up the street, if you really need to know," she said, her tone sharp and dismissive. "So you can keep it moving, 'cause I'm practically there already." Without waiting for a response, she quickened her pace, her stride firm and uninviting.

"Ain't no need to be nasty, baby—just tryin' to do you a favor. But hey, it's whatever." He spat the words out, his tone tinged with mock hurt as he waved a dismissive hand in her direction. With a rev of the engine, the car peeled off, the squeal of the tires echoing down the street as he sped away, his indignation trailing behind him like exhaust.

As the sleek, black Honda Accord finally sped off, its chrome rims catching the sun's glare, Victoria caught a glimpse of movement inside. Through the dark, almost impenetrable tint of the windows, she could just make out the shadowy outlines of two figures in the back seat—vague, hulking silhouettes that might have been male. A smirk tugged at her lips despite her irritation. Her eyes lingered on the license plate for a moment, the bold Wisconsin tag spelling out, "LDYSMN." The irony wasn't lost on her, and a dry chuckle escaped her throat.

Stepping into the grocery store, Victoria was momentarily struck by the blast of cool, air-conditioned relief, a sharp contrast to the oppressive ninety-degree heat outside. But the comfort barely registered. She had no time to savor it, her focus honed razor-sharp on the task at hand. Without hesitation, she darted through the aisles, her eyes scanning the shelves with frantic precision as she hunted for each ingredient. Her phone remained a constant presence in her hand, the glowing screen reminding her with every glance just how little time she had left.

Thankfully, the "12 Items or Less" line was short, sparking a flicker of hope that she might actually pull off this impossible mission. This was her halfway point, and every second counted. She stood in line, her impatience growing as the clerk lingered over a slow-moving conversation with a woman clutching an assortment of coupons. The chatter grated on her nerves, but before she could give it more than a passing glare, she felt someone step into line behind her—too close. Their warm breath brushed the back of her neck, and a subtle but unwelcome bump from their lower half pressed against her. A sharp wave of irritation shot through her. Tightening her grip on her basket, she shuffled forward, hastily placing her items on the counter and silently willing the unwanted presence to back off.

"Well, well... ain't you something else up close," a voice drawled from behind her, sudden and too familiar, dripping with the same unwelcome confidence she'd heard earlier.

Glancing over her left shoulder, she immediately recognized the intruder. It was the same baby-faced boy who had tried to offer her a ride earlier, now standing uncomfortably close. His loud-red custom tee screamed for attention, perfectly matched with equally obnoxious sneakers that looked fresh out of the box. His baggy blue jeans, slung so low they defied gravity, were held up by a belt fastened snugly around his thighs—an exaggerated display of the so-called "Saggin'" trend. To Victoria, the term was fitting; read backward, it described exactly the type of people she associated with this ridiculous fashion. The oversized clothes, at least two sizes too big, confirmed what she already knew: he was just a boy playing dress-up in a world he didn't yet understand. The smug expression on his face, complete with a bitten bottom lip and a hand rubbing his chin like some amateur model, only reinforced her first impression—this kid fancied himself a gift to womankind, and the thought made her stomach turn.

"Oh, hey, 'Mr. Lady's Man,'" she said, her voice laced with sarcasm as she threw him a sideways glance.

"The name's Clarence, but my people call me 'Clay,'" he replied, flashing a grin he probably thought was charming.

"I was talking about your license plate, but okay, 'Clarence.'" Her tone was sharp, cutting through his attempt at smoothness. She turned slightly, narrowing her eyes. "Do you mind backing the hell up and giving a bitch some space? I've got a lot of shit to handle, and I don't have time for your adolescent bullshit right now."

Pausing for effect, she clicked her wedding band against the counter, holding her hand up just enough for him to see the glint of the ring. "Besides, I'm already taken, so you can save your energy."

"What? Adolescent? Girl, I'm nineteen—ain't nothin' adolescent about this. And so what? He don't gotta know," Clay retorted, his voice dripping with misplaced confidence.

Victoria didn't miss a beat. She glanced over her shoulder with a sly smirk, her voice cool and cutting. "Who said it was a he?" With that, she handed the clerk her cash, her dismissive tone like a final nail in his bravado.

The clerk handed back her change, and Victoria, now wearing a faint smile, gathered her bags and headed for the exit. As she walked through the automatic doors, her stride confident and unbothered, Clay stood frozen in line. The cocky grin that had lit up his face moments ago was gone, replaced with a stunned expression of rejection. He watched her leave, his ego deflating like a balloon with a slow leak, as though the very idea of someone brushing him off was a foreign concept. For the first time, he looked less like a predator and more like a boy out of his depth.

As Clay stood frozen in the checkout line, another young man strolled up behind him, casually munching on a bag of chips he hadn't bothered to pay for yet. A smug grin spread across his face as he nudged Clay in the shoulder. "So, what's up? You get them digits or what?" he asked, his words muffled by a mouthful of crumbs.

Clay didn't bother responding. His friend's teasing and the clerk's increasingly impatient refrain of, "Did you find every-thing okay?" barely registered. His focus was locked on Victoria as she strode purposefully across the parking lot, heading back the way she had come. Her figure grew smaller in the distance, but the sting of her rejection lingered, dulling the confident swagger he'd worn moments earlier.

She pauses briefly, crouching down to reorganize her bags, shifting the spaghetti noodles, jars of sauce, chicken, and corn-meal to balance the weight more evenly between them. Her movements are quick but deliberate, the urgency in her chest pressing her forward. Straightening up, she fumbles through her pocket for her cell phone, the plastic of the bags digging into her fingers. Finally pulling it free, she glances at the screen to check the time, her heart sinking as the minutes continue to slip away.

(3:45 PM)

"Awwww... shit!" Victoria cursed under her breath as she picked up her pace, shoving her phone back into her pocket. She had barely made it another block and a half when one of the flimsy grocery bags gave out, the tear in the corner finally succumbing to the weight of its contents. Groceries tumbled to the ground, cans clinking against the pavement, and a jar of spaghetti sauce rolled precariously toward the curb, its glass catching the sunlight like a warning. She froze for a moment, her frustration bubbling over, before kneeling down to salvage what she could.

"Damnit!" she hissed, dropping to her knees to inspect the jars of spaghetti sauce, relieved to find them intact. Her hands moved frantically, scooping up the scattered groceries while cursing herself for not double-bagging them like she usually did. The memory of that annoying boy at the checkout flashed in her mind—his smug grin and unwanted attention. In her rush to escape him, she'd overlooked the simplest precaution, and now she was paying for it.

The roar of a car engine racing down the street snatched her attention. She turned just in time to catch the black, pimped-out Honda speeding past, its tinted windows revealing nothing of the driver or passengers. Unlike before, the car didn't slow, and the driver made no effort to acknowledge her.

Not that it mattered—Victoria barely gave it a second thought. Her focus was fixed on her mission, every step driven by the pressure of the ticking clock. The only thing looping through her mind was the tense phone call with her husband that had set this frantic chain of events into motion. As she neared the alley that led to her apartment, Will's words echoed in her head, sharp and relentless, refusing to let her forget what was at stake:

"I hope you got dinner about ready, 'cause I'm starving and might be coming home early tonight—if things go smooth," he said, his tone sharp with expectation.

"I thought you said you were working late... usually when you do, you grab something before coming home," she replied hesitantly, already sensing where the conversation was headed.

"How the hell am I supposed to grab something to eat when I gave you the last bit of money I had to get groceries? We went over this, Vee—this morning! Don't act like you forgot. There better be food on that damn table when I walk through the door. What exactly you been doing all day?"

"I'm sorry, baby. It just... slipped my mind," she stammered, her voice faltering. "I lost track of time with the doctor's appointment running late—"

"Don't give me that," he cut her off, his voice rising. "Vee, you let me walk in and there ain't no food? You know what's gonna happen. Don't play with me, girl."

"Okay—okay! I got it!" she said quickly, her voice tight with both fear and frustration, her hands trembling as she gripped the phone.

She frowned, resentment bubbling beneath her exhaustion. It was his fault she was running late. The trip to the doctor's office earlier had been necessary—she'd gone in complaining of abdominal pain. When asked how she'd been injured, she'd given the well-worn excuse of having fallen, a lie so common among women trapped in cycles of abuse that it barely sounded convincing even to her own ears. The doctor's skeptical expression had spoken volumes, her silence heavy with unspoken questions Victoria had no intention of answering.

Victoria's thoughts drifted to the better days she once shared with William Strong—days when his touch was tender, and the exchange of flowers between them was a common language of affection. She remembered their nights out as a young couple, losing themselves in music and laughter. During the upbeat songs, his hips pressed against her rhythmically, their bodies moving in sync as though they were the only two people in the room. When the tempo slowed, he would pull her close, his breath warm against the base of her neck. He would murmur compliments about her soft skin and the delicate scent of her perfume before placing gentle kisses that sent shivers down her spine. Those moments felt like magic, a love that once felt unshakable.

It was 1979 when she first laid eyes on him at Custer High School. He stood tall at six foot two, his athletic frame effortlessly commanding attention. His short-cropped hair rippled with neat waves, perfectly framing his flawless caramel complexion. His smile, bright and straight as polished ivory, had a way of disarming her completely. Back then, he was everything she dreamed of in a partner—a high school sweetheart who held doors open with a charming smile, showered her with daily compliments, and planned thoughtful dates that made her feel cherished. He embodied the ideal gentleman, and she fell hard for the version of him that seemed to exist only in those golden days of youth.

After high school graduation and their quick marriage, Will had been poised for a bright future, promised a secure, well-paying position in the family's thriving auto parts and repair business—a job perfectly suited to his passion for working with his hands. But that future went up in literal flames. One fateful night, the shop was consumed by fire, and Will's father, bound to a chair amidst a room filled with tires, perished in the inferno. Whispers in the neighborhood suggested it wasn't an accident. The blaze was rumored to be a grim warning, the price of an unpaid debt to dangerous men who had helped fuel his father's success. In the end, the cost wasn't just the business—it was a life.

She despised how life had unraveled after his father's brutal murder and the fiery destruction of their family business. The man she once knew began to fade, replaced by someone hardened and angry. His tenderness, once so natural, had become a rare and fleeting occurrence—just enough to make her laugh or remind her of the man she had fallen in love with. Those brief glimpses of his former self kept her clinging to hope, convincing herself that the kindness buried deep within him might someday return. She wanted to believe that the good in him wasn't gone—it was just lost, waiting to resurface.

With each passing year, his behavior spiraled further out of control. The man who once praised her slender, athletic frame now hurled cruel insults, calling her a "skinny, black bitch" whenever his temper flared. And his temper flared often, ignited by the most trivial of annoyances. He blamed her for everything—every failure, every setback, every disappointment in his life. On bad days, which came frequently, she became his scapegoat, his punching bag for frustrations he couldn't reconcile.

"If I'd never met you, I probably would've been there for Pop!" he'd shout, his voice dripping with venom. *"I'm sick of supporting your helpless ass!"* The irony was sharp and cutting—he wouldn't let her work, wouldn't let her contribute in the ways she wanted. Instead, he confined her, keeping her trapped under the weight of his anger and the suffocating cycle of his control.

In Will's mind, his unhappiness and lack of success were always someone else's fault. To him, "The Man" was the invisible oppressor holding him back from finding a decent job—a sentiment echoed by many unemployed Black men in the inner city, grappling with frustration and systemic obstacles that felt insurmountable.

Her mother's voice echoed in her mind, filled with the same warnings she had heard countless times. Her mom never trusted Will, always claiming he was no good or "probably out there cheating." She'd offer her usual brand of unsolicited, outlandish advice, like telling Victoria to watch him when he came home late. "Girl, if he ain't peein' straight, he ain't shootin' straight," her mother would say with a smirk, her tone half-joking but her message crystal clear.

Lost in her thoughts, Victoria's gaze stayed fixed on the cracked pavement beneath her feet, her surroundings blurring into insignificance. Her body moved on autopilot, each step guided by muscle memory rather than conscious thought, like a sleepwalker navigating a familiar but shadowy path. The ache in her chest was undeniable—a sorrowful weight pressing down as she grappled with the cruel reality that the man who had once been her sanctuary, her source of joy, was now the unpredictable storm she feared most.

Without warning, Victoria's world went dark, her body crumpling to the ground like a rag doll. When consciousness began to creep back in, pain radiated from the back of her head, sharp and relentless, as she lay sprawled on her stomach. Her thoughts were fragmented, struggling to piece together what had just happened. Blurry images swam before her—cans of corn rolling aimlessly across the cracked pavement, stopping near the shattered remains of a spaghetti sauce jar. She groaned, a weak and guttural sound escaping her lips. "Uuuugh... sssshit," she mumbled, the taste of dirt and grit invading the corner of her mouth, a grim reminder of how vulnerable she was in that moment.

An aluminum baseball bat clattered to the ground beside her face, its metallic surface glinting faintly in the dim light as it wobbled to a stop. Victoria's senses, dulled by pain and fear, were still sharp enough to detect the looming presence of someone standing over her, their shadow stretching menacingly across the ground. From a short distance away, a gruff voice cut through the air, commanding with chilling authority, "Hurry up... bring her ass over here."

Summoning the last ounce of strength she could muster, Victoria reached out toward the bat, her trembling fingers brushing against its handle. Before she could grip it, a blinding pain shot through her arm as an all-white sneaker crushed her wrist against the ground. Tiny shards of glass from the shattered spaghetti jar bit into her skin, embedding deeper with the relentless pressure. The searing agony was overwhelming, as if hundreds of needles were driving into her flesh all at once, leaving her breathless and paralyzed with pain.

Before she could cry out in pain, the man dropped to his knees, his hand pressing firmly against the back of her head, forcing her face into the dirt. His grip held her there, immobilized, leaving her unable to turn or catch even a glimpse of his identity.

Adrenaline coursed through her veins as the weight of her predicament sank in. She thrashed against his grip, but the effort only pressed the sharp gravel further into her cheek. Desperation surged, and she clawed at his wrist, her nails sinking deep into his flesh. A scream tore from her throat as she felt the warm slickness of his blood beneath her fingertips.

"Ow—shit!" he hissed, wrenching her hand away. His fingers twisted into her hair, lifting her head just enough before slamming it against the unforgiving surface, leaving her unconscious.

CHAPTER 2

Beast

(3:42 PM)

Across town, William Strong lingered at the edge of a bustling bus stop, his thoughts consumed by the crispy chicken and spaghetti waiting for him at home. His stomach growled in protest as his eyes locked on the billboard plastered across the side of the approaching bus. The image of a burger and fries looked so vivid, so tantalizingly real, he swore he could almost smell it. Mesmerized, he barely noticed the crowd surging forward, slipping past him to claim their places. By the time he snapped out of it, his spot at the front of the line was already gone.

"Move to the back, now!" the bus driver barks at the cluster of passengers loitering near the middle of the bus, their stubbornness as immovable as their feet. His voice, sharp and strained, slices through the steady hum of the engine. "We've got a crowd boarding, people! Let's keep it moving—back! Thank you!"

Will silently mouthed the "F" word, his lips forming the curse as he peered through the bus windows. Every seat was taken, packed shoulder to shoulder, with a crowd of unlucky passengers shoved toward the rear by the steady press of new arrivals. The thought of the long, grueling forty-five-minute ride home gnawed at him—a journey he'd have to endure standing, his small lunch box clutched tightly in one hand while the other gripped the cold chrome bar for balance.

People gave Will a wide berth as he settled into his spot, careful to avoid any chance of his grimy work uniform brushing against their pristine attire. The sharp tang of grease and oil clung to him, undercut by a faint edge of sweat, prompting those nearby to subtly shift away, their bodies angled to shield themselves from the unwelcome scent.

A little girl, no older than six, sat in the seat ahead of him. Her hair was done up in neat twists, each one capped with a colorful barrette that clicked softly as she moved, and a pink book bag rested on her lap, jostling with her every fidget. She wrinkled her nose and pulled her upper lip high enough to nearly seal her nostrils, fixing him with a look that said he was nothing less than a six-foot, rancid pile of trash wafting its stench in her direction.

"You stank," she says, wrinkling her nose as she scoots closer to her mother, who perches by the window with an air of quiet amusement.

"Real hard work ain't supposed to smell pretty, young lady," he replies with a broad grin, puffing his chest as if the sweat and grime were badges of honor.

"Then maybe you ought to get a 'real hard-working' car, so the rest of us don't have to suffer for it," a low voice mutters from the small crowd gathering behind him.

The stares and whispered remarks rolled off him without a second thought. He took no shame in his motor oil-slicked shirt and grease-darkened jeans; they were a testament to his hard day's work. Stepping off the bus at his stop, he moved with quiet confidence, his head high and his gait carrying a subtle swagger. He paused briefly to straighten his clothes, then continued down the familiar stretch of his neighborhood, undeterred.

"Heyyy, Will!"

Will turned toward the voice, spotting a girl perched on a porch, her hair being braided by another. "What's up, Trina—what's up, ladies?" he replied, nodding at two more girls who had just stepped out onto the porch, their eyes fixed on the rare sight of a fine, hard-working man strolling past.

"Mmm, just look at him," Trina drawled, her voice laced with admiration. "He knows he's fine, even rocking them raggedy clothes. Victoria's lucky as hell. You know he treats her right," she added, her words met with approving murmurs from the others as Will continued on his way.

He bounded up the steps to his apartment building, taking three at a time with a youthful swagger. As he reached the top, a young woman exited, brushing past him with a casual glance. Unable to resist, he turned on his heel, his eyes trailing her retreating figure. A sly squint and a sharp click of his tongue betrayed his appreciation, but his moment of admiration nearly cost him as he narrowly avoided walking face-first into the closing glass door. Catching it just in time, he looked up—only to find his landlord standing in the doorway, watching him with a raised brow.

"Well, hello there, Mister," she says.

"Hey, Ms. Flannigan. Damn, you're looking good! Bye, Mrs. Flannigan!" Will fires back, cutting her off mid-thought. His bold remark sends a flush to her cheeks, throwing her off balance just as she's about to ask about the rent. Instead, she's left standing silent and stunned at the foot of the stairwell. By the time the moment catches up to her, he's already vaulted up the stairs and out of reach.

The tenants all understood that Mrs. Denise Flannigan ruled the apartment complex with an iron fist. It was the sole thing her late husband had left behind, and she tended to it as if he were still by her side. The only real difference was how she had evolved—from a landlord into a relentless hellhound.

"First of the month's almost here, y'all," she'd bark, her keys jingling in her hand like chains in a dungeon. "Y'all knew it was coming last month, so don't act like it's some big surprise. No excuses!"

She'd always considered her late husband too soft, too willing to swallow the tenants' endless excuses for being months behind on rent. Their own finances had taken a hit because of it. So, she decided it was time for a change. A little "Foot-In-Ass" technique, as she liked to call it, would whip the place into shape—something he could never manage while letting the tenants walk all over him.

Will stormed in the way he always did, slamming the door so hard it sent a sharp gust across the room. The wind toppled the picture of Victoria and her mother from its spot on the end table, just as he'd intended. He had a knack for making that photo crash down, aiming for it to land face down so he wouldn't have to endure her mother's sour expression staring back at him. It wasn't just petty spite—it was a signal. The clatter would jolt Victoria, a reminder to have his dinner ready without delay.

He stopped, taking a slow, deliberate breath through his nose. The sharp tang of pine cleaner and synthetic air freshener filled his senses. Absent was the savory aroma of spaghetti sauce simmering, the sizzle of chicken frying, or the clatter of plates being set for dinner—nothing but silence.

"Vee? Victoria!" His voice echoed faintly, unanswered. "Aye!"

He marched into the kitchen, greeted by the stark absence of any hint of a meal—no simmering pots, no cluttered counters, just a pristine stove and neatly stacked dishes. As he turned toward the microwave to investigate further, a noise echoed from the bedroom at the end of the narrow hallway.

"Bitch, I swear, if you're back here sleeping..." he growled, kicking the door open. But the bed was empty, the covers pulled tight with military precision, corners crisp, and pillows stacked just so—large ones forming a perfect backdrop for the neat rows of smaller ones. The only imperfection was the closet door, left ajar, its knob tapping rhythmically against the wall as a cool breeze pushed in through the open window.

He slammed both fists into the door, the force driving the knob straight into the wall, splintering the plaster. Snatching his phone from the clip on his belt, he muttered a string of curses under his breath while jabbing her number.

The line rang on and on.

"I swear to GOD, if you don't pick up this *phone*!"

His words were cut short by Victoria's familiar voice: *"You-know-what-to-do--"* Beeeeep.

Holding the handset rigidly to his mouth, Will barked into the receiver, matching Victoria's sharp tone. ""Bitch, I know what Imma do! Imma break yo neck if you don't answer this phone. And if you walk through this door without a chicken dinner and biscuits, Imma act a fool!" Shoving the phone back into its holster, he turned to the bedroom window, his eyes scanning the sidewalk below, desperate to catch sight of her heading down the street.

Fuming with anger, he stormed into the living room, his chest thrust forward like a peacock who'd just conquered the gym. With a sharp grab, he snatched the remote off the coffee table and dropped onto the couch in a huff. The television blinked to life under his relentless button-mashing as he scrolled through channels, barking in frustration at the screen to deliver something worth his time.

"Fuck'n local channels! Why does Telemundo get all the good stuff? Damn Latinos taking over the neighborhood *and* my TV too," he grumbled, slamming the power button on the remote and tossing it carelessly into the corner of the couch. His fingers began an impatient rhythm against the armrest as he sat stewing. Finally, with a sharp breath, he got up and headed for the kitchen, his mood sour and his hunger gnawing. Rummaging through the cluttered pantry, he spotted an unopened bag of BBQ potato chips. Without hesitation, he tore into it, the sound of the crinkling bag the only relief to his restless agitation.

Leaning against the kitchen counter, he stuffed chip after chip into his mouth, the sharp crunch echoing in his head as his hand rummaged through the crackling bag for more. From the corner of his eye, a shadow slid across the living room wall, deliberate and slow. He froze for a moment, then tossed the bag onto the counter, clenched his fists, and charged into the living room, ready for a confrontation—only to halt abruptly, his tension evaporating as his bravado crumbled.

Victoria stood there, her head bowed to dodge any gaze, her appearance telling the tale of a struggle. Dirt clung to her like a second skin, her clothes ragged and smeared, forearms marked with raw scrapes and dark bruises. One hand gripped the waistband of her pants, keeping the broken zipper together, while the other steadied her trembling frame against the doorknob.

Without hesitation, he darted to her side, his hand swiftly covering hers as it trembled against the doorknob, steadying her fragile frame. Guiding her carefully to the couch, he bore the weight of her body with an urgency that matched the panic in his voice. "Come on, come on, I've got you, baby. What the hell happened—Vee?"

She didn't answer. She just sat on the couch, her gaze fixed on her knees, silent tears carving trails down her face and dripping onto her shirt.

He leaned closer, his index finger tilting her chin upward, his eyes narrowing as they took in the damage. Her cheek was scraped and bruised, the wounds laced with dirt and specks of embedded gravel. His jaw tightened, the muscles flexing and releasing as he scanned her from head to toe, the anger building with every detail he absorbed.

"You gonna answer me? Look at me, Vee," he commanded, his voice low but edged with steel.

"Yeah," she murmured, her head dipping in a hesitant nod.

Without hesitation, his hand clamped firmly around her jaw, ignoring the tender injuries. He turned her face toward him, his grip forcing her to meet his unwavering gaze.

"Who the fuck did this to you? Tell me!" Will demanded, his voice sharp with desperation. "Tell me!"

"I don't know who!" she snapped, jerking her face away from his grasp.

"Did you see they face? Anything?"

"I said I don't know!" Her voice cracked as tears spilled over, and she turned away, trembling. "I got hit from behind. When I woke up . . . my shirt was torn . . ." Her words faltered, and she buried her face in her hands, her shoulders shaking under the weight of it all.

Will's jaw tightened as he stared at her. "You woke up and what?" he pressed, his words cutting, his need for answers overriding his compassion.

"I don't want to talk about it! Leave me the fuck alone!" she yelled, her voice breaking under the strain. "Don't you get it? I didn't see who the motha-fuckas was!"

Will stepped back, his fists clenched at his sides. The fury boiling inside him was almost too much to contain. The thought of someone violating her space, her safety, made him feel powerless, and the lack of answers only deepened his frustration. He wanted to act, to fix, to punish—but there was nothing solid to fight against.

She turned her back to him completely, her frame still trembling, her breaths shallow and uneven. The silence stretched between them, heavy and suffocating, as they both wrestled with their own torment—hers rooted in fear and violation, his in helpless rage. He then drew his hand back, preparing to slap a confession out of her.

Buzzzz—Buzz—Buzz

The abrupt sound shattered the tense silence, jolting both of them. Will froze mid-motion, his breath caught as the buzzer echoed through the apartment. The interruption was sharp, jarring, pulling their attention to the secured entrance below.

Someone wanted in.

Will's hand lingered over the intercom, his posture rigid, his face unreadable. His finger pressed the button with deliberate caution, his ear tilted toward the static-tinged speaker. The faint hum of the apartment building's entranceway filled the room. He listened, his senses heightened, straining for anything recognizable—a voice, a familiar shuffle of footsteps, the clipped chatter of police radios.

The seconds dragged, heavy with tension. His eyes darted toward her, gauging her reaction as much as the sounds filtering through the speaker.

The quiet crackle of the intercom offered nothing. No voices. No clues. Just the muted sound of the glass door easing shut, the soft click sealing whatever or whoever had been there outside.

Will's jaw tightened, his grip on the intercom releasing. The air hung thick between them, weighted with what had been interrupted—and what still lingered unspoken in the wake of that sound.

"Hello?" Will's tone carried a sharp edge, his words bristling with attitude.

There was a pause before a woman's voice responded, calm but firm. "Yeah... where's Victoria?"

Will's brows knitted as he retorted, "Who is this?"

"This is her mother, Will. Don't act stupid."

At her words, Will turned toward Victoria, sitting casually on the couch. His expression twisted, more in disbelief than anything else. "Damn, girl, this yo momma!" The words escaped louder than intended, and for a moment, the air in the room seemed to tighten.

Victoria froze, her eyes wide before she frantically waved her hands. "Tell her I ain't here!" she hissed, her voice trembling with urgency.

Will gave a small, almost dismissive nod. He spoke into the intercom with a practiced ease. "She ain't here, Ms. Adams. You want me to have her call you when she gets home?"

The silence on the other end was palpable, thick and unsettling. It lingered just long enough to raise the tension before the quiet click of the inner door shutting broke it.

Will released the button, the buzz of the intercom fading into the stillness. For a moment, neither of them spoke, the weight of the exchange hanging heavily in the air.

"Hello!" he called out, leaning into the speaker, his finger pressing insistently on the button. Silence. He tried again, only to be met with the same empty void. "She must've left," he muttered, his shoulders sagging. Turning back to the couch, he barely had time to sit when a sudden, forceful knock rattled the door.

"Aw, hell—hope nobody let her in—DAMN!" he hissed to Victoria, his voice low and urgent. His eyes darted toward the door, and his body stiffened. Slowly, deliberately, he crept forward. Peeking through the peephole, he recoiled, throwing frustrated punches into the air as if trying to fight off invisible demons.

"Fuck-fuck-fuck," he mouthed silently, his fists slicing through the tension. He turned back toward Victoria, his voice barely above a whisper. "The last thing we need is your mom showing up right now. You know she's gonna start in, saying I've done something to you."

With a measured breath, he adjusted his posture, forcing calm into his movements. The door opened just a crack, his body wedged firmly in the gap. His presence blocked the view inside, but there was no escaping the sharp, unimpressed gaze of Ms. Agnes Adams. Her expression was a thundercloud of suspicion, a force as unyielding as her reputation.

Agnes didn't mince words, nor did she tolerate nonsense, especially from the man she openly dismissed as a "fool." Her disdain clung to the air, heavy and unmistakable, as her eyes searched his face, daring him to justify his existence in her daughter's life. He didn't flinch but knew any wrong move would fan her simmering disapproval into a full-blown storm.

Will's frown deepened as he regarded the woman before him, a mix of disbelief and irritation written across his face. She stood defiantly, arms crossed, her expression sharp and judgmental. Her outfit—a tight pink spandex ensemble paired with a cropped tee—seemed more about claiming confidence than fitting the moment, though her demeanor left little room for doubt about how she saw herself.

"Is that *you* smelling like that?" she demanded, her voice loud enough to carry through the quiet of the hallway. Her nose wrinkled as she flicked at it dramatically, like she'd stumbled into a cloud of something offensive. "I mean, I got it all up in my face when you opened the door. Ooo!" She gave an exaggerated shake of her head, as if warding off an invisible nuisance, her tone sharp with the promise of trouble.

Will rolled his eyes and leaned against the doorframe, clearly already exhausted by her presence. "Victoria's not here," he said flatly, his voice devoid of any warmth or patience.

The tension in the air thickened as she snapped her gum with a loud, deliberate pop that cut through the silence like a whip crack. She scratched at her wig with a pinky, her movements as pointed as her words. "Well, *where is she*?" she asked, her tone dripping with suspicion and challenge.

The weight of their long, strained history hung heavily between them, filling the space more than words ever could. It was clear this encounter was destined to spiral, just like the many times before.

Before Will could respond, a towering figure emerged from behind Agnes, stepping into view like a shadow stretching over the room. The man was immense, his presence as unyielding as the walls of the hallway. His sheer size—well over six feet—was matched by the intensity in his dark, piercing eyes, which seemed to burn with restrained fury. Tattoos crawled across his muscular arms and neck, lending him an air of quiet menace, while his broad chest heaved slightly, as though he had just stepped out of some unseen storm.

This was Mr. Truvon Adams, or "Tru" as he was known—a man whose name carried weight, both literally and figuratively. Agnes had told him everything during his time away, painting a picture of Will that filled him with disgust. Now, face to face with the man he'd only heard about, Tru's jaw tightened, and his fists clenched, his knuckles whitening with the pressure of barely contained rage. He didn't need to speak; his disdain for Will was palpable, an unspoken accusation hanging thick in the air.

Will, suddenly aware of how small he felt in comparison, stood his ground, though his knees threatened to betray him. His mind raced back to Victoria's words about her father—how he'd never see freedom again after his conviction. And yet, here he was, standing in Will's hallway, his presence a physical reminder of promises broken and threats unspoken.

Desperate to maintain some semblance of control, Will tried to block the doorway, rising onto his toes in a futile attempt to match Tru's towering height. But Tru simply leaned forward, pressing his palm against the door with measured force. Will pushed back, his hands trembling with the effort, but it was like trying to hold back an oncoming wave. Tru applied more pressure, his strength effortless, until Will had no choice but to stumble aside, the weight of the moment leaving him breathless and cornered.

The air between them felt electric, charged with tension that could ignite at any moment.

"She got jumped!" Will blurts out, his voice trembling as he instinctively steps back, his eyes darting between Victoria's parents.

"Daddy! When did you—?" Victoria shoots to her feet, but her words are swallowed by her mother's outburst.

"Now I see why you're covering for this fool—what did he do to my baby? Oh my God, Tru, *look at her*!" Agnes cries, her purse tumbling from her hand as she rushes to her daughter. Her eyes fill with anguish, scanning Victoria's face as though searching for answers in every mark and tear.

"I didn't do nothing to her!" Will protests, his voice cracking as he backs away. His steps falter as Tru's presence looms closer, the older man's fists clenching at his sides.

Tru's rage breaks like a storm, his sudden movement toppling the coffee table and sending it crashing to the floor. He vaults over the couch with a force that shakes the room.

Will scrambles back, his breath coming in shallow gasps as he presses against the wall. He drops to the ground, curling into himself, shielding his head with trembling arms. The distance between him and Tru seems to shrink with every heartbeat, and the air feels heavy with the weight of unspoken accusations and raw, unchecked emotion.

Victoria's voice cuts through the chaos, shaky but desperate, her plea echoing like a lifeline in the tense room. Agnes clutches her arm, her panic mirrored in Victoria's wide, tear-filled eyes. The family teeters on the edge of breaking, the consequences of this moment poised to ripple far beyond the walls of their home.

"Daddy, no! Stop! He didn't do it!" Victoria's voice cut through the chaos, trembling with desperation.

But Tru was beyond hearing. Consumed by fury, his fists flew, each blow fueled by anger rather than reason. Will staggered under the assault, unable to defend himself. The room seemed to shrink around them, heavy with the weight of shock and fear. Victoria's mother stood frozen, her hands clasped to her mouth, her face pale with disbelief.

Breaking free from her mother's hesitant grip, Victoria rushed forward. "Stop, Daddy! Stop—stop!" Her voice cracked as she grabbed his arm mid-swing, halting him with all the strength she could muster.

Tru froze, his chest heaving, his bloodied fist suspended in the air. Slowly, he turned his gaze toward her, his expression a mixture of anger and disbelief. "How dare you grab me?" he growled, yanking his arm free. His eyes burned as he stepped back. "You lost your mind, little girl? You don't need to cover for him. He's been asking for this for a long time. I've heard the stories! If he didn't do it, then who?"

Victoria's breath hitched as she met his gaze, her own eyes shining with unshed tears. Tru wiped his hand on Will's shirt, his voice low and venomous, but she refused to back down.

"I don't know, Daddy," she said, her voice breaking as she knelt beside her husband, cradling his battered face with trembling hands. The silence that followed was deafening, the weight of what had happened settling heavily in the air, a rift carved deep between father and daughter.

"Get your stuff now! You coming home with us!"

"But Daddy, I'm telling you he didn't do--"

"Don't argue with your father right now, baby—get your stuff and come on," Agnes interrupts, her voice sharp, a triumphant glint in her eyes as she briefly locks gazes with Will.

Will staggered upright, his body trembling as he pushed past the others without a word, his movements quick and unsteady. His chest heaved with suppressed rage as he stormed out, slamming the front door behind him. Down the stairwell and through the alleyway, he moved like a man driven, shoving the exit door open so hard it echoed in the narrow space.

In the dim light of the alley, Will paced in tight circles, his hands curling into fists at his sides. His breaths came in sharp, audible bursts as he muttered to himself, the words nearly unintelligible. " Imma kill that bitch-ass motha-fucka! This ain't over... I swear it ain't..." His voice trembled with fury, but there was a crack of something deeper—betrayal, desperation.

He caught his reflection in the dark glass of a parked car window. For a moment, he stared at the face staring back—unfamiliar, distorted, the strain of the night etched deeply into it. His left eye was starting to close, a reminder of how far things had gone, and how much further they could still go.

Tuesday afternoon, June 20, 2000.

Victoria stepped into the stifling heat of the apartment building's top floor, her senses immediately struck by the oppressive atmosphere. The air was heavy, not just with the unbearable heat and humidity, but with tension. Voices carried through the open doors of apartments, overlapping in frustrated tones.

"Mine just quit this morning," one tenant groaned to another, their voices muffled by the rhythmic hum of fans that seemed to struggle against the warmth. Another voice, sharper and tinged with exasperation, called out, "If this keeps up, I'm going to sleep in the stairwell."

Victoria's gaze swept over the corridor. The lucky few with working air conditioners had retreated behind closed doors, their cool refuges evident from the damp towels pressed beneath the frames to keep every bit of chilled air contained. For the rest, doors stood open, their homes filled with the droning sound of fans and the low buzz of televisions playing against the backdrop of discontent.

She moved further down the hall, catching snippets of conversation. Complaints overlapped like waves, building a collective wall of agitation. The air smelled faintly of sweat and desperation, and Victoria could feel her own nerves beginning to fray. It was the kind of tension that, left unchecked, could spark a fire of frustration among the tenants.

Her fingers trailed over the peeling paint of the walls as she walked, grounding herself. She knew the storm of complaints would soon reach her ears directly, but for now, she listened, trying to brace herself. It wasn't just the heat making the walls feel like they were closing in; it was the mood, simmering and ready to boil over.

The oppressive humidity clung to Victoria like a second skin, but it was the least of her worries as she made her way through the thick haze of emotions swirling in her chest. It had been over a week since she'd last seen Will, and their silence wasn't her choice. Her controlling mother, always meddling, had confiscated her phone, cutting off the lifeline between them. Victoria knew the damage this silence could cause. Not responding to Will wasn't just neglect—it was fuel to a fire that she'd have to face sooner or later.

Stepping into the apartment, she was greeted by a stifling wall of heat and stale air, a tangible marker of neglect. The kitchen sink overflowed with pots and pans, each one crusted with forgotten remnants of meals. The apartment reeked of abandonment, an eerie testament to how much had gone wrong in her absence.

"Oh my goodness, Lord!" Victoria exclaimed, the words tumbling out as she dropped her bag to the floor. The sight struck her deeper than she expected—not just messy, but symbolic. Will was nowhere to be seen, and his absence hung heavy in the room, amplifying the oppressive silence.

Without hesitation, she rolled up her sleeves and began to fill the sink with hot, soapy water. The task gave her hands something to do, but her mind churned with questions. Each dish she scrubbed was an outlet for the tension twisting inside her. Where was he? Why hadn't he cleaned up? And most troubling—what kind of state would he be in when he finally showed up?

The sound of the toilet flushing down the hall shattered the stillness, snapping Victoria out of her thoughts. Her movements quickened as she dried her hands and stepped toward the bathroom, ready to greet her husband. But as the door opened, it wasn't Will who emerged.

A woman—brown-haired, blue-eyed, and unfamiliar—strode out casually, oblivious to Victoria's presence. She adjusted her jeans with practiced indifference, popping her gum in a grating rhythm while smoothing her hair back into a ponytail. Her small lips, glossed to an almost artificial sheen, parted as she finally noticed Victoria standing there.

"Oh, umm... who is you?" the stranger asked, her tone carrying an unconvincing attempt at an urban accent. Her gaze swept over Victoria, an assessment more dismissive than curious.

Victoria's breath caught, then flared into indignation. "Who am I? This is my house, bitch! Who are you?" Her voice cracked through the air like a whip as she kicked off her shoes, the heat of betrayal roaring to life in her chest. Without thinking, she charged at the woman.

The stranger recoiled with a sharp intake of breath, her eyes wide as she darted back into the bathroom and slammed the door shut. The click of the lock punctuated the moment, leaving Victoria frozen with her hands pressed against the smooth wood. For a heartbeat, the hallway seemed to vibrate with her fury.

Before she could regroup, the bedroom door creaked open. Will stepped out, his shirt hanging open and his belt unfastened, his disheveled state telling a story Victoria didn't want to hear.

"Are you serious right now?" he barked, his voice heavy with frustration. "Coming home out of nowhere and start'n shit? What the hell are you even doing here, Victoria?" His words hit like cold water. "You don't answer my calls, don't return my texts, and now this? Really?"

Victoria barely heard him. Her focus was a single, furious purpose, her shoulder driving against the bathroom door as she tried to force it open. The only thing she felt more keenly than the resistance of the door was the slow crumbling of the life she thought she knew.

"You got some white bitch in my house asking me questions, Will? How dare you treat me like this!" Victoria's voice cut through the apartment like a blade. She jabbed her finger toward Will's face, her eyes blazing with fury, forcing him to retreat until his back met the wall.

"Get—yo—hand—out—ma—face!" Will said, his tone calm but edged with warning.

"I'm not moving *shit!*" she shot back, her voice trembling with anger. "You disrespect me by bringing this *bitch* in my house while I'm gone. I defended you—stood by you—"

"Get—yo—hand—out—ma—Vee!" Will repeated, his calm unraveling thread by thread.

Her lips curled in disdain. "I should've let Daddy beat the hell out of you some more. Maybe he'd have knocked some—"

"I ain't gonna tell you again!" Will's voice cracked like a whip, sharp and final. Victoria didn't stop.

His breathing deepened, his jaw tight as the tension in the room reached a boiling point. "I said, get your hand—" then, slapped Victoria so hard she bounced off of the opposite wall and fell to the floor.

The sudden movement startled the room into silence. Victoria stumbled and hit the floor, her shocked eyes meeting his for the briefest of moments before the weight of everything fell over them.

Through the crack in the door, the woman outside froze, her face pale as realization dawned. Without hesitation, she slipped out of the apartment, her footsteps fading into the hallway. Will didn't look after her. His focus remained on Victoria, a mix of regret and defiance flashing across his face as the storm they had unleashed finally settled into an uneasy calm.

"See what you make me do—*see*?" Will's voice was sharp, cutting through the thick silence as he helped Victoria to her feet. His thumb brushed her lip in a mockingly gentle gesture, his touch meant to comfort but only making her flinch. "I didn't want to hurt you! That girl was just a friend trying to help me out while you were gone, that's it. I missed you, baby—you know I did."

Victoria stood dazed, her breaths shallow as her back pressed against the cold wall. The words hit her harder than the earlier blow, each one twisting her confusion and fear tighter.

"So why'd you keep me waiting? Why didn't you answer my calls or my texts?" His body closed in, trapping her, the weight of his presence stifling. He leaned in, his breath hot and cloying, but when his lips sought hers, she turned away, her face jerking left and right in silent refusal.

His frustration bubbled over. Gripping her head with both hands, he forced a kiss, the intimacy twisted into an assertion of power. Victoria's resistance was wordless but palpable—her body rigid, her movements reluctant as he dragged her toward the bedroom.

The sound of his foot slamming the door shut behind them echoed like the sealing of a tomb.

CHAPTER 3

Yangu Mtoto

Two weeks had slipped by since Victoria had returned to her apartment. She stood in the dim light of the bathroom, staring into the mirror as if trying to recognize the woman reflected back at her. The faint hum of the city outside seemed distant, muffled by the thick weight in her chest. Tonight was supposed to be a celebration—Summer Fest's fireworks lighting up the lakefront, her favorite tradition for the Fourth of July.

The memory of that night with Will still clung to her, bittersweet and jagged. She could almost feel his arm around her as they glided on the sky ride, suspended between earth and stars. The fireworks had painted the night in bursts of gold and crimson, their brilliance mirrored in the water below. It had been the kind of moment that felt too perfect to be real, like something stolen from a romance film.

That was the night he had taken her hand, his voice low but brimming with promise. He hadn't needed a ring to make her heart race. His words had been enough. He'd spun dreams of a future together, built on the foundation of a fortune yet to come. "A ring that will outshine these fireworks," he had said, his eyes gleaming with conviction.

Now, standing alone in the harsh glow of the bathroom light, Victoria's chest tightened. The future they had spoken of seemed as distant as the stars that had watched over them that night. Something unspoken lingered in the air around her—an unease she couldn't quite shake, a sense that the promises made beneath the fireworks had scattered like ashes in the wind.

Tabitha pounded on the bathroom door again, her voice sharp and tinged with urgency. "Victoria, girl, let's go! Jarvis and Will are gonna be back any minute. You know I don't want to deal with no drama tonight."

Her tone carried the kind of no-nonsense authority that came naturally to Tabitha Boyd—a woman who balanced her sharp style with an unshakable sense of self. Her low-cut afro framed her face like a halo, glinting under the dim light of the hallway. She tugged at the hem of her wide-bottom jeans and adjusted her hoop earrings with a huff, the bedazzled American flag on her T-shirt catching the light as she leaned against the wall. Tabitha had a knack for staying calm in chaos, but even her patience had limits.

Inside the bathroom, Victoria's world was unraveling. She leaned against the sink, her back pressing into the cold porcelain. The mirror in front of her reflected not just her face, but the muted image of a framed picture of Jesus that hung on the opposite wall. His eyes seemed to meet hers in the glass, and she found herself whispering to the reflection.

"God," she murmured, her voice cracking under the strain. "If you love me, you'll fix this. Just... make it go away." Her lips trembled as she turned her gaze downward, breaking away from the silent judgment she imagined in His eyes. "I swear, no more cussing, no more messing around. Just, please..."

Her words trailed off into silence as she glanced at the small, innocuous strip of plastic lying on the sink. Two faint blue lines stared back at her, unassuming but definitive. Victoria's chest tightened, her breath catching in her throat as the reality of what those lines meant began to sink in. Her fingers tightened on the edge of the sink, nails digging into the cool ceramic as her mind raced.

The bathroom felt smaller now, the air heavier, as if the walls themselves were closing in around her. Every second felt like an eternity as she checked her watch again, the minute hand ticking with cruel indifference to the storm brewing in her chest. The muffled sounds of Tabitha's movements outside the door seemed distant, almost surreal, like the static of a radio in another room.

Victoria's reflection in the mirror was a stranger now—her wide eyes filled with a mixture of fear and disbelief. What would she say? What would Jarvis think? And Will? The questions came in rapid succession, one piling onto the other until they formed an insurmountable wall in her mind.

BANG—BANG—BANG

Victoria jolted as a sudden, urgent pounding rattled the bathroom door. The sound sent the delicate plastic strip tumbling from her trembling fingers to the floor. Her pulse raced, her thoughts scrambling to recover.

"Hellooooo? Girl, I gotta pee, and you're just in here chillen!" Tabitha's voice rang out, sharp with urgency. "Let me in before I go in your kitchen sink!" The telltale shuffle of her feet betrayed her struggle.

Victoria's breath hitched. "Shit," she muttered under her breath, panic clawing at her chest. Her voice wavered as she called out, "Umm... yeah, I'll be out in a minute! Just finishing up my makeup."

A scoff echoed through the door. "Bitch you ain't wore makeup in years—don't play me. Open up before I water this hallway!" Tabitha's voice held a teasing edge, but her patience was clearly wearing thin. Victoria saw the door creak slightly as Tabitha tried to peer through the gap.

Heart hammering, Victoria snatched up the plastic strip, wrapping it hastily in toilet paper. Her movements were frantic, hands fumbling as she buried it deep within the trash can, making sure no trace remained. Taking a steadying breath, she unlocked the door.

Tabitha wasted no time, brushing past Victoria with a quick shove, her movements a blur of urgency. Victoria stepped aside, her nerves frayed, as Tabitha claimed the toilet with the kind of confidence only desperation can provide.

"You might want to step out," Tabitha warned with a mischievous grin as she settled in, her words punctuated by an unmistakable, muffled airy sound from the toilet. The confined acoustics of the bathroom amplified the moment's awkwardness.

Victoria recoiled, her expression a mix of disgust and disbelief. "Oh my god, Tabby! I thought you had to pee!"

Tabitha shrugged, unapologetic. "Plans change."

"You so nasty!" Victoria snapped, storming out and slamming the door behind her. Outside, she leaned against the wall, her chest rising and falling as she tried to compose herself. The weight of what she had just hidden settled in her stomach like a stone, far heavier than Tabitha's antics could ever be.

Minutes later, the sharp blare of a car horn cut through the silence, its echoes bouncing off the towering brick facade of the apartment building. Down on the street, Will leaned hard on the steering wheel, his frustration mounting with every unanswered honk. Jarvis sat silently beside him, arms crossed, eyes flicking toward the upstairs window.

"They can't hear us," Jarvis muttered, almost to himself.

Will growled under his breath, slamming the door as he stepped out, storming toward the stairs leading to the main entrance.

Inside the apartment, Victoria stood frozen in the center of the living room, her arms wrapped tightly around herself. Silent tears carved trails down her cheeks as she stared at the worn carpet, her mind somewhere far from this moment. The sound of heavy footfalls traveling down the hall toward her door jolted her back to reality, and she quickly wiped her face. When the door flung open, she spun around, masking her emotions with a strained indifference.

"Y'all didn't hear us honking? We been downstairs for a minute—damn!" Will barked as he strode in, his voice sharp enough to make her flinch.

"How we supposed to hear you all the way up here?" she shot back, her tone defensive and raw.

Will glared at her for a moment, his frustration colliding with suspicion. "Yeah, whatever," he muttered. "Let's go. We need to get a good spot. Where's Tabby?"

"In the bathroom," Victoria replied curtly, keeping her back turned. Her voice cracked just slightly. "Can you grab the blanket from the bedroom? We'll need it."

Will narrowed his eyes, hesitating. Something was off, but he wasn't sure what. He finally shrugged and stomped toward the hallway.

Just as he reached the bathroom door, it swung open abruptly, and Tabitha emerged with deliberate force, her expression a mix of amusement and defiance.

"Hey, Will!" she said brightly, the grin on her face widening.

Will recoiled, instinctively covering his nose with his hand. "Oh, come on, Tabby! That's foul!"

"What?" she replied innocently, feigning ignorance.

"That's not right," he said, his voice muffled behind his hand. "Women aren't supposed to—"

"Shut up, boy" she cut him off, laughing. "Don't act like ya'll shit smell like flowers! Botha ya'll be stanking." Victoria's voice carried from the living room, sharp and biting. "Can we just go already?"

The tension in the air thickened as Will shook his head, retreating to the bedroom to grab the blanket. Tabitha's laughter faded as she glanced toward Victoria, her smile faltering for just a moment. Something unspoken passed between them—something brittle, fragile.

As Will, Victoria, and Tabitha stepped out of the building, the evening air was thick with humidity and the low hum of the city. Jarvis sat in the driver's seat, one hand lazily flipping through radio stations, searching for a groove that matched his mood. Will slid into the passenger side, the familiar creak of the old car welcoming him.

"What'd y'all grab?" Tabitha asked, climbing into the back-seat alongside Victoria. She leaned forward, her sharp eyes locked on the crinkled brown bag perched in Will's lap.

Jarvis smirked, glancing at her in the rearview mirror. "Everything we need, baby. Got us some drinks, sandwiches, the works."

"You didn't get no pork, did you? You *know* I can't stand pork," Tabitha said, her hand already rummaging through the bag.

"Nah, nah, I got you, girl," Jarvis said, his voice dripping with mock sweetness. "Beef only, just like you like it." With a sly grin, he shifted the bag onto his lap. "Dig deeper, though. You might find somethin' special."

Tabitha rolled her eyes. "Oh, you got jokes." Her hand closed around the neck of a heavy glass bottle. "This the 'special'? Crushed beef?" she teased, holding it up for effect.

Before Jarvis could respond, she dropped the bottle back into the bag with a dull *thud*. Jarvis yelped, his entire body jolting forward. "Damn, girl! That ain't funny!" He sucked in a sharp breath, gripping the wheel with one hand and cradling himself with the other. "If y'all knew how this really felt—"

"Yeah, yeah, we'd still play with y'all like that," Tabitha shot back, biting back a grin.

In the backseat, Victoria barely reacted. She sat still, staring blankly out the window, the city's neon glow reflecting off her profile. Will twisted in his seat to look at her.

"What's up with you?" he asked, his voice quiet but probing.

"Nothing," Victoria replied, her gaze fixed on something far away. "Just thinking."

Will studied her for a moment, his eyes narrowing slightly, but said nothing. He turned back around, the quiet tension lingering like an unspoken word.

"Looks like traffic's already a mess," Jarvis muttered, his eyes scanning the clogged streets ahead. "We ain't beating it this year, folks." He suddenly yanked the wheel, cutting into a U-turn to snag an open parking spot. The car jerked, throwing Tabitha and Victoria toward the passenger side.

"See, this is why I'm gonna start wearing a seatbelt," Tabitha grumbled, straightening herself out. "Gonna kill us over a parking space, Jarvis. For real."

Jarvis caught her glare in the rearview mirror and grinned. "You should be wearing it anyway, baby. Don't you wanna live a long, happy life with me?"

"Absolutely not," Tabitha deadpanned, crossing her arms.

Jarvis chuckled as he shifted the car into park. "Alright, let's do this."

The Summer Fest grounds buzzed with life, a sea of Milwaukee residents drifting through the warm twilight. The smoky aroma of brats and barbecue hung heavy in the air, mingling with the faint tang of lake water. After a two-block trek, they found a shady spot near an old oak tree, its gnarled branches stretching skyward. The soft hum of distant music promised an evening worth remembering—or enduring.

Victoria helped Tabitha spread out a couple of blankets, the laughter and chatter of the crowd a dull murmur in her ears. She kept her movements measured, her gaze flicking now and then toward Will, who was busy scanning their surroundings. When the coast seemed clear, he produced a paper bag from his jacket, passing it to Jarvis. The men moved quickly, filling Styrofoam cups with liquid courage and a hint of recklessness.

Tabitha handed Victoria a cup, her smile tight, knowing what was coming. "Here you go, girl," she said, her tone light but expectant.

Victoria shook her head gently, stretching out on the blanket and tucking her legs beneath her. "I'm good, thanks."

Will's head snapped toward her, his eyes narrowing. "The hell you mean, 'you're good'? You were the one hyping up getting a drink all day. Now it's here, and you're acting brand new?" He strode over, snatching the cup back from Tabitha and filling it to the brim. His movements were sharp, deliberate. "Here," he said, thrusting it into Victoria's hand. "Drink."

The air seemed to thicken between them. Victoria's fingers tightened around the cup, her jaw clenching. She forced herself to take it without a word, the sour scent of the liquor hitting her nose like a slap.

Her stomach turned, but she pressed the rim to her lips, taking a small sip. The liquid burned as it lingered on her tongue, but she didn't swallow. Instead, she let it sit, let it sting, before she leaned back and exhaled slowly. She glanced at Will, who was already distracted, cracking jokes with Jarvis and Tabitha.

The minutes stretched. Each time Will looked her way, she raised the cup to her lips, careful, deliberate. The ground beneath the blanket became her ally, swallowing little streams of liquor as she poured it out in increments, her movements subtle and practiced.

Tabitha caught her eye at one point, her brows knitting in concern. Victoria shook her head slightly, the smallest of gestures, but it carried weight. Tabitha looked away, her lips pressed into a thin line, and turned back to the group, her laughter forced now, higher-pitched.

As the evening wore on, the mood around them seemed to swell and pulse with the rhythm of the festival. But Victoria felt the isolation creeping in, each drink she faked a wedge between her and the group. She could feel Will's gaze now and then, sharp and assessing, and she braced herself for the inevitable fallout. For now, though, she played her part, quiet but compliant, hoping the act would be enough to keep the peace.

The night was just beginning, but already, she was counting down the hours until she could leave. The weight of Will's expectations—and her own defiance—pressed down on her like the summer heat, stifling, suffocating.

She swallowed the feeling, just as she had the liquor, and waited.

(9:14 PM)

The night air was thick, clinging to their skin like a wet sheet. Tabitha had dozed off on Jarvis's lap, her soft snores barely audible over the distant hum of festival music. Jarvis leaned back, nursing the last swig of his drink, his eyes half-closed. Will was out cold nearby, sprawled awkwardly on the ground with his hoodie bunched under his head.

Victoria stood off to the side, leaning heavily against a tree, her arms crossed tight over her chest like she was bracing against a storm no one else could feel. Her breaths came shallow and quick, her chest rising and falling as she struggled with something unspoken. Sweat slicked her brow, her face pale under the string lights flickering overhead.

Then, without warning, she bolted to the far side of the tree and doubled over. The sound of retching cut through the soft chatter of nearby festivalgoers. Gasps and murmurs erupted from the family sitting just a few feet away.

"Really? Seriously?" the mother snapped, yanking her picnic blanket away from the growing stain of bile and grass. She gathered her things in a flurry, her face twisted in disgust as she ushered her kids away.

Victoria wiped at her mouth with trembling hands, her teary eyes darting around in embarrassment. When she looked up,

Tabitha was standing there, a paper towel stretched out like a peace offering. Her expression was soft, but her eyes carried a weight that made Victoria squirm.

"Mmm, so *that's* what's going on," Tabitha said, her voice low but edged with suspicion.

"I just drank too much, that's all," Victoria mumbled, avoiding her gaze.

Tabitha's eyebrows lifted. "Girl, the only thing drunk tonight is that patch of grass you've been pouring your drinks into. Don't play me—I saw you. You were in that bathroom forever, and now you're acting all shaky. What's the real story? Does your coochie have an inmate with a nine-month sentence, or what? Mtoto?"

Victoria's head shot up, her face twisting in disbelief. "What? Girl, what are you even talking about?"

Tabitha folded her arms, her mouth twitching in amusement. "Mtoto," she said matter-of-factly. "It means 'baby' in Swahili. You know I've been taking that class. But I'm guessing he doesn't know, does he?" She tilted her head toward Jarvis, her tone sharpened by something more than curiosity.

Victoria opened her mouth to protest, but no words came. Tabitha stepped closer, dabbing the corners of Victoria's mouth with the folded paper towel, her movements gentle but deliberate.

"By the way," Tabitha said with a small, knowing smirk, "I'm calling it now—I'm gonna be the godmother."

Victoria's eyes widened, her breath hitching as the weight of the night crashed down on her.

Monday morning brought a sharp chill to the air, but Tabitha didn't seem to notice. She leaned against her car, her favorite hip-hop track pounding through the speakers like an anthem of defiance. The bass thumped against the stillness of the apartment complex parking lot, each beat a call to action.

Inside, Victoria stood frozen for a moment, her hand hovering over her purse. She checked and rechecked its contents—ID, social security card, a stray tube of lip gloss. Her keys jangled nervously as she snatched them up.

"Where you going?" Will's voice cut through the quiet like a warning bell. He glanced at his phone, squinting at the time.

"Me and Tab are hitting the mall," Victoria replied, her tone light, almost too light.

"With what money? And since when?" His tone carried that sharp edge, the one that could turn a casual conversation into a landmine. He stood there, his phone dangling in one hand, his gaze pinning her in place.

"We just window shopping," she shot back, her words a hurried shield. "I'll be back."

Before he could say another word, she turned and slammed the door, the echo of it ricocheting down the hallway. Her feet barely touched the stairs as she sprinted toward the parking lot. The early morning air felt heavy, pressing down on her chest as she slid into Tabitha's car.

"Go, go, go!" she hissed, yanking the door shut and fumbling to turn the music down. "I think he's coming."

Tabitha didn't need to be told twice. She shifted into drive, her eyes flicking to the rearview mirror. "What'd you say to him?"

"I told him we were going to the mall, and he started grilling me," Victoria muttered, leaning back in her seat, her arms crossed tightly over her chest.

Tabitha shot her a sidelong glance. "You should've told him sooner, Vick. Let him deal with it."

Victoria shook her head, her lips pressed into a thin line. "I couldn't. You know how he is. I need to be sure first. I can't risk the drama until I know for real. What if this doctor says—" She stopped herself, biting her lip hard enough to sting.

Tabitha didn't push. Instead, she tapped the steering wheel nervously, her knuckles white against the leather. The tension in the car was almost tangible, the unspoken fears hanging between them like a fog.

The mall wasn't their destination, but the truth weighed heavier than either of them could admit aloud. Whatever the doctor said would change everything. And Victoria wasn't ready for Will—or anyone—to know what kind of storm might be brewing.

Later that afternoon, Victoria stepped through the front door, the tension in the air hitting her like a wall. Will was at the kitchen table, sandwich in hand, his jaw tight and eyes sharp with an anger that seemed to buzz in the silence. She didn't say a word, just kept walking, her heels clicking faintly on the hardwood floor as she made her way to the bedroom.

"Where you really been?" His voice cut through the quiet like a blade, low and sharp.

She froze for a moment but didn't turn around. "I told you already," she said, her tone steady, almost defiant.

"That's not where you were." His chair scraped back as he stood, the sound scraping at her nerves. "Don't lie to me. I saw y'all peel off. Saw her car go south. Ain't no mall that way. So where you been, huh?"

Victoria let out a slow breath and stepped into the bedroom, unbuckling her shoes. She moved with deliberate calm, slipping one off, then the other, placing them neatly in the closet. Her silence was a refusal, an answer in itself.

"You think I'm playing?" His footsteps closed the distance, his shadow falling over her. "You just not gonna answer me?"

She barely had time to brace before he grabbed her arm, yanking her to face him. Her breath hitched as she stumbled back, her hand gripping the doorframe for balance.

"Let go of me, Will," she said, her voice trembling but firm.

But he didn't let go. His grip tightened, his frustration boiling over. The air between them felt suffocating, filled with words unsaid, accusations unspoken.

Her knees buckled as she pulled herself away, her back hitting the edge of the bed. She curled in on herself instinctively, her arms wrapping around her stomach, shielding, protecting.

"Stop!" she shouted, her voice shaking, her eyes wide with both fear and something more—resolve.

Will's breath came fast, his fists clenched, his body rigid like a coiled spring. But her words stopped him in his tracks.

"I'm pregnant," she said, her voice breaking on the last word.

The room fell into a tense silence, her confession hanging between them like a heavy curtain. His chest heaved as he stared down at her, the anger in his eyes shifting to something else. Confusion. Shock.

CHAPTER 4

BAMBAM

March 26, 2001. (10:00 PM)

Lenny's Bar buzzed with its usual hum—laughter, slurred banter, and the occasional clink of glasses. Tru leaned against the bar, turning up the volume on the ancient TV bolted in the corner, drowning out Agnes's lively chatter with the regulars.

On the screen, a grim-faced newscaster delivered the kind of story that made everyone pause.

"A man dies on the south side of Milwaukee from an unknown condition. Doctors speculate it could be a rare form of cancer, though nothing has been confirmed. The man, whose name is not being released, was admitted to St. Luke's hospital last week with severe abdominal pain. He passed away yesterday. The autopsy revealed signs of an unusual cancer in his large intestines."

Tru shook his head and let out a low whistle as the broadcast continued.

"Doctors report the man also suffered from Myasthenia Gravis, a rare neuromuscular disorder affecting muscle strength. This condition impacts roughly seventy thousand Americans."

Tru tilted his glass, studying the amber liquid at the bottom before knocking it back in one smooth motion. "Man, I swear," he called out to the bartender, his voice cutting through the room's din, "when I got locked up, all anyone worried about was AIDS. Now it's all this new stuff—things you can't even spell, let alone understand." He set the empty glass down with a clink, shaking his head. "The world's on its last leg, for real."

The bartender, polishing a glass, smirked. "Ain't that the truth. You want another one?"

"Nah, I'm straight. Just waitin' on the little lady to quit flappin' her gums over there." Tru glanced toward the corner, where Agnes was animatedly talking to a couple. "I got an early morning."

He pushed off the bar and approached Agnes, his broad shoulders cutting through the crowded space like a ship through water. Resting his hands on her shoulders, he leaned in close, his deep voice low but firm. "You ready, baby?"

Agnes turned, a smile playing on her lips. "A couple more minutes, shuga. It's still early. You sure you wanna bounce?"

"Yeah, I gotta roll. You know how it is." He brushed a kiss across her cheek. "Meet me out front. I'll warm up the car."

The cold night air hit him like a slap as he stepped outside. He shoved his hands into his jacket pockets, fishing out a skully cap. Tugging it down snug, he lit a cigar, the orange ember flaring against the darkness. He popped his jacket collar against the chill and took a long pull before heading toward the car parked in the shadowed alley.

The street was eerily quiet, the kind of silence that made the hairs on your neck stand up. Tru's heavy boots echoed off the brick walls as he walked, each step deliberate. His breath fogged in the cold as he reached the car, fishing the keys from his pocket.

Something shifted in the shadows. Tru froze, his senses prickling, every instinct screaming for him to be on guard. He turned, scanning the dimly lit alley, but it looked empty. Shaking it off, he unlocked the door and slid into the driver's seat.

Victoria shuffled through the fluorescent-lit aisles, wishing more than anything to be curled up in her bed instead of navigating this late-night grocery run. Her petite frame carried the unmistakable weight of a ninth-month belly—large, round, and commanding every ounce of her balance and patience.

The baby inside her, an apparent insomniac, flipped and tumbled like a gymnast every evening. Sleep? Forget about it. The only thing that seemed to calm the little daredevil was food. Real food. Doctor's orders about her sudden weight gain flickered in her mind briefly, but the man wasn't the one lying awake all night feeling like his insides were training for the Olympics. If her boy didn't eat, he'd make sure she felt it, and not in a gentle way.

Leaning over her cart, its handle snug against her belly, she rummaged through her purse for coupons. Her bag sat perfectly atop her baby bump—a handy, albeit temporary, side effect of pregnancy.

"Now where did I put those—" she mumbled, her voice trailing off as she noticed her cart sliding a few feet away. Her brow furrowed. Did she nudge it by mistake? With an annoyed sigh, she waddled after it and pulled it back into position.

At the checkout line, she pressed her belly against the cart handle again, half-focused on a display of candy bars. Her fingers hovered over a chocolate wrapper when a sharp voice cut through her thoughts.

"Excuse me!"

Victoria blinked, glancing up to see a woman in front of her turning with an exasperated look.

"What?" Victoria shot back, her tone defensive but confused. She shrugged and went back to the display.

"Ma'am", please. Do you *mind?*"

Victoria raised an eyebrow and looked down. Her cart had rolled forward again—this time bumping against the woman's rear. Mortified, she gasped, but then froze. She stared as the handle nudged forward on its own, a distinct *push* coming from her belly.

No way.

The baby kicked again, this time a solid jab, strong enough to make the cart move. Victoria slapped a hand over her stomach, feeling another defiant thump beneath her palm. A laugh bubbled out of her, unbidden and soft, as she realized what had happened.

"Oh, so that's how it is?" she whispered, rubbing the spot where his tiny foot had made contact. "My little Hercules, huh? Momma's strong little man."

The woman ahead of her huffed and adjusted her purse, clearly unimpressed with Victoria's revelation. But Victoria didn't care. She stood there, one hand steadying the cart and the other soothing her active little troublemaker, grinning through the chaos of late-night shopping and a restless baby determined to remind her who was boss.

"Damn! I done ran my mouth so much I forgot the time!" Agnes exclaimed, glancing at her phone. Tru had told her to meet him outside the bar nearly thirty minutes ago. She fumbled through her purse, tossing a few bills on the counter to cover her tab.

The bartender gave a knowing smirk to the couple seated nearby, who exchanged relieved looks as Agnes prepared to leave.

"Here you go, baby. Keep the change," she said, sliding the money across the counter. "I gotta make sure my man ain't left me stranded out here." She cast a quick glance out the window, frowning when she didn't see her car out front, warm, running, and waiting. "You didn't see him come back in here, did you?" she asked the bartender.

He leaned on the counter, shaking his head. "Nah, I keep track of who comes in and out. Trust me, I'd notice his big ass coming back through here."

Agnes chuckled, though her worry lingered. "Alright then. It was nice chattin' with y'all." She slung her rabbit-fur coat over her shoulders, clutching her matching purse as she stepped into the biting cold.

Outside, the air stung her cheeks as she scanned the block. The car was still there, parked exactly where she'd left it, but the engine wasn't running. She muttered under her breath, wobbling down the sidewalk in her heels. "Damn, Tru. Couldn't even warm the car up? Lazy ass."

The tinted windows, dark as midnight, made it impossible to see inside. Squinting, she cupped her hands to the windshield, trying to peer through. Tru's outline was faintly visible in the driver's seat, his broad shoulders slumped forward.

"Tru! Wake up, fool! It's freezing!" Agnes banged on the glass, her irritation mounting. Fishing in her purse, she pulled out a spare key. "Move over, big man. You ain't driving like this."

She unlocked the door, the hinges groaning as she opened it. The smell hit her first—metallic, thick, and wrong. She froze, her breath caught in her throat.

"Tru?" she whispered, leaning closer. Her hand touched his shoulder, stiff and unyielding. His head lolled to the side, revealing a dark crimson stain spread across his chest. His shirt clung to his body, soaked through. She gasped, stumbling backward as the sight fully registered: his throat was slashed, the gash wide and jagged. The half-burned cigar he'd been smoking had fallen onto his jeans, leaving an acrid scorch mark and a small, smoldering hole.

"Baby... no. No, no, no!" Agnes's voice cracked as panic overwhelmed her. She grabbed at his coat, shaking him desperately, but he didn't stir. Her knees buckled, and she collapsed onto the pavement, her hands trembling as they pressed against the cold ground.

Her screams tore through the quiet street, sharp and raw. Faces began to appear at the edges of the alley, drawn by the commotion. Whispers floated in the air, but Agnes couldn't hear them over the pounding in her ears.

She looked up, tears blurring her vision. The world felt colder, darker, and utterly unforgiving. The only thing louder than her cries was the dreadful silence from the man she loved.

The quiet of the night enveloped Victoria like a fragile cocoon. She sat in the dark at the dining table, the remnants of her midnight snack scattered before her. Resting a protective hand on her rounded belly, she hummed softly, the melody a lullaby for both herself and the baby. Her eyes began to flutter shut, the day's weariness pulling her under.

The sudden snap of a light switch shattered the peace.

"What are you doing?" Will's voice was sharp, cutting through the stillness.

Victoria blinked against the harsh glare, her hand instinctively tightening on her belly. "Just... just sitting here. Humming to the baby. I didn't mean to wake you."

Will leaned against the doorway, his tone hardening. "Well, I _am_ used to you being in bed next to me. So it's kinda hard to sleep when you ain't there. What're you eating, anyway?"

Her words came out haltingly. "I... I went to the store earlier, but I ended up finishing the fish instead. I've been craving meat."

The shift in his demeanor was instant. His brows furrowed, jaw tightening. "Aw, *hell—naw*...you ate my fish? I was saving that for work tomorrow—damn it!" He moved to the refrigerator, yanking the door open. "Damn it, Vic! I was saving that for work tomorrow!"

The refrigerator door slammed shut with a jarring clang. The baby shifted under Victoria's hand, pulling away as if sensing the tension.

Will's voice rose, the anger spilling over. "I don't get any respect in this house. I can't have shit for myself!"

The table jolted suddenly, the sound of wood scraping against wood reverberating through the room. The ornate vase in the center wobbled precariously.

Victoria's hands flew to her belly, shielding it instinctively.

Will spun to face her, his eyes dark and piercing. "I know you not pounding that table at me bitch. I'll still come over there and smack the shit out of you—pregnant or not! It's been a while since I have."

"I swear to God I wasn't, baby. My knee hit the table. I'm sorry." she stammered, her voice trembling. She rubbed her leg in mock pain, her breath quick and uneven.

He stared at her for a long moment, then scoffed, turning toward the bedroom. "Yeah. Well, I'm going back to bed. Now I have to get up early and figure out what I'm gonna eat tomorrow." His grumbling faded as he disappeared down the hall.

Victoria exhaled shakily. Her hand trembled as she rubbed the small bump on her belly, wincing at the tender bruise forming beneath her fingertips. "It's okay, baby," she whispered. "Shh... Momma's okay. You don't like Daddy's yelling, do you?"

Victoria's phone buzzed sharply against the table, the sound slicing through the quiet hum of the evening. Will froze mid-step in the hallway, his ears pricking instinctively. She glanced at the screen, her face lighting up briefly as she answered.

"Hey, Momma!" Her voice carried a casual warmth, but it quickly shifted as silence greeted her. She could hear the uneven rhythm of sniffling, the strained gasps for breath.

"Momma? What's wrong?" Her tone sharpened, a thread of unease unraveling in her chest.

"—Yo Daddy," Agnes choked out, her words fractured by sobs.

"What about Daddy? What happened?"

She took a hesitant step forward, her gaze drawn down the hallway where Will disappeared behind the bedroom door. Agnes's words came then, raw and shattering.

"Your daddy... he's gone, baby. He's—he's dead."

The phone slipped from her trembling fingers, landing with a dull thud on the floor. A sharp gasp escaped her lips as her knees buckled, her arms wrapping protectively around her stomach. She sank to the ground, her breath caught somewhere between a sob and a scream.

The phone lay face up, the call still connected. On the other end, Agnes's quiet sobs continued, a painful echo of the moment's grim reality.

"My baby... where's my baby!" Victoria's scream ripped through the quiet room, jolting Will from his sleep.

He sat up abruptly, his hand instinctively reaching for her shoulder. "Vee, calm the hell down!" he snapped, though his voice softened at the end, like he was trying to convince himself more than her.

Victoria's hands trembled as she tried to rip the IV from her arm, her voice shaking with desperation. "I need to see him, Will! I need to see my son!" Her body lurched forward, and her legs gave way the second she tried to stand.

Will caught her before she hit the floor, his grip firm and a little too tight as he hauled her back onto the bed. "What the hell are you doin'? You can't just get up like that!" He shoved the sheets over her legs, pressing her into the mattress as if he could keep her there by force of will alone.

"Don't tell me to calm down!" Victoria spat, her voice raw. "You don't understand—"

"I said it's cool!" Will cut her off, leaning in close, his tone a mix of annoyance and something darker. "The nurses got the baby. He's fine. Heavy as a goddamn rock, but fine. Now stop freakin' out before you rip somethin' else open." He stabbed the emergency button on the remote, his movements sharp, impatient.

The nurse entered without a word, her expression neutral as she began checking Victoria's vitals.

Victoria stared at her, her anger barely contained. "Hello? Can you at least say something?"

The nurse glanced up, startled. "Oh, I'm sorry. My name is Jackie. I'm just taking your vitals."

"I don't care about that," Victoria snapped. "Where is my baby?"

Jackie paused, her hands hesitating over the monitor. "The baby is fine, ma'am. You'll see him soon. The doctor had to perform a Cesarean because he was... well, let's just say he was in a hurry to meet the world. Big guy, too—set a hospital record at twenty-eight pounds, five ounces." She forced a nervous laugh, clearly trying to lighten the mood.

Victoria's eyes narrowed. "Can I *see* him now?"

Jackie nodded quickly. "As soon as the doctor comes in to speak with you. He'll explain everything. Shouldn't be more than thirty minutes." She ducked out of the room before Victoria could say another word.

Victoria sank back against the pillows, her chest heaving as she fought to keep the tears at bay. Frustration and exhaustion weighed on her like a heavy fog, pressing down until she closed her eyes, letting the darkness pull her under again.

When she woke, the light in the room had shifted. Will sat in the corner, slouched in the recliner, absently flipping through channels on the oversized hospital remote. The faint hum of the TV filled the silence, but it did little to mask the tension that hung thick between them.

"You didn't wake me," she murmured, her voice hoarse.

Will glanced at her, his face unreadable. "You needed rest," he said, his tone flat, distant.

Victoria's jaw tightened, but she didn't push. Not yet. She stared at the ceiling, her mind racing with questions she wasn't sure she wanted the answers to. The air between them crackled with unspoken words, and for a moment, she wondered if the baby's cry—when she finally heard it—would be enough to break the silence.

"Where your phone at? You heard from my momma?" Victoria asked, her voice sharp with just a hint of tiredness.

Will barely glanced her way, eyes fixed on the TV. "Yeah, she came by earlier. Said she was gonna see the baby, then left. Ain't been back in a while, so I figure she gone. Mentioned she was hungry, though—probably downstairs eatin' that sorry-ass cafeteria food."

Victoria sighed, already irritated. "Well, can I call her with your phone?"

Will waved a hand toward the other side of the bed. "Why you need my phone? Yours right there."

She grabbed her phone, jaw tightening. A missed call and a couple of picture messages from her mom flashed on the screen, but she didn't open them. Probably baby pictures. She shoved the phone back down with a frustrated flick of her wrist.

Before she could say anything else, the door swung open. "Good morning!" the doctor announced cheerily, stepping in like he was about to brighten someone's day.

Nobody responded.

The doctor, a short, white-haired man with an odd brace on his finger, didn't seem to notice the silence. He moved toward the bed, the faint squeak of his shoes—the only sound besides the TV. "When can I see my baby?" Victoria asked, her eyes trailing him suspiciously.

The doctor stopped beside her bed, his smile not faltering as he rested his braced hand carefully on the edge. "Well... as soon as we finish our chat, I'll have the nurse bring him in."

"Why do y'all keep sayin' 'big guy' and 'heavy' like something wrong with him?" Her tone was sharp now, her unease rising.

Will stood suddenly, muttering, "Gonna use the bathroom," before ducking out the door. The way he avoided her eyes made her stomach twist.

The doctor's expression softened. "Ms. Strong, I just have a few questions for my records. Nothing to worry about—your son is healthy and very strong. I just have some... concerns."

Victoria narrowed her eyes. "Concerns? Like what?"

The doctor hesitated, flipping open a folder. "First, let me say I'm sorry for your loss. I understand your father passed, and that's... incredibly difficult, especially today."

She blinked quickly, looking down. "Thank you."

The doctor cleared his throat. "Second, your son has a rare condition called Myostatin deficiency. It's very uncommon and causes significant muscle growth. But... your son's case is unprecedented. I've never seen muscles this dense in a newborn."

Her heart dropped. "Oh my God. My baby's deformed?" Tears welled up, her voice rising in panic. "Just tell me!"

"Ms. Strong, I promise, he looks like any other baby." The doctor leaned forward, his voice low, almost reverent. "But he's not like any other baby."

Victoria stared at him, confused and on edge. "What the hell you mean by that?"

The doctor raised his braced finger. "This? This is from him. Your son fractured and dislocated my finger when I tested his grip. His strength is extraordinary."

Victoria blinked, her tears forgotten for a moment. "You sayin' my baby broke your finger?"

The doctor nodded, smiling faintly. "The nurses have been calling him Bam Bam. Like from *The Flintstones*. He's a special boy."

Before she could respond, the door opened again. A nurse rolled in a baby cart, her face lit up with quiet admiration. "Here's your little guy, Ms. Strong," she said, carefully lifting the swaddled baby and placing him in Victoria's arms.

Victoria's breath hitched as she held him. His tiny hands curled into fists, his cheeks impossibly smooth. "My baby. My little William Strong," she whispered, brushing his cheek with her trembling finger before pressing a kiss to his forehead.

The doctor chuckled, flexing his injured finger. "Strong is right. That's a name he'll live up to, no doubt."

CHAPTER 5

Momma's Boy

June 2007

Six-year-old William Strong sat cross-legged on the living room floor, his Hulk action figure propped snugly between his little legs, staring wide-eyed at the TV. Around him lay the carnage of a plastic battlefield—broken action figures from every cartoon and movie imaginable, each victim of Hulk's imagined wrath, wielded by William's small but determined hands. His jaw hung open as he absorbed every detail of his favorite Saturday morning cartoon.

"Whoooa! Momma, lookit! Momma, come in here, lookit!" His voice shot out, brimming with awe.

From the kitchen, Victoria, elbow-deep in her morning routine, glanced toward the living room doorway. "Baby, Momma's on the phone! I can't watch that right now!" she hollered back, temporarily halting her conversation with her mother. Her focus shifted between flipping pancakes and the steady sizzle of bacon in the pan.

The cartoon switched to a commercial, and William sprang up, clutching his Hulk figure tightly. He dashed into the kitchen, excitement bubbling over.

"Momma, he was like *BAM!* ... *BOOM!* ... and then he did this—UGGGHHH!" He twisted the action figure's arms, reenacting Hulk's latest destructive rampage with dramatic flair.

"Uh-huh, baby," Victoria replied, balancing the phone against her shoulder while cracking another egg into the pan. "Go finish watching so I can finish cooking your food."

"Okay! But can I watch a movie if I eat all my food?" William asked, letting Hulk "jump" from the refrigerator handle to the microwave, then onto the tile floor with an exaggerated crash.

Victoria exhaled a quick laugh, rolling her eyes upward. "Let me guess... the Hulk movie? Again?"

"YEP!" he shouted, bouncing on the balls of his feet, his energy barely contained.

She shook her head with a half-smile. "I guess so, baby."

"Yes! I'm gonna eat *all* my food. Watch!" With that, he bolted back to the living room, his little feet slapping against the floor. The commercial had barely ended when he reclaimed his spot on the floor, already preparing Hulk for the next scene of destruction.

Will Sr. had picked up extra hours again, leaving Victoria and six-year-old William with the house to themselves most of the day. His recent promotion to manager had been a blessing, but it came with its own set of pressures—like renting a two-bedroom from Ms. Flannigan, who'd tacked on an extra eighty bucks a month for good measure.

"Sweetheart, Momma's just running downstairs to grab the mail. Stay put, okay?" Victoria called out as she hung up the phone. Her voice carried a practiced calm, though her thoughts were a tangled mess.

"K," William mumbled, eyes locked on the TV as his Hulk toy slammed into a plastic enemy.

Victoria grabbed her coat, her movements quick and purposeful, the kind of energy that comes from juggling too much. The cool air of the hallway was a brief reprieve, but it didn't last long. On her way back, flipping through overdue bills, she heard it—the telltale jingle of Ms. Flannigan's massive key ring echoing up the stairs. Victoria's stomach tightened. She quickened her pace, hoping to slip inside unnoticed, but it was too late.

"Well, well, Ms. Lady," came the familiar, singsong sarcasm. "How you doing today?"

Victoria turned slowly, forcing a tight smile that didn't reach her eyes. "Heeey, Ms. Flannigan. I'm good, how are you?" Her voice was sugary, but the undercurrent of tension was hard to mask.

"Oh, I'd be doing much better if my tenants paid their rent on time," Flannigan shot back, her tone cutting. She let the words hang in the air like a challenge.

Inside the apartment, William had grown bored with his show. Hulk was mid-smash when the sound of his mother's strained voice caught his attention. He crept closer to the door, his small frame blending into the shadows as he listened.

"I know, Ms. Flannigan," Victoria began, shifting the stack of envelopes from one hand to the other. "We just need a little more time. Will's been pulling extra shifts, and I promise, by the end of the week, you'll have it."

Flannigan tilted her head, her expression a mix of mock sympathy and thinly veiled annoyance. "Uh-huh. And what about next month, baby? You think this little overtime miracle is gonna cover you then?" She leaned in slightly, the keys jingling ominously in her hand like a warning bell.

Victoria's smile faltered. She glanced down at the mail in her hand, each envelope a reminder of just how far behind they were. Flannigan's words were harsh, but the truth they carried cut deeper than anything else.

William pressed his ear against the door, his small heart pounding. He didn't understand everything they were saying, but he could tell his mom was upset. He clutched Hulk tighter, wishing his favorite hero could do something to help.

"Well," Flannigan said, stepping back with a dramatic sigh. "First of the month is coming, Ms. Lady. Don't let me catch you slipping again." She walked off, the clinking of her keys fading with each step down the hall.

Victoria stood frozen for a moment, the weight of it all pressing down on her chest. She exhaled sharply, willing herself to hold it together as she unlocked the door and stepped inside.

William darted from the door back to his corner, pretending to rummage through the scattered blocks and action figures as if he'd been there all along. He kept his head low but watched out of the corner of his eye as Victoria stormed into the kitchen, tossing the stack of envelopes onto the counter with more force than she probably realized. Tears streamed down her face, smudging her makeup, but she didn't wipe them away.

She stood there for a moment, hands gripping the counter's edge, her shoulders trembling. Finally, she slumped into the chair, grabbed a pen, and started scrawling numbers onto a crumpled receipt. Her voice broke the quiet, raw and tired.

"I don't know how we're supposed to do this," she muttered to herself, her words heavy with defeat. "Every time I turn around, there's another damn bill. Faster than we can even breathe."

The sound of metal clinking down the hallway pulled her out of her thoughts. Little feet padded closer, and then, from the corner of her teary vision, a small, scuffed football-shaped piggy bank was hoisted onto the table. Coins rattled inside as it landed with a dull thud.

Victoria looked up, startled, to see William peeking just over the edge of the table. His wide eyes were serious, his lips pressed together like he was mimicking how grown-ups handled stress.

Her heart twisted. She reached for the bank and smiled weakly. "Oh, baby... my special little man." Her voice cracked, but she tried to steady it. "Thank you so much. But Momma can't take your money, sweetie. That's yours."

"But you're cryin', Momma," he said, his small voice fierce, like he was ready to take on the whole world if it meant making her smile again. "I don't need it. You need it."

Victoria closed her eyes, swallowing the lump in her throat. "You've helped me more than you know," she said, gently prying the bank open. She scooped out the mismatched coins and a few crumpled dollar bills, not because she needed the money, but because she needed to honor his gesture. "Thank you, baby. You're so good to Momma."

"Okay," he said, his chest puffing out. "Let me know if you need more, alright?"

She watched him march back to his room with all the determination of a little soldier, the weight of their struggles oblivious to him. Victoria sat back, staring at the loose change in her palm. It wasn't about the money. It was about what it meant.

A fresh wave of tears came, but this time, she let them fall. She'd figure it out somehow. She had to—for him.

Will pushed open the front door, his face lined with exhaustion from another long day. The weight of the world—or at least their bills—seemed to hit him before he even set his lunch bag on the counter. Victoria was already seated at the kitchen table, her arms folded over a sea of overdue notices, her eyes sharp and unwavering.

"Damnit, Vee," Will snapped, pulling a pack of M&Ms from his bag, the colorful candies rattling as he tore them open. "Can't I come home without hearing about what ain't paid? Let me get through the damn door before you start in. We can only do what we can do!"

Victoria didn't flinch, her voice steady but tired. "I can see if Tabby will watch our son so I can pick up a part-time job. At least that'll ease some of this."

Will shook his head, his jaw tightening. "I ain't trying to hear nothing about you working. We got enough problems without worrying about a damn babysitter. Once this new position pays out, we'll be alright. Just wait."

Her voice cut through his like a blade. "Wait? Will, I'm the one here, fielding the calls, dealing with Hell Hound stomping the hallways cause we owe her rent. We need the money. I need to work."

Their son, a quiet observer, was already gathering his toys. As if rehearsed, he disappeared into his room, shutting the door behind him. It wasn't fear—it was understanding. He knew the signs.

Will's body stiffened, his M&Ms forgotten on the counter. He leaned forward, his hand shooting out to the table, fingers splayed in warning. "I *know* you're not raising your voice at me right now, Vee."

Victoria sat straighter, but her eyes flickered briefly toward their son's door. "You're not listening to me—"

"Don't." Will's voice dropped, the air between them heavy.

Behind the thin door, William perched on his bed, headphones clamped tightly over his ears. He hit play on his favorite soundtrack—*The Lion King*. The swelling notes of "Circle of Life" drowned out the muffled tension from the other side. Or at least, they tried.

The sound of a dish breaking punctured the music, followed by the sharp fleshy crack of something unmistakable. William froze, his action figure limp in his hand. His chest tightened, but he cranked the volume up until Elton John's voice surged into his ears, drowning the chaos. He closed his eyes and rocked slightly, clinging to the illusion of safety that the music offered.

This wasn't new. He knew the pattern. The argument would burn hot, flaring like a wildfire, until the house fell silent again. But the silence was the worst part—it always came with consequences.

The hum of the tires filled the car, low and steady, as William stared at the grimy floorboard. His small fingers worked busily, picking through bits of trash—candy wrappers, a crumpled receipt, and the odd scraps that seemed to multiply in old vehicles like this. His mother's warning echoed in his head: *Stay buckled. Don't mess around near that hole.* But the ragged opening, big enough to swallow a soccer ball, drew his curiosity like a magnet. He watched the asphalt blur beneath it, alive and moving, and couldn't resist. An old kids' meal toy—a faded, limp plastic figure, became his experiment. He dropped it through the hole and craned his neck to watch it tumble and bounce from the back window, finally crushed under the wheel of the car behind them.

A small smile tugged at the corner of his lips, but he said nothing.

"Alright, baby, let's go," Victoria said as she eased the car into a parking spot in front of the doctor's office. She tilted the rearview mirror, smoothing her frazzled hair and adjusting her oversized bumblebee sunglasses. They did more than block the sunlight.

William hopped out first, skipping to catch up as Victoria shut the door behind her. Inside, the building was still, the soft hum of elevator music barely filling the sterile air.

"Good morning, Mrs. Strong," the receptionist greeted brightly as they approached the desk. Her eyes shifted briefly to

William, whose shy smile emerged as if on cue. "And how's my favorite little Strong man?"

"Goooood," William replied, voice small but warm.

"Here for his check-up?" The receptionist turned her attention to Victoria, her friendly tone unwavering.

"Yes, 7:30," Victoria answered, glancing at the clock. The waiting room yawned before them, empty and hushed, save for the faint click of keyboards from the office behind the desk. "Looks like we the first ones here."

The receptionist nodded. "Most folks come in later, so you've got the place to yourselves for a bit." Her gaze shifted, inadvertently catching the angle of Victoria's face under the shades. A flicker of recognition crossed her features—too quick to linger but impossible to ignore. "Go ahead and take a seat. Someone will call you in shortly."

Victoria's lips pressed into a thin line as she nodded, moving toward a corner seat as William lagged behind. He was already drawn to the neatly arranged toys in a bin against the wall, untouched and gleaming as if waiting just for him.

From the elevator, the metallic clatter of a snack dolly broke the silence. A stocky man maneuvered the cart toward the vending machines, humming faintly to himself. The crinkle of plastic and the clink of cans echoed across the room.

"Momma, can I have something?" William asked, his eyes darting toward the man with the snacks. His voice was hopeful but not demanding.

Victoria barely lifted her head from the wall where she had leaned back, her shoulders heavy with exhaustion. "No, baby. Not now," she said softly. "We don't have the money for that."

William didn't push further.

Victoria sighed, pulling her sunglasses tighter against her face as if the tinted lenses could shield her from more than just the morning light. But the ache of that bruise throbbed behind her eye, sharp and unyielding, a reminder of things she couldn't erase.

William sat on the play area floor, his small hands clutching his Hulk figure and matching backpack. His wide eyes followed the man refilling the vending machines, a parade of boxes coming and going with every trip to the elevator. As the doors finally slid shut behind the worker, William's gaze shifted to his mother slumped in the corner, arms crossed, mouth slack. He tilted his head, waiting for some sign of life, but she was deep in the kind of sleep that came with too much worry and not enough rest.

With a glance back at the now-unattended machines, William stood, his little sneakers squeaking against the tiled floor. The vending machines loomed like glassy skyscrapers, each one stuffed with treasures he'd only dreamed of holding in his hands. He swung his Hulk toy absentmindedly as he imagined the taste of the candies, the crunch of the chips. One careless flick of his wrist, though, and Hulk went flying, skittering across the floor before vanishing beneath the largest machine.

William dropped to his knees, peering under the machine. Dirt, crumpled receipts, and forgotten scraps cluttered the dark space, but there, near the back, was his toy. Stretching his small arms as far as they'd go, he clawed at the floor, his fingertips just brushing the edge of the figure. Close, but not close enough.

Frustration bubbled up, tightening his chest. He clenched his jaw, his baby teeth grinding audibly, and wrapped his hands around the edges of the vending machine. He wasn't about to leave without his Hulk. With all his strength, he yanked at the metal beast. It didn't budge. Undeterred, he tugged again, harder this time. The room filled with the groans of twisting metal and the sharp pops of bolts giving way. Still, his mother didn't stir, her exhaustion shielding her from the chaos unfolding a few feet away.

Finally, with a screech and a jarring metallic *pop*, the machine's heavy door swung open. William froze, blinking in disbelief at the glistening bounty inside. The rows of candy bars, chips, and sodas seemed to shimmer under the fluorescent lights like treasure in a pirate's chest. For a moment, he simply stared, wide-eyed. Then hunger and opportunity overtook him.

He reached for a Snickers bar, tearing the wrapper with feral enthusiasm and devouring it in messy bites. The chocolate smeared across his face, he cast a cautious glance at his mother, still fast asleep in her chair. Emboldened, he slipped off his backpack and began stuffing it with candy, his small hands working quickly and efficiently. But as his eyes wandered deeper into the machine, something caught his attention—something far more valuable than sugar.

"Whoa," he whispered to himself, his voice barely audible over the pounding of his heartbeat. "Look at all dat money."

His tiny fingers trembled as he pulled out rolls of bills and handfuls of coins, marveling at the weight of the currency. His mind raced, filling with half-formed thoughts and wishes. If he gave this to Momma, maybe Daddy wouldn't be so mad. Maybe the yelling and the hitting would stop. Maybe they could all be happy again.

Determined, he stuffed the money into his backpack, his resolve growing with each roll of cash. When one machine was empty, he moved to the next, prying it open with the same ferocity. The doors groaned in protest, but they gave way, spilling their contents to the mercy of his small but persistent hands.

By the time he was finished, the backpack was bulging. William zipped it up carefully, giving it a satisfied pat before turning his attention back to Hulk. Grabbing a broom propped against the wall, he jabbed at the toy, finally knocking it free. He clutched it tightly, relief washing over him like a warm blanket.

"William Strong? William Strong?" The nurse's voice echoed through the room.

William hurried to his mother, nudging her gently. With a startled snort, she jerked awake, her eyes darting around in confusion. She looked at her son, his face smeared with chocolate, his feet swinging innocently as he perched on the chair beside her.

"Ready, Momma?" he asked, his voice sweet and guileless. She blinked at him, her grogginess masking the storm he'd just unleashed. Smiling back, she rose, completely unaware of the weight of his backpack or the secrets it now carried.

Saturday, June 16, 2007

The air was thick with the smell of charred ribs and lighter fluid, laughter spilling out from every corner of Jarvis' backyard. Will's promotion to manager had everyone in good spirits, clinking bottles and swapping stories under the blazing summer sun. But William had carved out his own world at the edge of the celebration—a small table near the garage where his action figures were meticulously arranged.

Candy wrappers crinkled in his pocket as he adjusted his Main Man figure to stand guard over the rest. The Hulk was ready to smash anyone who dared cross him.

"Wow, you got a lot of toys! Can I play too?"

The voice startled him, and he whipped around, his eyes landing on a little girl. She couldn't have been older than six. Her black hair was braided back, clear beads catching the sunlight like tiny stars. Her smooth caramel skin glowed, and her hazel-green eyes locked onto his, warm and curious. She smelled faintly of something sweet—Barbie Doll perfume, maybe—and William froze, his mouth half-open, the sticky edge of a Jolly Rancher clinging to his lip.

"Can I play too?" she asked again, holding up a bag of Barbies like an offering.

"Uh... umm... yeah, okay," William stammered, snapping out of his daze. He shifted awkwardly to make room at the table. "Just don't mess up my stuff, 'kay?"

She grinned, the kind of smile that made him feel weirdly like he'd done something right. Leaning over, she reached for the Hulk, her small hand brushing his arm.

"Who's this?" she asked, curiosity lighting up her face.

"Hey!" William yelped, snatching the figure away so fast she blinked in surprise. "You can touch any of these—any of 'em—but not him. Got it?"

Her eyebrows shot up, and for a moment, William thought she might cry or storm off, but instead, she shrugged. "I wasn't gonna break it or nothing," she said, dumping her Barbies unceremoniously onto the grass. "You can play with mine if you want."

The small, colorful plastic world she emptied into the grass stood in stark contrast to his lineup of warriors. She was different, alright, but William didn't hate it. Still clutching the Hulk protectively, he eyed her collection. Some of the dolls were missing shoes, their hair tangled and stiff from too many backyard adventures.

"I don't play with Barbies," he muttered.

William couldn't take his eyes off her. Isabella sat cross-legged, meticulously arranging her collection of action figures and their tiny accessories. The afternoon light made her seem ethereal, like a little angel who'd wandered into the backyard. Her quiet focus was comforting—until it wasn't.

SMACK!

The sharp sting from a red tether ball exploded across William's cheek, and his candy—bright green and sticky—went flying into the grass. The world tilted for a moment. He staggered, pressing his hand to his face as laughter erupted nearby, growing louder with every second.

"Damn, my bad, little dude!" came a voice, thick with mockery. "Didn't mean to interrupt you and your girlfriend playin' house with your dolls."

William blinked hard and focused on the figure looming above him. Lamont Fields, a big seven-year-old who always seemed to have two shadows—his smaller, scrawny sidekicks. Lamont held the red tetherball, spinning it lazily in his hands as his pudgy cheeks lifted into a mean grin.

"They're not dolls," William said, straightening and fixing the toppled lineup. "They're action figures."

"Oh, yeah?" Lamont stepped closer, crowding William. "They look like dolls to me." His grin widened. "Watch this."

Before William could stop him, Lamont hurled the ball. It smashed through the table, scattering the carefully arranged figures. His favorite one, the Hulk, skidded into a muddy puddle by the garage. The impact chipped the green paint from its bicep revealing the pale plastic beneath.

William froze, staring at the ruined toy. Heat climbed up his neck as his fists clenched. That was his favorite one. His best one. The anger came fast and hot, threatening to burst out of him. He took a step toward Lamont, jaw tight, but a small hand grabbed his wrist.

Isabella.

Her touch was light, but it stopped him cold. When he looked at her, she wasn't looking back—her eyes were fixed on something distant, something behind him, or maybe inside him. And then she let go, pulling her hand away as if she'd touched a flame. The expression on her face wasn't fear. It was something worse.

"Yeah, what were you gonna do?" Lamont sneered, stepping forward. "Your little girlfriend saved your ass from gett'n whooped."

"She's not my girlfriend!" William shot back, his voice cracking. He darted over to the puddle, snatching up his action figure and wiping it off with his sleeve. His hands trembled as he worked, trying to clean the mud from its face. The toy seemed ruined.

Lamont snickered, leaning down to whisper to one of his friends. The two boys exchanged glances and nodded, their grins matching Lamont's.

"Aight, my bad," Lamont said, his tone fake-sincere. "Listen, me and the guys wanna play hide and seek. It's boring with just us three. Y'all wanna join?"

"No," Isabella said firmly, her voice sharp and clear for the first time.

Lamont's grin turned sly. "Oh, she speaks for you now too? Dang. Guess you don't do nothin' without her permission, huh?" His friends laughed on cue. "C'mon, it's just a game. If you don't like it, you can go back to playin' Barbies."

William hesitated. He could feel Isabella's eyes on him, hear the warning in her silence. But he also knew Lamont wasn't going to leave them alone. Not now.

"Fine," William said, his voice low. "We'll play."

Lamont's grin widened, and he tossed the ball into the air. "That's what I thought. I'll be 'it,' since I'm the best at finding people anyway."

Lamont turned toward the big oak tree, covering his eyes as he started counting. William and Isabella followed the boys, her footsteps slow and reluctant. The air felt heavier now, charged with something William couldn't name but knew he didn't like.

"One Mississippi, two Mississippi, three..." Lamont's voice echoed in the yard. William glanced at Isabella, hoping for reassurance, but her face was pale, her eyes distant again. She gripped her arm like she was holding herself together.

And for the first time, William wondered if playing along was the worst mistake he could make.

The kids scattered like startled pigeons, darting for hiding spots in the garage. Isabella ducked under a table in the far corner, curling up tight against the wall. Another boy darted to the opposite side and yanked an old chair in front of him, his breathing quick and shallow. The best hiding spot—the battered metal locker with colorful magnets clinging to its surface—caught the eye of one boy, who hesitated, cracked the door open, and then abandoned the idea. William didn't hesitate; he sprinted for the locker, shoving aside greasy rags before squeezing himself inside and pulling the heavy metal doors shut.

"Ready or not, here I come!" Lamont's voice rang out, smug and threatening.

Moments later, he appeared with one of his cronies in tow, the sidekick pointing eagerly toward the locker. Their giggles were muffled but distinct, a cruel prelude to whatever they had planned.

Lamont swaggered to a cluttered workbench, fingers skimming the tools until he picked up a long screwdriver. With a slow, deliberate motion, he slid it through the locker's padlock hole, jamming it in place. The two boys snickered, tiptoeing away like they'd pulled off the perfect crime. Their third friend emerged from hiding, joining them in the center of the garage.

Inside the locker, William could see them through a tiny hole in the door. They were pointing, laughing, relishing his helplessness.

Isabella crept out from her hiding spot, her heart thudding. "Why'd you lock him in there?" she demanded, marching toward the locker.

Lamont intercepted her, planting himself between her and the trapped boy. He crossed his arms, a wall of defiance.

"Move, Buddha, before I tell your momma," Isabella snapped, standing her ground.

The insult landed like a slap. Lamont's two sidekicks chuckled nervously until his glare silenced them. He stepped closer to Isabella, fists clenched, his chest puffed out.

Without warning, he shoved her hard. She hit the ground, the impact jarring but not enough to stop her.

"Leave her alone!" William's muffled voice roared from the locker. The handle rattled as he tried in vain to force it open. "Let me out!"

Isabella scrambled to her feet and ran out of the garage, yelling for help. Inside, William's cries grew louder, but Lamont and his crew drowned them out with laughter.

Lamont picked up William's prized Incredible Hulk action figure, holding it aloft like a trophy. "Hey, little dude, guess what?" His voice dripped with mockery.

William's heart sank as Lamont twisted the figure's head, snapping it off with a sickening crack. The boy tossed the pieces to the ground, stomping them into the dust.

"Nooooo!" William's scream reverberated through the locker, laced with anguish.

Lamont sneered, kicking the shattered pieces toward the locker. "What you gonna do, Hulk? Smash your way out?"

But something shifted within William—the air around them was quiet, like the calm before a storm.

BANG!

The locker door trembled as William struck it from inside. The magnets popped off, one zipping through the air and shattering a window. Another ricocheted across the garage, clattering into a pile of tools. A smiley-face magnet smacked Lamont square in the forehead, leaving a small, bleeding gash.

"Yo, what the—" Lamont staggered back, his bravado crumbling.

BAM! Another blow rocked the locker, scooting it across the dusty floor.

One of the sidekicks stammered, inching toward the exit.

Lamont hesitated, but the third strike sent a shudder through the metal that made them all flinch. Dust swirled around the room as the locker bent under William's relentless assault.

Suddenly, a hand shot out from the warped bottom of the locker, grabbing the remains of the Hulk.

"Yaaaaaaagh!" William's guttural roar sent the boys stumbling backward in terror.

Lamont tripped, falling hard at the feet of Isabella and her mother, Victoria, who had a firm hold of Isabella's hand seemingly in a trance and staring off to the distance.

"What happened to your face, Lamont?" Victoria demanded, her voice sharp with suspicion. But Lamont scrambled to his feet and bolted without a word, his friends following close behind.

Victoria turned toward the locker, her heart sinking at the sound of her son's muffled sobs. "Oh no, William? Baby, what did they do to you?"

She yanked the screwdriver free and pulled the door open. William's tear-streaked face emerged, his small hands cradling the shattered remains of his toy.

Victoria knelt, pulling him into her arms. "It's okay, baby. I'm here now. We'll fix it. We'll fix everything."

But William's gaze remained locked on the broken Hulk in his lap, his small shoulders trembling with rage and heartbreak.

CHAPTER 6

Black Sheep

September 2011

William sat on the cracked concrete steps outside the apartment complex, hood pulled low over his head. The oversized sweater his mother insisted he wear hung on him awkwardly, a feeble attempt to hide the broadness of his shoulders. He jabbed at a line of red ants with a stick, forcing them into disarray as they struggled to regroup. The sting of memory lingered sharper than the stick in his hand, pulling him back to the reason he was waiting for his mom to take him to this new school.

The echo of that day rang clear in his mind:

"Damn, dude, was your mom on steroids when she had you?" Bobby had said, his voice loud enough to cut through the classroom chatter.

William had ignored him, focusing on the stick-figure drawing he was sketching—just him and his mom, smiling.

"Maybe he's some kind of protein baby," a little girl volunteers.

Collin had leaned in next, jabbing a finger into William's arm. "What are you, some kinda science experiment? Look at these biceps!"

"Don't touch me," William had warned, his voice low.

"What you gonna do, freak?" Collin had sneered, finger hovering just above William's arm. "You can't take all of us."

Thomas had leaned over his desk, grabbing William's drawing. "Let me fix this for you." He'd scribbled circles where muscles should be, the class roaring with laughter.

What happened next was a blur of yelling, desks screeching, and fists flying. By the time the teacher returned, three boys lay sprawled on the floor. William had stood in the middle, fists trembling, chest heaving, tears cutting streaks down his face. The silence that followed was louder than the chaos.

"Hi, William!" Isabella's voice snapped him back to the present.

He turned, finding her standing there with her usual sunny grin, the sweet scent of her Barbie Doll perfume floating in the humid air. She was the one bright spot in this mess of a new school.

"Hi, Bella," he said, forcing a smile as he dropped the stick and shoved his hood back.

Isabella leered down at him with mild disgust. "What are you doing? We leaving or what?"

"Yeah, my mom's coming," William muttered, glancing toward the building.

Isabella snatched the stick from the ground and hurled it into a nearby bush. "Stop bullying the ants!"

William frowned. "Why'd you do that?"

"'Cause! You're picking on those ants and all they want to do is go home. What if someone picked on you on your way home, huh—and all you wanted to do was go watch cartoons? That's probably what they want to do," Isabella explains, watching the ants reorganize.

"Ants don't watch cartoons, Bella," he retorted, shaking his head. "They're just dumb little bugs."

Before she could respond, a beat-up car pulled up, its screechy brakes drawing their attention. A man and a woman sat in the front seat, their lips locked in a sloppy kiss.

"Ew," Isabella muttered, scrunching her nose.

The woman hopped out, flashing them a too-bright smile. She patted their heads like they were pets before skipping into the building.

The man lingered, his phone ringing. His face twisted into a scowl as he answered, voice tight. "I told you I was at the store. Damn, why you blowin' up my phone like this?" He sighed. "Yeah, I worry about you too, baby, but—" His words faded as the car rolled away.

William and Isabella stared after the car, their earlier conversation momentarily forgotten.

"You ever wonder what that feels like?" William asked, breaking the silence.

"What?"

He hesitated, "To kiss somebody."

Isabella wrinkled her nose. "Like kissing a boy?"

"Well, yeah."

"Nope. I heard my Daddy tell my Momma that if he caught some little boy touching on me he was gonna snatch they nuts off."

William's eyes widened as he instinctively looked down between his own legs. He shifted uncomfortably at the thought.

Isabella giggled at his reaction. "Why? You think about it?"

William hesitated, the weight of her father's words hanging heavy. "What would you do if I kissed you?" he finally asked, attempting to sound bold, yet casual.

"I'd punch you in the face!" she said, balling her fist for emphasis.

William laughed nervously, scratching the back of his head.

"My daddy says men don't value rocks; they value diamonds," Isabella said proudly.

"What? I like rocks better. You can't do anything with diamonds but look at'em."

"But when you get done with the rock, what do you do with it?" she smiles, her head held higher.

"I just throw it back and-" William choked on his words, suddenly realizing her intended message.

She recited a poem her father had shared with her, each word settling over William like a lesson he didn't fully understand yet:

Boys toss and play with stones they find,
No meaning held, no worth in mind.
They kick, they throw, with little care,
For plenty lie scattered everywhere.
But then one day, a stone appeared,
So pure, so bright, it drew him near.
Its beauty shone, unlike the rest,
A rarest gem, the earth's bequest.

Not every man can claim to own,
A treasure so unique, so finely honed.
For few will hold, and fewer find,
A treasure so precious—a diamond divine.

"You kids ready?" William's mom, Victoria, called out as she stumbled out the door, her coffee sloshing in one hand, keys jangling in the other.

"Yes, ma'am," Isabella chirped.

The three of them climbed into the old car, its engine sputtering like it might give out at any moment.

The chalk screeched faintly against the board as Ms. Kutsmode wrote her name in precise, looping cursive. The chatter behind her swelled—snickers, whispers, a few rogue claps. She could feel the energy shifting, but she kept writing, determined to maintain her routine. Fourth graders were like sharks; they could smell hesitation.

"Scuze me, ma'am!" a voice cut through the noise, sharp and brash.

Ms. Kutsmode turned, marker still in hand, and spotted a young man. Chubby cheeks flushed pink, a mop of frosty blonde hair framing his wide-eyed grin. He had the look of a kid who lived for attention—and the classroom was his stage.

"Yes?" she asked, voice steady but firm.

"What kind of name is that?" he said, pointing a stubby finger at the board. Laughter rippled through the room.

Ms. Kutsmode didn't flinch. "And your name is?"

"Billy," he muttered, shrinking slightly as the attention turned on him.

"Ah, Billy Prescott?" she confirmed, scanning her roster. He nodded, and she continued, "Well, Mr. Prescott, my name is pronounced *Kutsmode*—like 'cuts the lawn, mowed the lawn.' Easy enough, yes?"

Billy nodded again, but the smirk lingered as he leaned back in his chair, triumphant. The giggles hadn't stopped entirely, but Ms. Kutsmode decided it was enough—for now.

Just as the teacher wrapped up her explanation, the classroom door creaked open, catching everyone's attention. Victoria and Isabella stepped into the room, their presence immediately drawing curious glances. Pausing in the doorway, Victoria glanced back into the hall, her brow furrowing as she spotted her son lingering outside. Reaching out, she gently tugged his sleeve, coaxing him forward with a mix of patience and insistence.

The students' stifled giggles filled the air as William reluctantly shuffled inside, his hood drawn low over his face, his gaze firmly fixed on the polished floor.

"Well, good morning! And who might we have here?" Ms. Kutsmode asked warmly, crouching slightly to meet the newcomers at eye level. Her voice was light and soothing, a deliberate contrast to the rising whispers around the room. "Don't mind the others," she added with a conspiratorial smile. "We've got quite the giggly bunch today."

"My name is Bella," Isabella said confidently, her voice carrying just enough sweetness to draw attention.

"Well, hello, Bella! And what lovely eyes you have—absolutely stunning," Ms. Kutsmode replied, her expression softening as she took in the girl's glittering pink gloves and the books cradled protectively against her chest. Isabella beamed in response, her smile lighting up her delicate features.

Ms. Kutsmode turned her attention to the boy standing silently beside her. "And what's your name?" she asked gently. William hesitated, his body rigid as he lifted his head just enough to take in the sea of curious faces watching him. His mother's subtle nudge broke his paralysis.

"William," he mumbled, his voice barely above a whisper.

"Well, it's lovely to meet you, William," Ms. Kutsmode said, straightening and placing her hands on her hips. "You two can leave your jackets in the hall on the hooks and then come back to find your seats."

As Ms. Kutsmode and Victoria fell into quiet conversation, the children complied with the teacher's instructions. When they returned, Isabella's pink gloves glittered even brighter in the morning light, but William's hoodie remained stubbornly in place, its oversized fabric shielding him from the world.

"William, you'll need to take your jacket off, dear," Ms. Kutsmode reminded him, her tone gentle but firm. "Did you forget?"

Before William could respond, a voice rang out from the middle of the room. "Why are your clothes so big?!" Billy Prescott blurted, his remark sparking another round of titters from the students.

"Okay, class! That's enough," Ms. Kutsmode said sharply, her reprimand cutting through the laughter.

William's eyes darted to his mother, silently pleading for her intervention. But Victoria remained by the door, her hands folded, as if waiting for him to muster the courage on his own.

The silence stretched, heavy with expectation, until William hesitantly began pulling back his hood, his movements slow and deliberate. Just as his fingers brushed the hem of the jacket, his mother interjected.

"Oh, he really loves that hoodie," Victoria said quickly, her tone breezy as she offered Ms. Kutsmode a subtle wink. "I think he'll be fine keeping it on."

William exhaled quietly, relief softening the tension in his shoulders. He moved to an empty desk near the back, sliding into the seat behind Billy Prescott. His mother lingered a moment longer, her eyes meeting his with a reassuring glimmer. She blew a quick kiss to both children before stepping out, leaving the room to Ms. Kutsmode's capable hands as the lesson began.

Meanwhile, the school janitor, Mr. Moreno, stowed away a pale mop bucket in the shadowy confines of the cramped supply closet. The air in the small space was thick with the acrid cocktail of cleaning agents and chemicals, their sharp odors mingling like a bitter orchestra. He shoved the bucket into a corner with an impatient grunt, the motion sending a shiver through the shelves, where precariously perched bottles of flammable liquids clinked together ominously.

Cracking the closet door, he leaned forward, his weathered face illuminated faintly by the sterile hallway lights. His dark eyes scanned the empty corridor, ensuring his privacy. Satisfied, he pulled the door shut with a quiet click, pressed his back against it, and fished a crumpled, half-smoked cigarette from his pocket. The tiny spark of his lighter flared briefly, casting flickering shadows across the cramped space.

Inhaling deeply, he savored the forbidden reprieve, a stolen moment of defiance against school regulations. The faint haze of smoke curled upward, mingling with the chemical haze. The thought of walking all the way off school grounds for a mere two puffs felt absurd.

Bang—Bang—Bang!

The sudden pounding on the door sent his heart racing, the cigarette trembling between his fingers. He stubbed it out hastily against the wall, leaving a faint charred smudge, and flicked the still-warm butt onto the floor. Waving his hand frantically to disperse the telltale smoke, he barely caught his breath before a voice shouted from the other side.

"Mr. Moreno, we need your assistance!" one of the teachers called, their tone fraught with urgency. "The toilets are over-flowing and spilling into the hallways!"

Muttering a curse under his breath, he yanked the door open and stepped into the hallway, letting it slam shut behind him. The vibration sent a bottle tumbling from the shelf, its lid rattling loose as it struck the floor. A thin, sinister stream of liquid began to seep out, winding its way in a glistening path toward the discarded, still-smoldering cigarette butt.

William's class swarmed the playground, their laughter and shouts mingling with the creak of swings and the clatter of sneakers on the monkey bars. The air was crisp, carrying the faint scent of autumn leaves. On the edge of the chaos, William perched on a weathered wooden beam, his hoodie pulled low over his face, a stick in hand as he doodled absentmindedly in the sand. His attention, however, wasn't on his drawings but on the lively chatter between Billy Prescott and Isabella, their voices rising above the din of recess.

Billy swung lazily from a metal bar, his grip firm but casual. "But it's not even cold outside," he said, his tone brimming with boyish incredulity.

Isabella, hanging upside down from the bar opposite him, her hair swaying like a curtain of dark silk, shrugged with defiant nonchalance. "So what? I like them. I think they're pretty."

"Whatever," Billy muttered, his lips curling into a mischievous smirk. Then, out of nowhere, he blurted, "Do you have a boyfriend?"

The question hung in the air like a fragile thread, causing William to lift his gaze from the sand. Hidden beneath his hood, his eyes sharpened with curiosity, a pang of something unnamed prickling at his chest.

"Yep," Isabella replied, her voice steady and unflinching.

Billy's eyes widened, his grip tightening on the bar. "Who?"

Isabella rolled her eyes dramatically, a playful smile dancing on her lips. "For me to know and you to find out. But it's not you, that's for sure."

William's fingers loosened around the stick, a small, satisfied smile creeping onto his face. Isabella's words were enough to extinguish the flicker of jealousy in his chest. Billy Prescott was no threat.

Billy squinted at her, his tone sharp with teasing disbelief. "I bet it's that boy over there with the baggy clothes, huh?"

Isabella tilted her head, her upside-down face unreadable as she replied coolly, "Do you always blurt stuff out? You should really learn to keep things to yourself sometimes, or people won't like you. But to answer your question... maybe, maybe not!"

William's smile deepened just as the school bell shattered the playground's symphony. The children scurried to their teachers, forming untidy lines that straightened under stern gazes. Back in the classroom, they settled into their seats, the hum of their chatter softening into the subdued energy of focused work.

Isabella, however, made a beeline for Ms. Kutsmode, her steps urgent. "Ms. Kutsmode, I have to go really bad. Can I have a hall pass for the bathroom?" she asked, her legs crossing in exaggerated discomfort.

Ms. Kutsmode chuckled lightly, retrieving a laminated pass. "Okay, sweetie, but hurry back!"

By this time, the liquid in the janitor's closet had already caught fire, its sinister orange glow licking hungrily at the walls. The flames crept like living vines, their heat intensifying as the bottles of chemicals began to tremble under the growing pressure.

Isabella darted out of her classroom, her sneakers squeaking faintly against the polished tile floor, heading toward the nearest bathroom. But as she pushed open the door, she was greeted by a chaotic scene: water cascaded over the edges of the toilets, forming shimmering puddles that reflected the flickering overhead lights. In the middle of the mess stood Mr. Moreno, mop in hand, looking both exasperated and resigned.

"Honey, you'll have to find another bathroom," he said, pinching his nose as he sidestepped a growing stream. "As you can see, this one's out of order."

"Ewwww, okay!" Isabella exclaimed, wrinkling her nose as she backed away. She turned and bolted down the hallway.

After weaving through the maze of corridors, she reached another bathroom, this one tucked on the far side of the school. It was directly across from the janitor's small, cramped room—now an unholy furnace where the flames had reached their tipping point. As Isabella slipped into the bathroom, the chemicals across the hall combusted with a deafening roar. A burst of fire surged outward, shattering the door and sending it clattering against the walls. The blast echoed like thunder through the halls, making Isabella freeze in her tracks.

The shrill wail of the fire alarm erupted immediately, its piercing tone slicing through the air. In the classrooms, the children erupted into cheers, their innocent excitement mistaking the alarm for a mere fire drill. Teachers quickly moved to action, their practiced calmness guiding the chaotic energy of the children.

"Okay, okay, children! Get in line and hold hands!" Ms. Kutsmode called, her voice steady as she scanned the room to ensure everyone was accounted for. Once satisfied, she began herding the students toward the door in an orderly line.

But William lingered, his brow furrowed as his eyes darted around the classroom. "Ms. Kutsmode, where's Bella?" he asked, his small voice edged with worry.

Ms. Kutsmode offered him a reassuring smile. "Bella will be fine, sweetie. She went to the bathroom when we started. During fire drills, someone always checks the bathrooms and makes sure everyone gets out safely."

William nodded reluctantly, though his gaze still lingered on the empty space where Bella should have been.

Isabella reached for the bathroom door handle, her gloved hand meeting the blistering heat of the metal. She recoiled with a startled gasp, yanking her hand back as wisps of smoke curled from the singed fabric of her pink glove. Impulsively, she stripped it off and flung it to the floor, where it landed in a limp heap.

Her wide eyes darted toward the source of the heat: the janitor's closet. Its door, now a blackened slab consumed by flickering flames, had collapsed in the hallway, igniting the bathroom door. Flames licked hungrily at the edges of the wood, spreading closer to where she stood frozen.

The unpleasant scent of burning filled her nostrils as Isabella stepped back, her heart hammering in her chest. She cast a desperate glance around the room. The windows—her one possible escape—were cracked open just enough to tease the promise of fresh air, but not enough to offer salvation. Beyond the glass, iron bars loomed like silent sentinels, impenetrable and unyielding.

Outside, the teachers' alarm had shifted into grim realization as they observed dark plumes of smoke curling ominously from the roof of the school. The shrill cries of the fire alarm filled the air, but the fire trucks had not yet arrived. Ms. Kutsmode, her face pale and drawn, paced anxiously among the gathered students, her heart sinking with dread. Isabella was still unaccounted for.

"Did they find anyone in the bathrooms?" she asked another teacher, her voice thin and brittle.

"I haven't heard anything," came the uncertain reply.

Nearby, William caught the exchange, his expression hardening with resolve. Tugging his hood over his head, he slipped away from the clusters of murmuring students. With deliberate steps, he moved toward the school's back entrance, his small frame weaving through the chaos like a shadow.

Inside, Isabella was fighting her own battle. The bathroom had become a stifling prison, smoke creeping insidiously under the door and licking at the walls. Frantic, she crammed wads of toilet paper and paper towels into the toilets, flushing desperately in an attempt to create a flood. The suction prevented her efforts. Shifting tactics, she turned to the sinks, blocking the drains and twisting the faucets to their maximum flow. At last, water began to spill over the rims, pooling on the tiled floor and slithering toward the encroaching fire.

Meanwhile, William crept down a hallway thick with smoke, his heartbeat hammering in his ears. He had just rounded a corner when a hand clamped down on his shoulder.

"Young man! You're not supposed to be in here!" Mr. Moreno barked, his face grim with worry. "Come with me. It's not safe."

"Let me go! I gotta find Bella!" William protested, his voice cracking with urgency. He strained against the janitor's grip, his eyes darting toward the smoke-choked corridor beyond.

"You're gonna get yourself hurt, and I won't allow it!" Mr. Moreno insisted, tightening his hold.

But William's determination was unyielding. Summoning strength beyond his years, he wrenched free, his small hands clutching the janitor's arm with surprising force. Moreno gasped, his face contorted in pain as the boy's grip crushed his forearm. Reluctantly, he let go, staggering back as William darted toward the smoke.

In the bathroom, Isabella was cornered. Flames crept closer, their fiery tendrils licking at the walls above her head. She sat huddled on the wet floor, knees pulled to her chest, as tears streamed down her soot-streaked face.

"Help me!" she screamed, her voice hoarse from the acrid air. "I'm in the bathroom!"

The water she'd summoned was evaporating rapidly, offering no solace against the searing heat. She rose shakily, pressing herself into the corner as the flames roared louder.

Then, a sharp crack interrupted the chaos. The wall beside her bulged inward, plaster crumbling under some unseen force.

"Help! Please!" Isabella cried again, her voice barely a whisper now.

The wall buckled once more, and this time, a jagged hole appeared.

"Bella!" William's voice rang through the haze, clear and steady.

"William?" she called back, a spark of hope flickering in her chest.

Chunks of plaster and tile flew as William tore at the wall with his bare hands, determination etched into his young face. At last, he broke through, his eyes locking with Isabella's terrified gaze.

"Come on!" he shouted, vaulting into the bathroom. The flames bit at him, singeing his clothes, but he pressed on, swatting away embers. He soaked his pullover in the last remnants of water around her feet and draped it over her head. Without hesitation, he scooped her into his arms, his muscles straining as he leapt through the flames and back into the safety of the adjacent room.

Outside, the first firetruck screeched to a halt, but not before a cloud of dense smoke erupted from the school's entrance, racing across the lot like a living shadow. A firefighter threw a fireproof blanket over the two children as they collapsed, coughing and trembling.

When the blanket was lifted, Isabella clung to William, her small body shaking with sobs. His shirt was charred, clinging to his sweat-slicked skin, revealing a startlingly muscular frame for his age.

The gathered students and teachers froze, their voices silenced by the surreal sight. Whispers and gasps rippled through the crowd, but no one dared step forward.

Then, breaking the uneasy stillness, Billy Prescott pushed his way to the front, his wide eyes fixed on William.

"Why are your muscles so big?" he asked, his tone a mix of awe and disbelief.

William didn't answer, his gaze shifting back to Isabella, who clung to him tightly. The awkward silence returned, heavy and unbroken, as the flames inside the school continued their grim work.

CHAPTER 7

Silence is Golden

October 2011.

Two months had slipped by since William's act of bravery, and now his class was exploring a sprawling forest on a crisp autumn day. The air was tinged with the earthy scent of fallen leaves, and sunlight cascaded through the canopy, setting the woods aglow with fiery reds, brilliant oranges, and warm yellows. Their teacher had tasked them with collecting leaves, an assignment that most students approached with tepid enthusiasm.

"William, slow down!" Isabella called out, breathless as she chased after him. The two veered off from the group, their laughter blending with the distant rustle of leaves. "If we go too far, we're going to get lost."

"Here's a good spot," William announced, stopping beneath an ancient oak with a sprawling trunk. Its gnarled branches stretched skyward, adorned with a kaleidoscope of autumn hues.

"Why did you want to come all the way out here?" Isabella asked, brushing a stray curl from her face.

"Because it's cool," he replied, craning his neck to take in the tree's grandeur. "Come here and look."

The pair lay down at the base of the tree, their feet pressing against its sturdy trunk. They stared upwards, where sunlight filtered through the leaves, casting a shimmering mosaic of colors onto their faces.

"That's amazing, isn't it?" William said, his voice softer now. "The way the light shines through like that. I saw it earlier and thought this tree deserved a closer look."

"Yeah," Isabella agreed, her voice tinged with wonder. "It looks like a Grandpa Tree. Like it's been here forever, and all these smaller trees are its kids." She giggled at her own fanciful thought, her eyes twinkling.

William turned his gaze to her, watching as she smiled, caught up in the moment.

"Can I tell you something, Bella?" he asked after a pause.

"Yeah, what is it?"

"I have a secret—well, kind of," he began, his eyes returning to the golden canopy above. "I'm stronger than people know, and it scares me. I can do things other kids can't."

She turned her head toward him, her expression unreadable. "I know. I've always known, stupid."

"You knew I was strong, but did you know it scares me?" he asked, his voice tinged with vulnerability.

"I know more about you than you think, William," Isabella said, sitting up and hugging her knees. "Remember when Buddha and us were playing hide-and-seek at that barbecue a few years ago?"

"Yeah," William replied, wincing at the memory.

"You were about to fight him. I grabbed your arm to stop you, remember?"

"Yeah," he admitted reluctantly.

"Well..." Isabella hesitated, her voice dropping to a near whisper. "If I tell you this, you have to promise not to laugh—or tell anyone. Swear it."

"Alright, alright. I swear on my mother," William said with an exaggerated sigh. "Now spill."

She looked at him intently. "I can do stuff too."

William raised an eyebrow. "What, like your grip's strong?"

"No," Isabella said, glancing upward. "I can see things."

"Like ghosts?" he asked, his skepticism clear.

"No," she said firmly. "When I touch someone's skin, I can see things they've done... or things they're going to do."

William laughed, a sharp, disbelieving sound. "You're trying to say you're psychic? That's—"

Before he could finish, Isabella grabbed his arm, her fingers pressing into his skin. Her eyes fluttered shut, and her breathing quickened as her body twitched. When she released him, she looked pale and shaken.

"What was that? Why did you grab me?" William asked, scooting away, his voice tinged with alarm.

She looked at the ground, her voice barely audible. "You hide a lot, don't you? When things go wrong at home, you hide and play your music so you don't have to listen. But you have a plan, don't you? You know it's wrong, but you do it anyway."

"Stop it!" he shouted, pressing his back against the tree. "You don't know what you're talking about!"

"I'm sorry, Will," Isabella said quickly, her eyes filling with regret. "I just wanted to show you—"

Silence settled between them, heavy and awkward. For ten long minutes, they sat there, each lost in thought, fiddling with leaves and twigs. Finally, Isabella broke the tension.

"We should collect some leaves. If we go back empty-handed, we'll get in trouble."

William sighed in relief at the change in subject. "You want some leaves?" he asked, a mischievous grin spreading across his face.

Rolling onto his back, he placed his feet against the tree trunk and stomped hard. A cascade of golden leaves rained down, catching the sunlight as they fell. Isabella laughed, standing and twirling with her arms outstretched, her joy infectious as she danced beneath the shimmering downpour.

CHAPTER 8

How The Ball Bounces

William sat slumped against the gym wall, his knees drawn up, eyes fixed on the supply closet doors like they might reveal a terrible secret. Around him, the low hum of restless fifth graders filled the air, their chatter bouncing off the high, echoing ceilings of the gym.

Next to him, Isabella jabbered on, her hands moving like she was telling the best story in the world. "...and then my little cousin tried to ride the dog like a pony—William? Hellooooo?" She waved a glove-covered hand in front of his face, her bracelets jingling. "Dude, why are you staring at that door like it owes you money?"

William blinked, dragging his attention away with effort. "I'm not," he muttered, his voice low. "I'm just... thinkin' about stuff."

"Uh-huh." Isabella squinted at him like she could see right through his excuses. "You look like you're scared your momma's gonna come through that door with a belt and whoop yo butt."

"Can you not?" he snapped, his words cutting through her teasing. "I'm fine. Just don't wanna play dodgeball, that's all."

Isabella snorted. "That's it? Dodgeball? Man, just tell Mrs. Richards you ain't feelin' it today."

"I can't. I'll get a zero," William said, his voice sharpening.

"Then play, dummy. Let someone hit you and get you out. Bam—done."

He glared at her, but before he could argue, the gym door creaked open. Mrs. Richards emerged, pushing a cart full of shiny red tetherballs that seemed to gleam like warning lights.

"Aww, hell no," William groaned, turning to thud his head softly against the wall.

Mrs. Richards stopped at the center line, her voice cutting through the room like a whistle. "All right, I need two volunteers to help me set up the balls."

The gym erupted in chaos as hands shot up. Everyone wanted to be part of the action—except William, who kept his arms firmly crossed. He wasn't about to make this worse for himself.

"Hmm..." Mrs. Richards scanned the crowd. "Isabella and Lamont, come on up."

William's stomach dropped. Lamont strutted to the center like he owned the place, his forehead still showing the faint smiley-face imprint of that magnet from the barbecue incident—a reminder of just how much Lamont loved making trouble. The kid turned and shot William a grin, full of teeth and mischief, like he was already planning his next move.

William groaned again and slumped deeper, his head hanging between his knees. The worst-case scenario was playing out in slow motion. Everyone knew the rule: whoever set up the balls became the team captains.

Lamont as captain? That spelled disaster. And Isabella—she'd probably pick William first just to mess with him. He couldn't even hope to be the last pick and land on Buddha's team by default. No way Isabella would let that happen.

As the tetherballs clunked onto the court, William's mind raced, searching for a way out. But all he could see was Lamont's smug grin and Isabella's relentless teasing. His heart thudded against his ribs like it was bracing for impact.

And dodgeball hadn't even started yet.

Isabella won the coin toss and immediately pointed to her best buddy as her first pick.

"Oh, crap," William muttered, dragging himself to his feet. He shot Isabella a look of mild betrayal before shifting his gaze to Lamont, who stood on the other side of the gym with a smirk that could curdle milk. Lamont rubbed his hands together deliberately, his grin widening as if he were savoring his next move.

William trudged to his team's side, shoulders slumped, already wishing he were anywhere else. The teams quickly lined up at the far walls, hands pressed against the cool surface, their sneakers squeaking on the polished floor as they shifted in anticipation. William, however, took his time, dragging each step as if he were wading through molasses.

"William! Let's go!" Mrs. Richards barked, her whistle dangling from her neck. "Get the lead out, or you're sitting out!"

William rolled his eyes and touched the wall, barely lifting his hand before stepping back again. His movements were sluggish, his energy practically nonexistent, as if delaying the game could somehow save him from the inevitable.

Mrs. Richards blew her whistle, sharp and commanding, and chaos erupted. The kids surged forward like a stampede, shoes pounding against the gym floor. The tetherballs scattered as eager hands grabbed at them, the gym filling with shrieks and laughter.

William lingered at the back of the group, arms folded, watching the frenzy with a mix of apathy and dread. He hoped to be taken out early—anything to get off the court without having to engage.

Balls whipped back and forth across the center line, slicing through the air with loud, rubbery snaps. The slower kids who failed to grab a ball scurried backward, ducking and dodging the projectiles that ricocheted off the walls or smacked into unfortunate targets.

William stood still, rooted to the back of his side, barely moving as the game unfolded. His eyes tracked the action half-heartedly, silently praying that a ball would hit him soon so he could sit down and fade into the background.

But the game didn't give him an out. The kids around him scrambled, dodged, and shouted, while William stood apart, a quiet island in the middle of the storm. For now, he was safe. But he knew it wouldn't last.

The red rubber balls whizzed across the court like missiles, their sharp *thwacks* echoing through the gym. One by one, players fell out, leaving only four on each side: Isabella's team against Lamont's. The tension grew thicker with every throw, every dodge, every near miss.

Billy Prescott, a powerhouse on Isabella's team, hurled his ball with enough force to make the air hum, but Lamont caught it cleanly, his grin smug as ever. The crowd on the sidelines erupted, half cheering, half groaning. Billy clenched his jaw, stomped off the court, and Lamont basked in the attention, immediately using the ball he'd caught to bring a teammate back into play.

Without missing a beat, Lamont turned and launched the ball directly at William. It came fast and low, like it had been aimed with laser precision. William could see it coming, knew this was the moment he'd been dreading—but there was no way he'd let Lamont have the satisfaction. At the last second, he pivoted, the ball whipping past him harmlessly and bouncing off the back wall.

"Missed me," William muttered under his breath, though his heart raced like he'd just dodged a bullet.

"Will! Grab a ball! Come on, dude!" Jordan shouted, clutching one himself and looking frazzled. He shot William a pleading look, his face red with exertion. "We're getting killed out here!"

Before Jordan could say anything else, a ball slammed into the back of his head with a loud *smack*. He stumbled forward, eyes wide with shock, before slamming his own ball to the ground in frustration. His glare locked on William. "Really, man?" he muttered before storming off the court, shaking his head.

The kids on the sidelines were yelling now, their voices blending into a chorus of frustration.

"Come on, William!"

"Do something!"

"What are you even doing out there?!"

Isabella, still in the game, snatched up a ball and hurled it with precision, her throw landing square on the hip of one of Lamont's players. The girl yelped in surprise before reluctantly stepping off the court. Isabella turned to William, her expression a mix of determination and exasperation.

"William!" she barked, dodging a ball thrown at her with quick reflexes. "Do something! Anything!"

William froze, his eyes darting between the remaining players on Lamont's side and Isabella, who was giving everything she had to keep their team in the game. She caught another ball aimed at her, her movements sharp, focused, but there was no hiding the frustration in her gaze when she glanced his way.

The players on the sidelines weren't helping. "Pick up a ball, Will!" someone shouted. "Stop just standing there!"

But William couldn't bring himself to move. His feet felt rooted to the floor, the weight of everyone's expectations pressing down on him. Even Isabella—his closest friend—shook her head in disappointment before turning back to the game, her resolve hardening.

It was down to the two of them now, but to everyone watching, it looked like Isabella was fighting alone.

"Just pick it up and throw it, Will!" Isabella shouted, deflecting a ball with a quick flick of her wrist. Without missing a beat, she hurled her ball with surprising accuracy, striking Lamont square in the shoulder.

"Yeah!" she cheered, fists clenched in triumph, turning to William with a bright smile. For the first time, he managed a small grin back. For a moment, the game didn't feel so bad.

But Lamont's expression darkened, his grin twisting into a snarl. He looked down at his forearm, veins slightly bulging as his fist tightened around the ball as if he were willing it. Without warning, he charged the center line, the tetherball gripped tightly in his hand.

Neither William nor Isabella noticed his move until it was too late. Isabella had just turned to face the game when Lamont unleashed his throw with all his strength. The ball slammed into her stomach with a loud *thud*, dropping her to the ground like a rag doll.

"Isabella!" William shouted, his heart sinking as she curled up on the floor, clutching her stomach. Tears streamed down her face, her cries of pain silencing the chaotic gym.

"BOOOOOO!" the sidelines erupted. "Cheater! You were out, Lamont!"

"That was unnecessary, Mr. Fields!" Mrs. Richards stormed onto the court, her voice sharp and cutting. "Off the court, now!" She knelt by Isabella, helping her to her feet with the assistance of another student.

Some of Lamont's teammates snickered, their laughter rippling through the gym. Lamont threw his head back, laughing louder than anyone, exaggerating every chuckle like it was part of some cruel performance. His eyes darted to William, his smirk widening.

"Did I hurt your girlfriend?" he mocked, his voice dripping with sarcasm. "Go kiss her boo-boo and make it all better." He puckered his lips and made obnoxious kissy faces, earning more laughs from his crowd.

William's fists clenched at his sides, his jaw tightening as he watched Isabella limp off the court, supported by Mrs. Richards.

His anger burned hotter with every passing second, his focus narrowing on Lamont.

Out of nowhere, one of Lamont's remaining teammates, thinking the game was still on, tossed a loose ball at William. It struck him in the chest and bounced off harmlessly, as though it had hit a brick wall. William didn't flinch. He didn't blink.

"Aaaaaa-haaaa! You're out, and we won!" Lamont crowed, throwing his hands in the air as his team erupted in cheers.

But William wasn't listening. Slowly, he bent down and picked up a ball, his fingers squeaking against the rubber as he gripped it tightly. His gaze locked onto Lamont, who was now preening for his crowd like a comedian on stage.

"You're out, Will!" one of Lamont's teammates called. "Game's over!"

William didn't care. He stepped toward the center line, his expression cold and unrelenting. Lamont, oblivious, held a ball in front of his face, knees shaking comically as he pretended to cower.

"Oh, no! Please don't hurt me, Mr. Strong!" Lamont jeered, lowering the ball just enough to pull faces at the laughing crowd.

William didn't hesitate. He wound up and hurled the ball with everything he had. The rubber missile flew straight and true. Lamont, distracted by his own antics, didn't notice until the last second.

The ball connected with a resounding *crack*, slamming into the side of Lamont's face. The force sent him stumbling backward, his arms flailing as he landed flat on the floor. The gym erupted with laughter as the ball ricocheted upward, perfectly arching into the basketball hoop above.

Lamont groaned, clutching his throbbing face as the ball fell back through the hoop—this time landing directly on his groin. The laughter shifted to collective gasps, followed by cringing "Ooohs" and empathetic groans from the boys on the sidelines, many of whom instinctively shielded their own sensitive areas.

Lamont writhed on the floor, one hand covering his face, the other cradling his injured pride. His moans of pain echoed through the gym, his earlier bravado reduced to pitiful whimpers.

William stood still, his chest heaving as the adrenaline coursed through him. His expression softened slightly, the faintest flicker of satisfaction crossing his face before he took a deep breath and let it go.

"You two—principal's office, now!" Mrs. Richards barked, her voice cutting through the chaos like a knife. She pointed at the door, her eyes blazing.

CHAPTER 9

Weight A Minute

January 2016

After fifteen long years in that dingy, suffocating apartment, Victoria had finally tasted a slice of what she called freedom. The new house wasn't a dream home—not by a long shot. No grand staircase, no sunroom for her afternoon escapes into a good book, no deck where she could host summer barbecues. But it was theirs. A private backyard. A basement. A garage. And best of all, no more run-ins with the landlord, aka Hell Hound, from the old neighborhood.

Her son, William Strong, had grown into a mountain of a teenager. At fifteen, he stood six-foot-one, all muscle and presence, though his oversized clothes swallowed most of that. He was polite, a bit reserved, but carried himself with a quiet confidence that filled the room.

That afternoon, William lounged on the couch, flipping through channels and inhaling a plate of meatloaf sandwiches. The faint hum of the TV filled the room when his father, Will, walked through the door. Tension hit the air like a thunderclap.

"I'm sick of this shit," Will grumbled, tossing his keys onto the counter as he made his way to the kitchen. "I come home from working my ass off all day, and you can't even acknowledge me? Boy, you better speak when I walk in."

William didn't glance up, chewing with deliberate slowness.

Will's frustration bubbled over as he yanked open the fridge door. "Damn, where's that meatloaf I saved? And the mashed potatoes? Don't tell me y'all left me with nothing again."

William glanced at his plate, then back at the TV, a brief flicker of guilt crossing his face before he muttered, "I ate it. There wasn't nothing else."

Will's voice grew louder, his tone sharp enough to cut glass. "You ate my food, boy? All I do is work to keep this roof over our heads, and you eat my shit without even asking?"

"It's not that serious," William replied, his jaw tightening as he stared at the screen. "I was hungry."

"HUNGRY? Boy, you eat like a damn vacuum! You gonna eat me outta house and home." Will's voice cracked with frustration as he slammed the fridge shut. "Where's your momma? She couldn't at least leave something warm for me?"

William wiped his hands on his shirt and shrugged. "She's at Tabby's. Said it was an emergency. She'll be back soon."

Will paced behind the couch, running a hand over his face as he tried to calm the storm building in his chest. Watching William finish the last bite of his sandwich only stoked the fire.

"You know what, William?" he said, pointing a finger at his son. "You're getting a damn job. I'm not about to let you sit here eating and doing nothing while I bust my ass every day."

William's face hardened, his posture stiffening as he finally looked up at his father. "I didn't ask you to do all that. You chose this life, not me."

The words hit Will like a slap, and for a moment, the room fell silent except for the low hum of the TV. The weight of unspoken resentment lingered between them, thick and suffocating.

"I'm trying to teach you something," Will said, his voice quieter now, though no less intense. "Life ain't gonna hand you shit, boy. You gotta work for it."

"Yeah?" William stood, towering over his father now. "Then maybe you should've taught me how to live it instead of always telling me what I'm doing wrong."

Will stared up at his son, his jaw working as he searched for words that wouldn't come. The tension lingered, an unsteady truce hovering in the air.

"Clean this shit up," Will muttered finally, retreating to his bedroom and slamming the door behind him.

William sank back onto the couch, his jaw clenched, the sandwich suddenly heavy in his stomach. The TV droned on, but William wasn't listening anymore.

The cold wind howled through the partially open window, waking William from a restless sleep. He wiped the grogginess from his eyes, squinting at his digital clock. Almost time for school. The chill bit at his skin as he stumbled over to the window and slammed it shut. The sudden silence brought a new noise into focus: muffled voices rising from the basement.

William tilted his head, his father's sharp tone cutting through the air even though the words were indistinct. Curiosity tugged at him, and he shuffled over to the vent in his bedroom floor. The conversation came into focus like tuning into a radio station mid-argument.

"I don't care. You better have a talk with him 'cause I ain't putting up with this shit no more," Will's voice growled, thick with frustration.

Victoria's softer voice followed, trying to keep calm as she folded clothes. "I'll talk to him, Will, but you know how he feels about sports since that thing in elementary school. It's not just something he can forget."

"I don't give a damn about what happened back then," Will barked. "He needs to get over it. Play football, get a job—hell, anything! All he does is eat and lay around like he owns the place. Shit, little nigga eatin' every got-damn thang in the house, and I'm the one paying for it."

There was a pause, then the sound of fabric being slapped onto the folding table. Victoria's tone shifted, steely but controlled. "Stop calling your son a 'nigga,' Will. And lower your voice. He's upstairs; he could hear you."

"That boy ain't hearing nothing," Will shot back, his voice laced with contempt. "All he do is eat, shit, and sleep. He's probably snoring right now. And don't pull that 'my son' mess on me. You know how I feel about that."

Victoria's voice dropped to a dangerous whisper. "I swear, Will, don't you start with this again."

"What? What you gonna do, Vee?" Will's voice climbed, dripping with mockery. "I told you a million times—he don't look a damn *thang* like me. Style, maybe. Face? Hell no. If Maury wasn't canceled, we'd be on there today, and I'd get that sweet 'You are NOT the father!'"

"Shut up, Will!" Victoria hissed. "If you doubt it so much, just get the damn DNA test like I told you. Walgreens sells them."

"And how the hell am I supposed to pull that off without him knowing? I can't even afford that shit. Are my pants dry or what? I gotta go."

The dryer door clanged, and then the sound of tossed clothing. "Here," Victoria snapped. "Take 'em, but don't burn yourself."

"Ow, damn it! Zipper hot as hell! You trying to burn me alive, woman?" Will grumbled, yanking on the pants. "Talk to that boy, Vee. He needs to do something. I'm gone." The stomp of his boots faded as he ascended the stairs.

William leaned against the wall, rolling his eyes. "I can't stand his ass," he muttered to himself. "I hope he ain't my dad." He wandered over to the window and peered outside, watching as Will loaded the car. With a smirk, he traced two butt cheeks and a dot in the center using the fogged glass and added an arrow pointing to his father outside before stepping away.

Hearing the soft hum of his mother's tune drifting upstairs, William decided to head down. He hesitated at the base of the stairs, watching her move about the room. Even in the face of everything, she carried herself with grace, her smile untouched by the morning's drama.

"Good morning, Mister," Victoria greeted warmly, her voice light despite the tension.

"Morning, Momma," he mumbled, his tone heavy.

She tilted her head, a knowing look in her eyes. "What's wrong? That's a sorry 'good morning.'"

"Nothing." He paused. "Just... I heard you and Pop talking earlier."

Victoria froze mid-fold, then placed the shirt on the table with a sigh. "Damnit, I told him to lower his voice." She shook her head, folding with renewed determination. "Listen, don't let your father get to you. Sometimes he talks crazy, but it's just him venting. Don't pay him no mind, okay?"

"But why does he gotta talk like that, though?" William pressed, his fists clenched at his sides. "He's always finding ways to hurt you. If I ever catch him putting his hands on you, I swear—"

"Enough!" Victoria's voice was firm, but her eyes softened. "I told you, I'll handle your father. You're not grown yet, so stay in your lane. He's still the one keeping this roof over our heads, and that's more than I can do alone."

William's jaw tightened. "I'm gonna get you out of this, Momma. I know you try to hide it, but I see it. He's wrong."

Victoria smiled sadly, lifting the basket of clothes. "Don't you worry about me, baby. I've been handling myself a long time. Everything I do, I do for you." She paused, looking down at him with warmth that belied the morning's tension. "Now, come on upstairs so I can cook you something before school. You're not leaving here starving."

William followed her up, the weight of his father's words still lingering, but his mother's resolve shining like a shield against it all.

"William Strong, where are your manners!" Victoria exclaimed, dropping the warm skillet into the soapy dishwater with a loud clatter.

She glanced over her shoulder at the sight of her son, hunched over his plate in a feeding frenzy. His fork scraped the plate with every bite, cutting massive chunks of pancakes and cramming them into his mouth like he hadn't eaten in weeks.

"'Forry, Romma, Immo be rate, I gotta hurry!" William mumbled through a mouthful of food, barely looking up.

"That has *nothing* to do with you being late," she snapped, hands on her hips. "Boy, you eat like this every morning. Now slow down before you choke yourself."

"K." William gave a dismissive nod, finishing off the last bites of bacon and pancakes in record time. He stood, kissed her cheek with sticky lips, and snatched his backpack from the floor.

"Ugh, William Strong!" Victoria hollered, swiping her cheek with her shoulder as he bolted toward the door. "Wipe your lips before kissing me! You got syrup all over my damn cheek!"

"Sorry, Momma—love you!" William shouted, the door slamming behind him before she could respond.

Victoria sighed, a mixture of exasperation and affection settling on her face. "Love you too, baby," she murmured, knowing full well he was too far to hear her. A proud smile lingered on her lips as she turned back to the sink.

Meanwhile, William ducked low beneath the back kitchen window, his movements quick and calculated. The snow crunched softly beneath his boots as he crept toward the backyard, careful to stay out of sight. In the far corner of the yard, behind the garage, lay the spot he'd been returning to for months. His backpack hit the ground next to the massive rock that bore the words *In God We Trust*, a remnant of the previous owners' landscaping.

William knelt beside the stone, glancing over his shoulder to ensure no one was watching. The cold bit at his exposed hands as he slipped off his gloves. Hugging the rock tightly, he heaved it across the snow-dusted grass with a grunt. Despite its immense weight, he moved it with ease, revealing a carefully hidden stash beneath.

Underneath the rock was a black garbage bag, its edges slightly frosted from the cold. He pulled it out, untying the knot with practiced precision. Inside were three shoeboxes packed with change and crumpled bills. One of the boxes stood out—green and purple, with the face of the Incredible Hulk emblazoned on it, a remnant of his childhood favorite sneakers.

William pulled a wad of cash from his front pocket, the result of weeks spent quietly pilfering from vending machines all over Milwaukee. He smirked to himself, shoving the money into one of the boxes and taking a moment to admire his growing fortune. The stacks of coins and crumpled bills filled him with a sense of satisfaction, a small rebellion against the world that always seemed stacked against him.

"Almost there," he murmured, his voice low but resolute.

Quickly, he rewrapped the boxes in the garbage bag, sliding it back into its hiding place. He grabbed the rock and rolled it into position, ensuring no sign of disturbance remained. Dusting off his pants, he glanced around one last time before grabbing his backpack and heading for the street, the faint trace of a smirk still on his face.

Taking a shortcut through the neighbors' frost-covered yards, William moved briskly, the snow crunching beneath his boots as he tried to make up for lost time. His backpack bounced against his shoulder with each hurried step. As he reached the edge of the block, he spotted Isabella standing on the corner, her breath visible in the chilly morning air. She shifted her weight impatiently, glancing at the cars whizzing by.

"Bella!" William called out, waving to grab her attention as he jogged toward her.

She turned, her dark curls catching the light of the rising sun. "Hey, Will!" she shouted back, her voice carrying easily over the hum of traffic. "Come on, hurry up! We're already running late."

"I know, I know," he panted, closing the gap between them.

When he reached her side, Isabella playfully shoved his shoulder. "What took you so long? Oversleep again?"

William smirked, adjusting his backpack. "Something like that. Let's just go before we're stuck out here forever."

The two stepped off the curb as the light changed, hurrying across the street together, their banter blending with the noise of the city waking up around them.

The final bell rang, releasing a tide of students into the hallways. The air buzzed with energy as kids rushed to leave the building or head to their after-school activities. William stood at his locker, methodically stuffing his books and supplies into his backpack. He moved with deliberate focus, his mind still racing with thoughts of the stash hidden in his backyard.

As he slammed his locker shut, a flash of movement caught his eye. Over by the school bulletin board, a student was taping up a flyer. The bold letters caught his attention immediately:

LOOKING FOR EXTRA MONEY??

THERE IS A JOB OPPORTUNITY FOR A HARD-WORKING STUDENT WHO CAN BE ON TIME AFTER SCHOOL 5 DAYS A WEEK.PLEASE SEE MR. KLINE FOR DETAILS IF INTERESTED!!!

The words practically jumped off the page. William froze for a moment, his gaze narrowing as he considered the implications.

Without a second thought, he strode over and snatched the notice from the board, crumpling it slightly in his grip. His mind churned as he read the flyer again, weighing his options.

A job? It wasn't the first time he'd thought about getting one, but this felt...different. The words *extra money* rang loud in his head. With his father's complaints about him "eating everything in the house" still fresh, the idea had a sharp edge to it.

Tucking the flyer into his backpack, William set his jaw and headed for the door.

Coach Kline sat at his desk, flipping through his worn playbook, his brow furrowed in concentration. The heavyset man had the demeanor of someone who'd seen it all, his Marine Corps discipline evident in his no-nonsense posture and the high-and-tight haircut he'd maintained for years. Despite the belly that tipped the scales at over 270 pounds, his sharp eyes and authoritative presence remained intact.

"Coach Kline?" William said, standing hesitantly in the doorway.

Coach glanced up, his expression neutral as he studied the young man. "I suppose you're here about the job?" Without waiting for a response, he returned his attention to his playbook. "That was fast. I only told the office I needed someone thirty minutes ago."

William blinked, slightly thrown. "Yes, sir, but how did you know that's why I'm here?"

Coach gestured lazily at the crumpled flyer in William's hand. "Just a hunch. That notice you're holding kinda gives it away."

"Oh." William unfolded the flyer, smoothing it out before tossing it onto the desk. "So, what's the job?"

Coach leaned back in his chair, crossing his arms over his chest. "Here's the deal. My athletes use the gym after practice, which means by the time they're done, the place is trashed. We're talking sweat everywhere, weights scattered, the smell of teenage hormones and bad decisions hanging in the air."

William raised an eyebrow. "And you need someone to clean all that up?"

"Exactly." Coach nodded. "By morning, it smells like two-week-old hard-boiled eggs sealed in a jar. Since I can't trust those juice-heads to clean up after themselves, I need someone responsible to handle it. Think you're up for it?"

"Yes, sir. Without a doubt," William said confidently.

Coach narrowed his eyes but smirked. "First off, stop calling me 'sir.' I work for a living."

William didn't miss a beat. "Only if you stop calling me 'son.'"

Coach let out a low chuckle, leaning forward on his desk. "Fair enough. We've got a deal. But it'd help if I knew your name."

"William. William Strong." He extended a hand.

Coach took it, nodding appreciatively. "Nice grip, William Strong. You play sports?"

"Nope."

Coach raised an eyebrow. "Why not?"

"Just don't. I've got other stuff to do."

"Fair enough." Coach shrugged, leaning back in his chair. "We've all got our reasons for doing what we do, right?" He reached into his desk drawer, pulling out a pad of sticky notes. "The job pays forty bucks for two hours a day. It shouldn't take you that long, but everything has to be locked up by twenty hundred hours."

William frowned. "What?"

Coach smirked. "Eight p.m., William. Military time. You'll get used to it. Here." He tore off a sticky note and handed it over. "That's my number. If you need anything, call. Can you start today?"

"Yes!" William said, his enthusiasm breaking through.

"Good. I'd give you a tour, but it's a weight room. Not much to see. The supply closet's in the back—towels, disinfectant, a mop bucket, everything you'll need to make this place smell halfway decent."

"Got it," William said. "What about gloves?"

Coach grinned, his sarcasm coming out in full force. "Plenty of those in a white box. Don't want you ruining your pretty hands with those harsh chemicals, Princess."

William didn't flinch, his expression flat as he stared back. "Anything else I need to know?"

Coach shook his head, a flicker of amusement crossing his face. He opened a drawer, pulling out a gold key with a white tag. "Here's the spare key to the weight room. It also works on the supply closet. It's one of those fancy keys you can't duplicate, so don't lose it." He tossed it to William, who caught it mid-air.

William tucked the key into his pocket. "Got it. Thanks, Coach."

Coach nodded, watching the boy leave with steady steps. Something about the kid intrigued him—quiet confidence, maybe, or the way he seemed to carry more weight on his shoulders than his age should allow. Either way, Coach was eager to see if William was up to the task.

The varsity football team burst into the weight room, their voices loud and filled with post-practice adrenaline. Their laughter and shouts echoed off the walls as they moved toward the equipment. William stood near the supply closet, quietly preparing his cleaning supplies, his focus unwavering despite the noise.

One of the players nudged his teammate, motioning toward William with a smirk. "Yo, is that the new cleaning lady or what?"

William turned slowly, recognizing the voice. There, with arms folded and a smug grin plastered across his face, stood Lamont "Buddha" Carter—his childhood rival. William's eyes narrowed for a moment before he straightened and met Lamont's gaze.

"What's up, Buddha—oops, I mean Lamont?" William said, his voice calm but cutting. "Still running your mouth whenever you've got a crowd, huh?" Without waiting for a response, he turned back to the table, pouring disinfectant into spray bottles. "How's that scar? That magnet really did a number on you, didn't it? Still pretty obvious. Oh, and the lazy eye? Tether balls can be brutal, huh?"

The room erupted in a mix of laughter and "oohs," Lamont's teammates clearly amused. Lamont's grin faltered, and his face darkened.

"This right here," Lamont said, pointing to his forehead, "was a freak accident from back when we were kids. But trust me, I've grown since then." He flexed a massive bicep, his muscles bulging under his jersey. "That shit ain't happening again."

William didn't flinch. Instead, he finished pouring the solution and calmly screwed the cap back onto the bottle. His back still to

Lamont, he said with a quiet confidence, "So, you wanna work on another scar?"

Lamont's expression shifted from annoyance to anger in an instant. "What?" He stepped forward, fists raised, but before he could get close, his teammates grabbed him, holding him back.

"Chill, Lamont!" one of them said. "It's not worth it, man."

"Fuck you, little Willy!" Lamont shouted, struggling against their grip. "I got something for you, boy. We ain't kids no more!"

William turned slightly, just enough to glance at Lamont over his shoulder, his expression calm and unbothered. "Then act like it," he said, his tone even.

Before Lamont could break free, a voice boomed from the doorway. "What the hell is going on in here?" Coach Kline bellowed, his eyes sweeping the room. The team immediately froze, releasing Lamont as Coach strode inside, his presence commanding.

"You ladies either start working out or get the hell out of my weight room!" Coach barked, glaring at each of them. "And that goes for you too, Lamont. You got energy to fight? Use it on the bench press."

Lamont muttered something under his breath but didn't dare defy Coach. He shot one last glare at William before heading toward the weights with his teammates.

William smirked faintly to himself, picking up his supplies and continuing his work, unfazed. Coach lingered for a moment, watching him, then nodded slightly before turning his attention back to the team. The tension in the room dissipated, replaced by the clatter of weights and the sound of grunts as the players got back to their workout.

The weight room buzzed with energy as Lamont pumped out his fifth repetition, the bar clanging loudly as he slammed 250 pounds back onto the rack. He wiped the sweat from his brow and turned his attention toward William, who was quietly cleaning equipment and doing his best to stay out of the team's antics.

"You better put those weights back when we're done," Lamont called out with a smirk. "Cleaning lady might not be able to handle it."

The team erupted into laughter, their jeers echoing across the gym.

William ignored him, focused on spraying down a bench, but Coach Kline had heard enough. Stepping into the weight room, he marched over to Lamont, standing over him as he prepared for another set.

"I happen to think he can handle it just fine," Coach said, turning toward William with a knowing grin. "What do you say, William?"

William paused, mid-spray, clearly reluctant to engage. "I'm just here to clean," he said, his voice even.

"Oh, come on now," Coach said, walking over to him and lowering his voice so only William could hear. "If you beat this guy, I'll pay you double for two weeks."

William shook his head. "Coach, I've never even lifted weights before. That dude's huge. You're setting yourself up for disappointment."

"Okay, triple," Coach countered, leaning in conspiratorially.

William sighed, setting down the spray bottle. "Coach, I—"

"Look, if you *try*, I'll pay you double for a week. But if you *win*—triple. Deal?"

The offer dangled in the air, and William hesitated, thinking of what the extra money could do for his mom. Finally, he gave a small nod. "Fine. I'll try. But if I lose, you leave me alone."

Coach clapped him on the shoulder. "Deal."

As William walked toward the bench, his foot accidentally landed on a digital scale. One of the nearby players noticed the numbers on the display spike rapidly, peaking at 321 pounds before William stepped off. The boy blinked, rubbing his eyes. "Ain't no way he weighs that much," he muttered, shaking his head.

William sat down at the bench, sliding beneath the bar. He noticed Lamont to his right, grinning with anticipation, and Coach to his left, watching closely. Taking a deep breath, William gripped the bar above him, his mind racing.

What are you doing? You don't need this attention. But... that money could really help Momma. Just don't overdo it.

Expecting the weight to challenge him, William tensed his arms and pushed—but the bar shot upward with almost no effort, as if he were lifting a broomstick. Realizing his mistake, he quickly slammed the bar back onto the rack, pretending to adjust his grip. The ruse seemed to work; Lamont smirked, clearly convinced William was struggling.

"See?" Lamont sneered, nudging a teammate. "Ain't no way he's pushing that twice."

William let out a mock grunt as he lifted the bar again, mimicking the others' strained efforts. He eased the bar down to his chest, pressed it back up, and repeated the motion. Satisfied, he set the weight back on the rack and stepped aside.

Lamont laughed. "Man, he struggled with that! Did you see it? That was embarrassing." He turned to William. "Yeah, you didn't know you had to push that shit twice for it to count, huh? Make sure it touches your chest next time, little man."

Now it was Lamont's turn to show off. He motioned for his teammates to load three 45-pound plates on each side, bringing the total to 315 pounds. "Watch and learn, baby," he taunted, flexing for good measure.

Without a spotter, Lamont hoisted the bar off the rack and cranked out three quick reps, the third accompanied by a triumphant grunt. Slamming the bar back into place, he bent the already rickety rack further. "That last one was for you, sweetheart," he said, blowing a mock kiss toward William before high-fiving his teammates.

William approached the bench again, this time rolling up his sleeves as he adjusted the bar. His exposed arms caught the attention of the players.

"Yo, look at his arms," one whispered. "Damn..."

William pressed the bar upward, this time deliberately slower, his biceps flexing visibly. As the weight reached its peak, the safety lip on the rack gave way, sending the bar—and its massive load—plummeting.

Instinctively, William caught the bar with one hand, halting it midair.

The room went silent.

Lamont's jaw dropped, his folded arms slackening. A Gatorade bottle tumbled from another player's hand, spilling onto the floor. Even Coach Kline stared his mouth slightly agape. Everyone watched in silence and disbelief as William paused, lying on the bench, holding three hundred and fifteen pounds in a single grip

William, realizing the spectacle he'd created, quickly slid from under the bar, dropping it and spilling the weights at the feet of the onlookers, then rose to his feet, his face burning with embarrassment.

"I'd call that a win," Coach finally said, breaking the silence.

The team's stunned eyes followed William as he grabbed his belongings and pushed his way through the crowd. Without a word, he exited the weight room through the rear doors, leaving behind a room full of wide-eyed players and a bent, broken rack.

CHAPTER 10

Gifted

February 2016.

Victoria sat across from Tabitha, the warm buzz of the coffee shop masking the weight in her chest. The hum of chatter, the hiss of the espresso machine, and the occasional burst of laughter blended into a soothing white noise. The slice of banana bread on her plate remained untouched, her salted hazelnut Frappuccino now a cold, neglected pool.

Tabitha, in stark contrast, was mid-story, recounting her chaotic Friday night with animated fervor.

"And girl, these heifers were out there wildin'. Big as linebackers, fighting right in the middle of traffic! Skirts flying up like broken blinds, showing all kinds of ass and thongs. I swear, it was like an episode of *Hood Gone Wild*. Dead weave everywhere. I pulled out my phone and recorded the whole thing. Told myself, never again. Center Avenue clubs are for the birds—triflin' hoes." She chuckled, sipping her plain black coffee.

Victoria didn't even crack a smile. Her gaze was distant, her hand mechanically stirring her Frappuccino. Tabitha's laughter faded, replaced by a furrowed brow.

"Vee, you good?" she asked, leaning forward.

Victoria blinked as if snapping out of a trance. Her voice came soft, but heavy. "I don't know who his father is."

Tabitha froze mid-sip. The statement hit like a jolt of static in a quiet room. She coughed, nearly spilling her coffee, and grabbed a napkin to wipe her mouth. "Come again?"

"I said..." Victoria's voice trembled, her eyes glossy with un-shed tears. "I don't know who the father of my son is."

Tabitha's mouth fell open, but no words came. The silence between them was thick and charged. Finally, she slid her coffee aside and reached for Victoria's hand. "What's going on? Why are you saying that?"

Victoria took a shaky breath, swirling her straw as if searching for the right words in the bottom of her cup. "I've never said this out loud before, Tabs. Not to anyone. But I need to now."

Tabitha nodded, her expression firm but gentle, bracing for whatever came next.

"I was... attacked. A couple of times. The week William was conceived." The words came out haltingly, each one heavier than the last. "So... I don't know who his father is."

Tabitha's gasp was audible. "Oh my God, Victoria—what?!" She scrambled around the table and wrapped her arms tightly around her friend. The scent of Tabitha's faint perfume mingled with the lingering aroma of coffee beans, grounding Victoria in the moment. "Who did this to you?"

"I don't know," Victoria whispered, the tears now spilling freely. "I couldn't tell anyone back then. You had your own stuff going on, and I just... I kept it to myself. I thought if I stayed quiet, there'd be no questions, no drama. But now..." She trailed off, staring blankly at her untouched banana bread.

Tabitha returned to her seat but kept a firm grip on Victoria's hand. "Did you go to the police?"

Victoria nodded, wiping her cheeks with the back of her hand. "My mom made me. They questioned me, did tests. I told them about these guys I ran into at the grocery store, but I didn't know for sure. I was a mess. Crying so hard I couldn't even see straight. They tested the guys, but..." Her voice cracked. "One of them died before they could even finish the investigation. It was in the news. I was giving birth when I saw it."

Tabitha's grip tightened. "And Will? He doesn't know?"

Victoria shook her head, her voice barely audible. "He's always saying how William doesn't look like him. And I give him hell for it, but... what if he's right? If he finds out, Tabs, he might leave us with nothing. What am I supposed to do?"

Tabitha sat back, exhaling sharply, her face a mix of compassion and resolve. "Baby, this is heavy. But if you really need to know, you've got options. They've got those home DNA kits now. Simple, discreet. You prick your finger, prick your kid's finger, and boom—results. Technology's a trip, but it's also a Pandora's box. Once you open it, there's no closing it. You need to think about what this means for William."

Victoria's shoulders slumped, the weight of the world pressing her further into her seat. "I just want this nightmare to end. It's eating me alive. But please, Tabs, promise me—don't tell Jarvis."

Tabitha reached out, pulling Victoria into another hug. "You've got my word. But, girl, whatever you decide, you don't have to do this alone. I got you."

The two friends sat there in a tight embrace, the world outside the coffee shop moving on without them. Inside, the air was thick with the unspoken, the unresolved. But for the first time in years, Victoria didn't feel entirely alone.

The gym was quiet, the early morning light filtering through the high windows as Coach Kline unlocked the front doors. The faint echo of his footsteps accompanied him to his office, where he flicked on the lights and placed his thermos of coffee on the desk. He eased into his chair, sipping the steaming brew as he logged into his email. A few mundane messages, one from the athletic director, and a couple from parents. Nothing out of the ordinary.

His gaze wandered to the bottom drawer of his desk. A smile tugged at his lips as he opened it, revealing a small, velvet-lined box nestled inside. He pulled it out and clicked it open, marveling at the bracelet he had chosen for his wife. The ruby, emerald, and sapphire caught the light, glinting against the white gold band. Her favorite colors, her favorite gemstones, all in one. Perfect. His fingers traced the edges of the box as he imagined the look on her face when he gives it to her tonight, on their anniversary.

Shaking himself from his thoughts, he carefully returned the bracelet to the drawer, locked it, and stood up. Time to get moving.

Coach Kline headed to the weight room, the smell of fresh cleaning solution hitting him as he flipped on the lights. He nodded approvingly. The room looked immaculate—equipment polished, floors spotless. His new custodian was already earning his keep.

But his satisfaction was short-lived. As he moved toward the benches, his eyes narrowed at the sight before him. On his brand-new weight bench, twelve forty-five-pound plates were racked on a bar, six on each side, as if someone had left them, mocking his specific instructions to rerack the weights.

"Are you freakin' kidding me?" he muttered under his breath, placing his coffee cup on the bench's edge as he examined the setup. His jaw tightened as he stood over the bar, hands on his hips. "What the hell were you gym clowns doing with this?" he mumbled to himself.

He carefully began unloading the plates, one by one, muttering under his breath the whole time. His frustration wasn't just about the plates—it was about the principle. The gym was his sanctuary, a place where order and discipline reigned. Carelessness like this rubbed him the wrong way.

Once the plates were properly racked, he wiped his hands on his pants and took a deep breath, glancing around the room. The new weight bench gleamed under the lights, unmarred now. He picked up his coffee cup, took a long sip, and exhaled. "We'll talk about this later, fellas," he said to the empty room, shaking his head as he left to continue his morning rounds.

William walked into the gym later than usual, his steps tentative as he glanced around the quiet building. The after-school rush had passed, and the place was nearly empty. He appreciated the stillness; it gave him space to do his work without dodging the usual chaos.

He was mid-step toward the weight room when Coach Kline's voice boomed from his office. "William! Come here, man. I need to talk to you."

William dropped his backpack by the wall and jogged toward the office. "Yeah, Coach?"

Coach Kline leaned back in his chair, gesturing for William to come closer. "Hey, I just wanted to say you're doing a great job cleaning up in there. Seriously, it looks and smells great—better than it has in years. I'm impressed."

A smile spread across William's face. "Thank you, Coach."

"But..." Coach's tone shifted slightly, and William's smile faltered. "Those weights have to go back where they belong, okay? You can't leave them stacked on the bar like that. It's dangerous, and it's not good for the equipment."

For a moment, William looked confused. Then it hit him. But instead of finding an excuse, he nodded. "Oh, umm... yeah, Coach. Sorry about that. It won't happen again."

"Good man." Coach stood, grabbing his things. "The place is all yours tonight. The guys have cleared out, so you shouldn't have any trouble. Oh, and check the back of the closet—there are some new cleaning supplies in the boxes. Use whatever you need."

"Okay."

Coach paused at the door, turning back with a firm reminder. "Don't forget to lock everything up. Once that door closes behind you, it's locked for the night."

"Got it, Coach. Thanks."

"Alright, have a good one. I'll see you tomorrow." With that, the heavy gym door swung shut behind him.

The moment Coach was gone, William darted to the window, peeking through the blinds to watch his car pull away. Once satisfied the coast was clear, he made a quick sweep of the gym to ensure no one else was lingering. Finding it empty, he returned to the weight room, grabbed his backpack, and pulled out his black weightlifting gloves and a towel.

Meanwhile, Coach Kline was a few minutes into his drive, humming along to the radio as he approached a stoplight. The rumble of bass-heavy music caught his attention as a car full of young women pulled up beside him. He glanced over briefly.

"Wooooo! Hey there, Devil Dog!" the passenger yelled, leaning halfway out the window, her rave music blaring. The driver, smirking, turned the volume down slightly.

Coach gave a polite smile, avoiding eye contact. He could already tell where this was going.

"Are you a Marine? Your sticker says Marine Corps! I *love* Marines," the passenger continued, shimmying to the beat of the still-audible music.

"Girl, leave him alone," the driver chimed in, rolling her eyes. "Can't you see the big ol' ring on his finger? Bet his wife's at home fixing dinner or something."

Coach stared straight ahead, pretending not to hear. The light turned green, and he was about to accelerate when it hit him like a freight train.

"The bracelet!" he blurted, slamming on the brakes. He had left the anniversary gift—the white gold bracelet, the one with all her favorite stones—locked in his desk drawer.

"Damn it, Kline," he muttered to himself, gripping the wheel. As the light changed from yellow to red again, he made a sharp, illegal U-turn, cutting in front of the girls' car. Their honks faded into the background as he sped back toward the gym, cursing under his breath.

"How could you forget something like that? Stupid, stupid, stupid," he growled, his knuckles whitening as he gripped the wheel. The bracelet had been the perfect gift—there was no way he was leaving it behind tonight.

Coach Kline parked his car hastily, the engine still clicking as he stepped out and jogged to the side entrance of the school. He tugged on the handle—locked. Of course, it was. He groaned, weighing his options. Walking all the way around to the front entrance would take too long, so he wandered over to the nearest window instead, wiping a grimy layer of dust off the glass with his sleeve.

Squinting through the cleaned patch, he could only see part of the weight room: a sliver of the weight bench and the faint gleam of the new equipment under the fluorescent lights. His eyes narrowed as he leaned closer, trying to make out more. Then he froze.

"Son of a bitch," he muttered under his breath. The bar on the weight bench was loaded again, plates stacked on each side just as he'd warned William not to do. His irritation flared, but before he could move, something caught his eye.

The bar moved. Smoothly. Rhythmically. It wasn't just sitting there—it was being pressed. His jaw slackened as he pressed his face harder against the glass, the cold pane squeaking under the pressure. He couldn't see the lifter fully, but the bar was rising and falling with perfect control.

Eager to figure out what was happening without alerting whoever was inside, Coach decided to make his way to the front entrance. He walked briskly around the building, keyed himself in, and stepped into the dimly lit hallway. His shoes echoed softly as he approached the gym doors, now moving with deliberate care.

The faint sound of clanging weights grew louder as he neared the weight room. He paused just outside the entrance, peeking in cautiously. His breath caught in his throat.

From his vantage point, he could see the loaded bar in motion again, and he quickly counted the plates on one end. His heart skipped. "Five hundred and eighty-five pounds," he whispered to himself. "And he's on his ninth rep? Are you kidding me?"

As the bar went up for another repetition, the lifter came into view. It was William.

Coach blinked, stunned. The kid had stripped down to just his gym shorts, sneakers, and weightlifting gloves. His baggy cleaning clothes, it seemed, had hidden an extraordinary physique. William's body looked like something out of a superhero comic—broad shoulders, carved arms, and a chest that seemed to defy gravity. Sweat shimmered on his skin, running down the grooves and cuts of his back like rivulets of water down a polished statue.

Coach stood frozen, the memory of William catching that 315-pound bar with one hand flashing through his mind. He'd chalked it up to adrenaline at the time, but now... this was something else entirely.

Before William could turn and spot him, Coach snapped back to the present. The weight room was William's domain now, and Kline didn't want to interrupt or risk an awkward encounter. His goal was simple: retrieve his wife's bracelet and slip out unnoticed.

With William still at the water fountain, his back turned, Coach seized the opportunity. Moving quickly and quietly, he ducked into his office, retrieved the velvet box from his desk drawer, and stuffed it into his pocket.

He glanced once more at William through the crack in the office door, the young man now back at the bench, adding another plate to each side. Coach shook his head in disbelief.

"Whatever he's made of," Kline thought to himself as he exited the gym, "it's not the same stuff as the rest of us."

The heavy door closed softly behind him as he slipped back into the night, the bracelet safe in his pocket and his mind racing with questions about the quiet kid who had been hiding in plain sight.

CHAPTER 11

Chicken Dance

September 2018.

It was late September, and the buzz of Homecoming was thick in the air. Posters for the dance hung lopsided on every hallway wall, marked with scribbled hearts and barely legible signatures. William knew this was his shot. Senior year. No excuses. Isabella wasn't just any girl; she was *the* girl. And tonight, he'd figure out how to ask her to the dance—or die trying.

In his cramped bedroom, the mirror stood as his silent coach. He squared his shoulders, licked his lips with exaggerated drama, and pointed finger guns at his reflection.

"Yo, Isabella, you already know what's up," he said, adding a slow wink. "Homecoming. You and me. Done deal."

He cringed. Too cocky.

Switching gears, he leaned against the wall, one arm propped up like he was starring in a cheap rom-com. His voice dropped an octave. "Look, girl. The dance is gonna be fire. And you? You're my plus-one. Period."

He glanced at himself, eyebrows raised, waiting for approval from the mirror version of Isabella that didn't exist. Nothing but silence and regret stared back.

"Man, this is weak," he muttered, running a hand over his face. Frustrated, he checked his watch. "Oh, hell no. I'm late!"

He bolted, snatching his battered backpack off the bed. Before heading out, he made a pit stop in the kitchen. Moving fast and quiet—like the ninja he definitely wasn't—he eased the fridge door open. His eyes darted between the half-empty ketchup bottle and a sad stick of butter before landing on the jackpot: a pack of bologna. He grabbed it, tucked it under his arm like a football, and slipped out the kitchen door into the evening air.

The weight of the night ahead pressed against him. He still didn't have the right words for Isabella, and time was running out. As he trudged toward the bus stop, his mind raced. Would he nail it, or would he blow it in front of half the school? Either way, the clock was ticking.

And William wasn't ready. Not yet.

Coach Kline sat hunched over his desk, flipping through the pages of his battered playbook. His pen tapped rhythmically against the edge, the sound echoing in the quiet of the office. Outside, faint grunts and the clanging of weights filled the gym, the soundtrack of another practice day.

When William finally yanked open the heavy gym door and strode in, he made a direct line for the weight room, his backpack slung lazily over one shoulder. He had barely made it past the office door when Coach's voice cut through the air.

"Hey, Strong, get over here for a second," Coach called, waving him in with a mix of authority and familiarity.

William hesitated, then popped his head into the office. "Yo, my bad, CK. I got held up at home, had to help my mom out." He dropped his bag on the floor and leaned against the doorframe, casual but restless.

Coach leaned back in his chair, the creak of the old springs making him grimace. "It's cool. Just come here. Sit down. I need to talk to you."

William slid into the chair across from him, bouncing his knee up and down as he fiddled with the zipper on his hoodie. "Before you start—can I ask you something real quick?"

Coach raised an eyebrow. "Alright. Shoot."

"So, uh, I was hearing some of the guys talk in the weight room..." William paused, scratching the back of his head. "And, uh, they were saying we need more weights. You know, so they don't gotta wait forever for a turn on the bench."

Coach smirked, leaning forward and lacing his fingers together. "More weights? What are they asking for? Ten-pound plates? Maybe some baby dumbbells?" His tone was teasing, but his eyes stayed sharp, testing William's angle.

"Nah, nothing like that," William said, his words quick and nervous. "Like, forty-five-pound plates. Maybe some dumbbells heavier than 110 pounds." His voice picked up as he spoke, a flicker of excitement breaking through.

Coach chuckled, shaking his head. "*We* need heavier dumbbells now, huh? Since when do you even lift, Strong?"

William's face flushed. "I'm not saying *me*—I just, you know, I see this stuff since I clean up in there all the time. Feels like my space, you know?" He trailed off, looking away. His eyes caught something on the desk. "Hey, what's that, CK?"

"What's what?" Coach asked, glancing down at the clutter.

"That bookmark in your playbook. What's it mean?" William leaned forward, reaching for the laminated card before Coach could protest.

Coach sighed but let him have a look. "It's called an 'Okodee Mmowere.' It's an African symbol—the talons of the eagle. Strength, bravery, power. Picked it up during my time in the Corps."

William studied the symbol, his brow furrowed. "Looks more like one of those inkblot test things. Why do you still keep it?"

Coach leaned back, folding his arms. "It's a reminder. The Oyoko clan used this emblem in their military. Back in the 17th century, they defeated the Denkyira clan, earned respect and fear across the coast of Africa. I keep it here because it's about strategy, strength, and not backing down. Helps me plan for our games—and maybe win that damn championship."

William handed it back, smirking. "Didn't you say you weren't gonna bore me?"

Coach snatched the bookmark and slid it back into his playbook, slamming it shut. "Alright, comedian. Don't you have something better to do?"

William laughed and grabbed his bag, heading for the door. Before he made it out, Coach called after him.

"Hey, you like fried chicken?"

William froze, turning slowly to look at him. "Yo, CK, for real? I clown on you about your story, and you gotta come at me with that?"

Coach threw his hands up, laughing. "No, no! I didn't mean it like that. My wife's cooking up a big batch tomorrow, and we've got way too much. You want to come over for dinner?"

William raised an eyebrow. "Can your wife throw down?"

"What's that supposed to mean?"

"Nothing," William said, grinning. "Yeah, I'm down. What time?"

"After you finish here. Ride with me, and we'll head over."

"Bet," William said, slinging his bag over his shoulder.

Coach shook his head, laughing to himself as William disappeared down the hall.

"How long until the Homecoming dance, baby?" Victoria asked, her hands moving rhythmically under the stream of soapy water as she scrubbed the dinner plates.

"Next Friday," William replied, handing her the last plate from the table. "Think you can help me find something to wear?"

She gave him a side-eye, her lips curving into a smirk. "Only if you dry and put the dishes away while I wash them."

"Deal." William grabbed a towel and took his place beside her, eagerly taking the first plate.

"So," Victoria said, her tone turning playful. "Who's the lucky girl you're taking to the dance?"

William hesitated, a little too long for her liking. "I didn't ask anybody yet. I might just go by myself." He tried to sound confident, but the crack in his voice betrayed him.

"Uh-huh," she said, her hands pausing in the soapy water. "Okay, but let's just say you *did* want to take someone. Who would it be?"

He fidgeted with the towel, avoiding her gaze. "Uh... Isabella, I think."

Her head snapped up, soap suds dripping onto her wrist. "You *think?*"

"Yeah, 'cause I ain't asked her yet!" William admitted, his voice rising in self-defense.

She rolled her eyes, flinging a handful of suds at his head. "Boy, what's wrong with you? The dance is next week, and you haven't even asked her yet? Are you trying to let somebody else snatch her up?"

"It's not that easy, Momma!" he groaned, ducking to avoid the suds. "She's my friend, and I don't even know if she sees me like that. And I don't know how to ask her!"

Victoria laughed, shaking her head. "With all that practice you've been putting in front of that mirror, I'd think you'd have it down by now."

William's jaw dropped. "Wait—you've been listening to me? God, Momma, can I get some privacy?"

"First of all," she said, her voice laced with mock sternness, "I didn't *see* you. But just because you hear everything from the basement doesn't mean we can't hear *you*!" She nudged him with her elbow, her grin mischievous. "Second, if you splash water on my hair, I don't care how grown you are—I'll beat your behind."

William burst out laughing. "Momma, you just bought that wig! Ain't nothing gonna happen to it—it's not even yours!" He reached up to tug at a strand, but before he could, she jabbed him in the side, making him flinch.

"This *is* my hair, boy," she snapped, her voice tinged with mock indignation. "I bought it, so it's mine. Same way that car in the driveway is mine, even though I didn't build it. Now hush."

"Okay, okay, I got you," William said, chuckling.

"And don't try to change the subject." She pointed a soapy hand at him. "Has she said anything about the dance? Dropped any hints?"

William shrugged, his confidence faltering again. "She talks about it sometimes, but she's never said anything about wanting to go with me."

Victoria sighed, shaking her head. "Listen, son. That's a pretty little girl, and I promise you, there are plenty of boys lining up to ask her. You better pick up that phone before someone else beats you to it. Girls don't always say things outright—they hint and hope the guy is man enough to hear it and do something about it."

"But what do I even say?" William asked, his voice tinged with frustration. "Every time I think about it, my heart gets all stupid, my vision gets blurry, and I can't even breathe."

Victoria placed a soapy hand on his arm, her tone softening. "Relax, baby. Just be yourself. She's been your friend all this time for a reason. If it's meant to be, it'll happen. But don't let the chance slip away—you'll regret it later if you do."

William smiled, her words sinking in. "You're right, Momma." He put down the towel and turned to leave.

But Victoria grabbed his wrist before he could take another step. "Oh no, you don't," she said, giving him a pointed look. "*After* you help me finish these dishes."

"Yes, ma'am," William said with a grin, grabbing the next plate.

They both laughed, the moment filled with the kind of love and warmth only a mother and son could share.

Later that evening, William lay sprawled on his bed, staring at the small, dark dot nestled in the corner of the ceiling. His mind buzzed, thoughts of Homecoming swirling like static. Instead of calling Isabella, he had wasted another night running through endless what-ifs. His stomach twisted as he imagined her rejecting him.

"What's the worst that could happen, huh?" he muttered to himself, his voice breaking the quiet. "It's just Bella."

He reached into the nightstand, pulling out a tiny bottle of BBs. Pouring a few into his palm, he rolled one between his fingers, settling it against the crook of his thumb and forefinger. He took careful aim at the dot.

"Man, just ask her. If she says no, it's not the end of the world."
FLING

The BB zipped through the air, landing just right of the target. The sharp *plink* of chipped paint echoed, and a small crater formed in the plaster.

"See? Just like that—missed, but no big deal." He smirked, grabbing another BB.

FLING

This one ricocheted wildly, skipping off the wall and pinging toward the door just as his mother walked in. The BB clipped the bulb of the reading lamp beside her, shattering it with a pop. Victoria screamed, throwing her hands up and dropping the cordless phone she was holding.

"Oh my God! *William Strong!* Boy, what the hell are you doing in here?"

William shot up, spilling BBs across the bed and floor. His wide eyes darted to the corner where the little black bug he'd been aiming at scuttled across the wall and disappeared out the window.

"Momma, I'm sorry, I was just—"

"Save it!" she snapped, her expression torn between anger and amusement. "I'll deal with you later. Right now, you've got a phone call." She grinned, holding the phone out to him.

"Who is it?" he whispered.

"Someone you should've called weeks ago."

His stomach flipped as he took the phone, holding it to his ear without saying a word. Victoria's eyebrows shot up, silently urging him to speak.

"Uh, hello?" he croaked.

"Heeeey William!" Isabella's familiar, bubbly voice burst through the receiver, instantly lighting his face with a smile.

That smile quickly disappeared as his mother, grinning ear to ear, started slow dancing in the doorway.

"Come on, Momma. Please, go away!" he whispered, covering the phone with his hand.

Victoria ignored him, spinning and twirling her imaginary partner with exaggerated flair.

"Momma! *Seriously!*"

She laughed, giving a final dramatic dip before sashaying out of the room.

William shut the door behind her, sighing as he brought the phone back to his ear. "Hey, Bella, what's up?" he asked, trying to sound casual.

"Not much! Everything okay over there? Sounded a little crazy."

"Yeah, yeah," he said, rubbing the back of his neck. "Momma's just being funny. You know how she is."

"She's hilarious. I love her," Isabella said, giggling. "Anyway, I wanted to ask you something—if you've got a few minutes. I need your advice."

"Yeah, sure," William said, his heart already thudding in his chest. "I've got a question for you too, actually."

"Oh? What is it?"

"Nah, you go first. Mine can wait."

"Alright," she said, her voice softening. "So, you know the dance is coming up, right?"

"Yeah," he replied, swallowing hard.

"Well... I think Devon wants to ask me. But he's really shy, and I don't know how to get him to actually do it. I mean, he's soooo cute, and I really want to go with him. You're my best friend, so I thought you'd know what to say to a guy like him."

The words hit him like a punch to the gut. His chest tightened as the hope he'd built crumbled in an instant. Isabella kept talking—about what she'd wear, how she'd style her hair, how perfect they'd look together—but her voice became distant, drowned out by the weight of her words.

William slumped back onto his bed, the phone slipping from his hand to his lap. His fingers brushed against the scattered BBs, one of which he idly rolled between his fingers. He closed his eyes, trying to steady his breathing, but his heart pounded relentlessly.

"Will? You there?" Isabella's voice broke through his thoughts.

"Yeah," he said, forcing a weak laugh. "Sorry. Just... got distracted. Devon, huh? Yeah, um... I'll think of something to help you out."

"Thanks, Will! You're the best," she said cheerfully.

"Yeah," he murmured, staring at the chipped plaster on the ceiling. "The best."

CHAPTER 12

Coach

The next evening, Coach Kline's car eased into the driveway of his Mequon home, the engine's low rumble settling into the quiet suburban night. The house was the picture of serenity—a neat, ranch-style home with a wraparound porch and a back-yard big enough to fit a whole squad running laps. It felt almost too perfect for someone like William, who was more used to the grit of the city.

Coach hadn't even shut the door when a massive jet-black German shepherd barreled out of the shadows, tail whipping like a propeller. The dog leapt up, its paws resting on Coach's chest as it licked his face with wild enthusiasm.

"Alright, alright, Guss! Damn, man, lemme breathe!" Coach laughed, playfully grappling with the dog's thick neck. He turned to William, a grin breaking through the gruff exterior. "Hey

Strong, don't just stand there, man. Come meet the toughest dog in the neighborhood. He's all bark, no bite."

William hesitated for a second, sticking out his hand cautiously. "What's his name?"

"Guss," Coach said, giving the dog a hearty pat on the side.

Guss sniffed at William's hand, then, apparently unimpressed, bolted toward the front door. The screen door creaked open, and out stepped a woman who could only be described as stunning. She leaned on the frame, her smile sharp and confident, like she was fully aware of the effect she had on people.

"So y'all just gonna stand out here admiring the view, or you coming in to eat?" Her tone was playful but carried an edge, a subtle reminder of who ran things here.

Coach waved a hand toward her as he headed inside. "Strong, meet my wife, Jada. Now, fair warning—she bites."

William, trying to keep it cool but fumbling anyway, managed, "How you doin', Ms. Coach Kline?"

The couple stopped dead, exchanging a look. Jada raised an eyebrow while Coach shook his head like he couldn't believe what he just heard.

"You serious right now?" Coach said, half-laughing. "Relax, man. Mi casa es su casa, alright? And lose that Ms. Coach Kline nonsense. Ain't nobody trying to be that formal." He muttered something about washing his hands and disappeared inside.

Jada stayed, her gaze warm but cutting. "Don't let him rattle you, baby. He's just gettin' old and cranky," she said, gently guiding William by the shoulder into the house. "And for the record, it's Jada. No Ms., no Coach, just Jada. Got it?"

William nodded, feeling the weight of her presence. She was nothing like he'd imagined. He'd pictured some frumpy woman who spent her days gardening or fussing over casseroles. Instead, she was a showstopper—five-six, with long dark hair that shimmered under the porch light, a figure that could turn heads, and an effortless swagger that demanded respect.

The air inside the house was thick with the rich aroma of home cooking—spices, fried chicken, and the faintest hint of something sweet. William tried to act natural, but his mind was still catching up.

Jada gave him a once-over and smiled knowingly. "You hungry? Good. I got more than enough to feed a whole damn team."

And just like that, the tension eased, but William knew one thing for sure: nothing about this night was going to be ordinary.

Time passed as the three of them worked through the meal, the table filled with the comforting warmth of fried chicken, mashed potatoes, and rich gravy. William leaned back slightly in his chair, expertly picking the last bits of meat off a drumstick, while Coach stretched out, one hand resting contentedly over his stomach. In the kitchen, Jada moved with an effortless grace, rifling through cabinets and drawers for plates and forks.

Coach tilted his head toward William, his tone casual but carrying that ever-present edge of amusement. "So?"

William glanced up, mid-bite, his brow furrowing. "So what?"

"The wife can throw down, huh?"

Before William could answer, Jada swept back into the room, balancing a perfect apple pie on one hand and a stack of small plates in the other. She caught just enough of the exchange to smirk.

"Hell yeah—oh, damn! My bad, Ms. Kline," William said, his excitement over the pie cutting straight through his manners. "Wait—oooh, is that pie?" He slid his dinner plate aside as fast as he could.

Jada shook her head, the smirk growing wider. "Looks like someone might outdo the eating machine over there." Her eyes flicked toward Coach, who was already looking a little too satisfied with himself.

Coach patted his belly dramatically. "What can I say? Gotta maintain this perfect form. All that cooking you do, baby, it's got me losing my abs of steel."

Jada didn't even miss a beat. "Baby, if abs stood for 'A Big Stomach,' you'd be in perfect shape." She dropped a slice of pie in front of him with flair, leaning down to kiss his cheek.

Coach gasped, his hand clutching his chest like she'd mortally wounded him. "Whoa, that was low, babe. Low blow! Uncalled for!"

William tried to hold it together but couldn't. A laugh bubbled out, and he quickly covered his mouth with his hand, his shoulders shaking. Coach caught the look and shook his head, grinning despite himself. "Told you she bites," he muttered, giving William a knowing nod.

The two men tucked into their pie without another word, the room filled only with the sounds of forks scraping plates and satisfied chewing. Then, out of nowhere, Guss appeared at the edge of the table, a heavy black glove clutched between his teeth. He nudged it insistently against Coach's leg, his tail wagging like he was proud of his find.

William paused mid-bite, eyebrows raised. "Okay, I get a ball, maybe a Frisbee, even a stick—but a glove? What's your dog doing bringing you that, C.K.?"

Coach grabbed the glove, inspecting it like it was the most natural thing in the world. "Nah, this ain't for fetch, my friend. This here's a different kind of catch." He tossed the glove onto the table with a grin that practically screamed mischief.

William leaned back, intrigued. "Alright then. What's the deal?"

Coach stood, pushing his chair back with an exaggerated scrape. "Finish your pie and find out. We're heading to the garage."

The tone shifted, the easygoing laughter replaced by a quiet anticipation. William couldn't help but wonder what kind of "catch" was waiting for him on the other side of that door.

After a few more quick bites of pie, the three made their way through the side door into the garage. The space was cluttered with storage boxes, old yard tools, and the faint smell of motor oil hanging in the air. Coach Kline moved with purpose, heading straight to a tall cabinet near the back wall. He opened it, reached inside, and grabbed a set of keys hanging from a hook.

"Alright, come on. Out this way," he said, holding the door open that led to the backyard.

But William's attention had already been snagged by something glinting in a nearby box. Curiosity got the better of him, and he reached in, pulling out a shiny gold trophy. He read the engraving aloud, his voice filled with disbelief: "National Championship Shotokan Karate, 2nd Place."

He turned to Coach, eyes wide. "Yo, C.K., you a ninja or somethin'?!"

William dug deeper into the box, uncovering more trophies, ribbons, and old photos. It was like a treasure trove of a completely different version of Coach Kline. "Or are you some kinda kung fu master?"

Coach turned, shaking his head with a look that said he'd heard it all before. "First of all, Kung Fu and Karate? Two completely different styles. Shotokan's the art of breaking bones, not flipping around on wires like in the movies. Second, that was back when I was younger—way younger. And third, get your hands outta my stuff before I have to show you a couple moves. Now bring your nosy ass out back. Guss is waiting!"

William hesitated for a second before putting everything back in the box. He couldn't shake the mental image of Coach taking down opponents in some intense tournament. "Okay, okay—but, real talk, what kinda karate you know?"

"Shotokan Karate," Coach replied over his shoulder. "Picked it up in the Corps. It came in handy a few times."

"Man, that's tight! Why you never told me you could whoop ass like that?" William grinned, throwing a couple of exaggerated punches and kicks, his moves straight out of a bad martial arts flick.

Coach glanced back, smirking. "Some men got secrets they don't feel like sharing. You should know somethin' about that, huh?"

William froze mid-pose, puzzled by the comment. Coach didn't elaborate, just shot him a sly look before heading out to a small shed in the backyard.

"Watch your step," Coach said as they entered the dark, cramped space. "It's a mess in here."

William stumbled over a bucket near the doorway, catching himself on the wall. Coach yanked the thin cord hanging from the ceiling, and a single bulb flickered to life, casting a dim glow over the room.

Guss was already there, his tail wagging wildly as he sat in front of a large, army-green footlocker. The dog was tense with anticipation, his focus locked on the box as though it held something sacred.

Coach crouched down, the keys jingling in his hand. As soon as he began unlocking the chest, Guss rose to his feet and froze, his body rigid, eyes glued to the scene.

William watched, his curiosity mounting. "What's in there?"

Coach didn't answer immediately. He reached into the chest, grunting slightly as he pulled out what looked like a large, heavy body suit. The material gleamed faintly under the weak light, its bulk almost menacing.

"What the hell is that?" William asked, his voice tinged with awe and confusion.

Coach stood, holding the suit up for a moment before slinging it over his shoulder like it weighed nothing. He shot William a grin. "Something to help you learn the meaning of 'different kind of catch.' You ready, or you wanna keep playing kung fu movie out here?"

William gulped, suddenly unsure about what he'd gotten himself into. "Uh... yeah, let's do this."

Coach chuckled, Guss letting out a sharp bark as if to punctuate the moment. Whatever was about to happen, William knew one thing for sure—it was about to get real.

"This, my friend, is a bite suit." Coach Kline held up the bulky, armored suit like it was a trophy. As if on cue, Guss growled low and deep in his throat, his hackles rising.

Coach shook the suit playfully in the dog's face. "Oh yeah, Guss hates this thing, don't you, boy? It's a love-hate kinda deal. Now, come on, fellas. Let's take this outside. And Strong—grab that other glove over there. Trust me, you're gonna need it."

William froze mid-step, his face twisting in disbelief. "What the hell am I gonna need gloves for? You ain't stickin' me in that thing so your dog can chew me up. No way, C.K.!"

Coach smirked. "Come on, man. Don't be a punk. Guss ain't gonna hurt you in this. He's just gonna show off a few tricks. You'll be fine."

William gestured at the suit with both hands. "Why don't you put that thing on and show me first, huh? I can't see no tricks if I'm too busy gettin' mauled by Killer Guss over here! Seriously, what's this about?"

Coach sighed, dropping the suit on the ground as he adjusted the gloves. "Look, I trained him this way. Back in the Corps, I worked with K-9 units. Trust me, I know what I'm doing. Here's the deal: I'll suit up first, show you how it works, and then it's your turn. Deal?"

William eyed Guss, who looked more like a happy, panting house dog than a deadly weapon at the moment. "Alright," William said cautiously. "But only if you show me some of those ShotoCAN moves afterward. Deal?"

Coach chuckled. "It's ShotoKAN, like 'CON.' And fine—if you can handle Guss, I'll show you some moves. But no crying like a baby, or no deal."

William puffed up his chest. "You got it. But I want the real stuff, man—something I can use if I gotta throw hands."

Coach suited up with exaggerated movements, hiding a mischievous grin. "Oh, you're gonna get the real stuff. Let's do this!"

He stomped his gloves together, the dust puffing off them like smoke. Coach then led Guss to the far side of the yard and commanded him to stay, using a sharp downward motion with his open palm. Guss dropped instantly, lying still except for his wagging tail.

"Alright, I'm gonna teach you some basic commands first," Coach explained. He demonstrated another hand signal, bringing Guss back to a sitting position.

"Aww, man, that's impressive!" William said, nodding.

Coach rolled his eyes. "You think that's impressive? Watch this."

He walked over to Guss, turned him around so his back was to them, and returned to William's side. "Now, how do I give him a hand command if he can't see me?"

William shrugged. "I guess you'd have to call him, right?"

"Nope. I don't do verbal commands. Watch this." Coach rubbed his thumb and fingers together, creating a faint scratching noise. Guss's ears perked, and he turned to face them. Then, with a sharp point to the ground, Guss bolted over and laid down at Coach's feet.

William's jaw dropped. "Yo, that was insane! I've never seen anything like that!"

Coach grinned. "You ready to give it a shot?"

William stepped forward, confidence brimming. "Yeah, let's do this."

Coach guided Guss back into position and handed the reins over to William. But when William tried the downward hand command, Guss just sat there, panting with an amused tilt of his head.

"Yo, what's up with this? He ain't doing nothin'!"

Coach smirked. "You want a hint?"

"Yeah, man. Please."

"Well, for starters, he's already lying down. Try getting him up instead."

William groaned and switched to the upward motion. But Guss still didn't budge, his tongue lolling lazily out of his mouth.

"C'mon, man!" William threw his hands in the air. "What's the deal?"

Coach burst into laughter. "It's 'cause you're black!"

William froze, then flipped him off. "Man, you play too much."

"Relax. It's 'cause it's your first time here. He doesn't know you yet. Guess that means you're gonna have to suit up." Coach started peeling off the bite suit, tossing it at William's feet.

"This is some bullshit, C.K., and you know it," William grumbled, slipping into the oversized gear. William's gaze settled on Guss, the dog's powerful frame relaxed yet brimming with quiet energy. His tongue lolled lazily to one side, glistening in the faint light, each pant a steady rhythm of calm anticipation.

"You better not hurt me, you stupid dog," William muttered, his voice laced with half-joking bravado.

At the sound of his words, Guss's tongue slipped back into his mouth, his ears pivoting upward like radar dishes locking onto a signal. He tilted his head, a sharp, inquisitive motion that gave him an almost human air of comprehension. For a brief moment, the dog's amber eyes met William's, gleaming with a peculiar mix of mischief and understanding, as if silently asking, *Who's the stupid one here?*

Once suited up, William looked like a clumsy, camo-covered sumo wrestler. Coach stepped back into the shed, reappearing with a helmet.

"What the hell is that?" William asked.

Coach grinned. "Bite suit helmet. Trust me, you're gonna need it." He plopped it on William's head and fastened it.

"Alright, Guss, let's show him what you got!" Coach yelled, slashing his hand across his throat.

Guss exploded into motion, tearing across the yard like a furry missile. William's eyes widened behind the helmet, and he stumbled backward, flailing like a scarecrow.

"Don't run—it makes it worse!" Coach called out, laughing as Guss closed the

distance.

CHAPTER 13

Fugitive Strong

PART ONE

It was Friday morning, the kind of day that already felt like it was moving too fast. William darted across the street, weaving between impatient drivers leaning on their horns, the asphalt shimmering with the threat of rain. Ahead, Isabella was halfway down the block, her books clutched to her chest like armor.

"Yo, wait up!" William called, slinging his backpack higher on his shoulder. He jammed his index finger in his mouth, gnawing at it absentmindedly as he jogged to catch up.

Isabella slowed, glancing back with an annoyed but familiar look. "I waited for you, but you're always late," she said, her voice edged with the kind of exasperation only close friends can get away with.

"My bad, I'm here now." He rubbed his thumb over the tip of his finger, the irritation distracting him. "So, you're still going to the dance with Bones?"

Isabella rolled her eyes, her pace steady. "Yes, *William*, I'm still going with him. And don't call him that. He's not that skinny."

"Not that skinny?" William scoffed, barely missing a crack in the sidewalk as he caught up to her. "That boy's so skinny his shadow's ashamed to follow him. And, real talk, I heard he puts Band-Aids on his nipples, so they don't poke through his tight-ass shirts".

Isabella shot him a glare, her lips twitching like she wanted to laugh but refused to give him the satisfaction. "You done? Or is your job today to roast my date to death before third period?"

"Just saying," William muttered, raising his hands like he was innocent. But his grin faltered. "Wait, so... nobody else asked you? Not one dude?"

Isabella stopped, whipping around to face him, her books shifting precariously. "No. Nobody. Not even you," she snapped, her tone sharper than a broken pencil. "My mom kept hyping me up, saying I'd have all these boys lined up to ask me, but guess what? Nothing. Just Bones."

William's stride faltered. He stood there, his finger back in his mouth as if chewing it would help him swallow the knot in his chest.

"What's wrong with you?" Isabella asked, her frustration softening just a little. "And seriously, why do you keep sucking on your finger?"

He pulled his hand away and shook his head, staring at her like she'd just admitted the world was flat. "I thought... I thought someone—anyone—would've asked you. Hell, I—" He stopped himself, his voice catching like a shirt snagged on a nail.

Isabella glanced at him, the tension between them thick as the morning fog. "Yeah, well, you didn't," she said quietly, turning back to the crosswalk as traffic whizzed by.

William didn't follow right away. He leaned against a stop sign, tapping his shoe to shake loose a pebble rattling inside. Her words hung in the air, heavy and unforgiving, and when she stepped off the curb, he realized too late what she'd meant.

"I'm really disappointed in you, William," she called over her shoulder. "If anyone was gonna ask me, I thought it'd be you."

His chest tightened, the truth in her words hitting harder than he wanted to admit. His hand gripped the stop sign pole as he watched her walk away, the weight of what he'd let slip through his fingers sinking in. The metal groaned beneath his grip, bending slightly under the pressure. He shoved his foot back into his shoe and took off after her.

"Isabella, wait!" he shouted, but she didn't stop.

Behind him, the stop sign wobbled, then fell, crashing into the grass like some kind of grim punctuation. He didn't look back.

Instead, he chased her down, the sound of his sneakers pounding against the pavement almost loud enough to drown out the voice in his head whispering that he'd blown it.

Back at home, Victoria moved through the kitchen with the determination of someone trying to outrun her own thoughts. The mess William had left after one of his chaotic morning feasts was scattered across the counter—a half-eaten bagel here, an abandoned cereal bowl there. She sighed, scooping the leftovers into a Tupperware dish and stacking it in the fridge.

The hum of the dishwasher filled the space as she crammed the last of the plates inside and hit the start button, the low rumble doing little to drown out the background noise of the TV in the living room.

"Crime rates across the city have seen a sharp increase over the last two years," the anchor droned, their voice as monotonous as the stats they read. Victoria barely paid attention, her focus on wiping down the counter and restoring some semblance of order.

Her phone buzzed sharply in her pocket, cutting through the moment. She hesitated before pulling it out, already bracing for the kind of distraction she didn't need. The screen lit up with a text from her husband:

"We got some serious things to discuss when I get home."

Her brow furrowed as she read it, her cleaning forgotten. Typing back quickly, she asked, **"Tell me what we gotta talk about that's so serious?"**

She waited, her thumb hovering over the screen, but no reply came. The seconds stretched into minutes, and when she tried calling, the line went straight to voicemail. Again. And again.

Her irritation bubbled over. "Uh-uh, no, sir. You ain't about to have me sitting here all day stressed out over some vague-ass, bullshit message," she muttered, shaking her head as she set the phone on the counter.

Still, she felt the weight of the words, heavy and unsettling, like a storm cloud on the horizon. Her fingers twitched, tempted to turn the phone back on, but she forced herself to take a step back.

"Not today," she declared, her voice firm as if she were talking to someone other than herself. "Ms. Victoria is gonna have a good day. Just me and the TV. No interruptions, no nonsense."

She picked up the remote and sank onto the couch, flipping through channels with practiced indifference. But the phone sat on the counter, silent and foreboding, its dark screen a reminder that whatever her husband had to say wasn't going to wait forever.

Later that day, William pushed through the front door, the faint crunch of a protein bar audible as he chewed. He kicked off his sneakers halfway into the hall and shrugged off his backpack, letting it fall to the floor with a thud before heading straight to the kitchen.

"Momma! What we got to eat?" he called, already yanking open the refrigerator door. The cool air wafted out as he scanned the shelves, but there was no reply.

Closing the door with a huff, he noticed a neatly folded note stuck to the fridge with a magnet. His mom's familiar handwriting greeted him:

I knew this would be the first place you'd look when you got home. I left you something in your bedroom.

Love,
Momma

A grin tugged at his lips as he crumpled the note in one hand, curiosity pulling him toward the stairs. He climbed them two at a time, the protein bar forgotten in his other hand, and pushed open the door to his room.

On his bed lay a black tuxedo, sharp and pristine, with satin peak lapels. The white shirt and bow tie were perfectly arranged, as though they belonged in a shop window. Beneath the bed, a pair of glossy black dress shoes gleamed in the light. The scent of fresh fabric lingered in the air, faint but unmistakable.

Something poked out from the breast pocket of the tuxedo jacket—a second note. William plucked it out, his grin widening as he read:

Boy, you gonna look good in this!!!

He let out a low whistle, lifting the tuxedo carefully off the bed and holding it up. The fabric felt expensive, smooth beneath his fingers. Turning to the mirror, he pressed the jacket against his chest and tilted his head, inspecting his reflection.

"Damn, this is clean!" he said, the excitement spilling out in his voice. "Thank you, Momma. Thank you!"

For a moment, the room felt different—lighter. He ran his hands down the sleek lines of the jacket again, a mix of pride and gratitude bubbling inside him. He imagined himself at the dance, looking like he belonged on a magazine cover, and for the first time in weeks, he felt ready to face the evening ahead.

PART TWO

The gym pulsed with energy, every surface drenched in the school's bold colors of red and white. Streamers crisscrossed overhead, banners hung from the walls, and tables were draped in matching tablecloths. Even the punch bowl, trembling slightly with every beat of DJ Boom's latest track, seemed alive with the atmosphere. The gym floor was a sea of teenagers, a chaotic mix of dancing, shouting, and raised cups sloshing with sugary red punch.

William stepped inside, his polished shoes clicking softly on the gym's hardwood floor. A couple of girls near the entrance caught sight of him, their eyes traveling from his sharp tuxedo to his confident stride. They exchanged looks and giggled appreciatively before moving on. But William didn't notice. His focus was razor-sharp, scanning the crowd for one person and one person only.

Rising onto his toes, he craned his neck to peer over the shifting crowd. The tuxedo hugged his frame perfectly, tailored just enough to highlight his athletic build without being showy. Every detail of his appearance, from the shine of his shoes to the crisp bow tie, was meticulously in place. He wanted Isabella to see him like this, to notice the effort he'd made. He didn't care that she was there with someone else. Tonight, he needed her to realize what she'd missed by choosing that "stick figure" over him.

As he wove through the crowd, his senses were assaulted by the thrum of bass and the buzz of voices. Then, out of nowhere, he flinched at a poke to his side. His hand shot out reflexively, catching the culprit's wrist. When he looked down, he saw a small hand in a white glove.

"Gotcha!" came Isabella's teasing voice.

William turned, his breath catching for a moment. There she was, standing inches away, dressed in a sleek white gown that shimmered under the gym's flashing lights. The dress fit her like it was painted on, accentuating every curve in a way that made her look effortlessly grown. A faint sparkle dusted her shoulders and collarbone, her caramel skin glowing as if lit from within.

"Damn," he muttered, stepping back slightly.

Isabella's laugh rang out, light and warm. "Whatever, but I could say the same about you, boy. Look at you! All dressed up like some kind of GQ model." She bumped him playfully with her shoulder.

"Oh, is that funny?" he teased, his smirk creeping across his face.

"Not funny, just... different," she admitted, her eyes sweeping over him again. "You've always got those baggy clothes on. It's about time you let people see what's underneath."

For a moment, they stood there, caught in an unspoken tension. The music and the crowd around them faded, and it was just the two of them, unsure of what to say next.

Finally, William broke the silence. "So... did you come with Sticks?"

Isabella's playful expression vanished, replaced with a warning glare. "What did I tell you, Will?" She pushed him lightly, her tone somewhere between exasperation and amusement.

"What?" He grinned, leaning into his usual mischievous charm.

"Stop it, that's what. Don't be an asshole tonight. Please?"

Before he could respond, a tall, wiry figure emerged behind her, draping a possessive arm over her shoulders. Devon. His presence cast a long shadow, and the smug confidence on his face sent a ripple of annoyance through William.

"Is everything okay, baby?" Devon asked, his gaze shifting between Isabella and William.

"No, he didn't," Isabella thought, her stomach sinking.

William's grin widened into something sharper, more pointed. "Yeah, baby," he said, mimicking Devon's tone. "Is everything alright?"

Isabella shot him a warning glance before stepping back slightly. "Devon, this is William. William, this is Devon." She motioned for the two to shake hands, but the air between them was already thick with unspoken tension.

William extended his hand, his grin frozen in place, trying to play the part of the bigger man. But Devon didn't move. He simply looked at the outstretched hand with faint disdain.

"I got some friends I want to introduce you to," Devon said, ignoring the gesture entirely as he steered Isabella away. "Come on, you need to upgrade your company anyway."

Isabella glanced over her shoulder, her eyes meeting William's for a brief moment. Her lips parted, as if she wanted to say something, but the words never came. Instead, she disappeared into the crowd, her white dress vanishing like a ghost among the swirling reds and whites.

William stood there, his hand still hanging in the air, his grin finally fading. He let it drop to his side and exhaled slowly, his jaw tightening. The music thumped on, but the room suddenly felt much emptier.

The gym buzzed with energy, but William wasn't feeling it. His sharp tuxedo, which had boosted his confidence earlier, now felt like a costume masking his frustration. As he leaned against the wall, lost in his thoughts, Coach C.K. appeared out of nowhere, clapping him on the shoulder.

"Strong! Hey, man, looking snappy!" Coach said, grinning as he eyed William's suit.

William shot him a half-hearted smirk. "Snappy? Really, C.K.? You're showing your age with that one. But thanks."

"Hey, take it easy," Coach chuckled, taking a sip from his cup and offering it to William. "Here, try some of this."

William eyed the cup suspiciously, swirling the contents and catching a whiff of something sharp and unmistakably alcoholic. "What is it?"

"Just a little something to spice up this dull-ass punch. Gotta keep it interesting, surrounded by all these kids whining about the homecoming game," Coach said, glancing around like a guilty conspirator. "Just a sip, though. Small ones. Don't make a scene."

Without hesitation, William tipped the cup and downed it in one go. The burn hit him immediately, scorching his throat and leaving a bitter aftertaste that made his eyes water.

"Holy shit, dude, I said *sip*! What part of that didn't you understand?" Coach grabbed the cup back, glaring at the empty bottom. "Do you even know what a sip is?"

"Ughhh." William grimaced, fanning his tongue as the alcohol spread through him like wildfire. "What the hell was that?"

"Something you're *definitely* not getting any more of. Damn, Strong, you're gonna get us both busted. And while I've got you—have you seen Buddha? He's been MIA, and people are asking questions."

William shook his head, the warmth of the alcohol making it harder to focus. "Nah, haven't seen him in a minute. And I'm good with that."

Coach sighed, rubbing the back of his neck. "Figures. He's my best nose tackle, and I hear rumors he's in trouble. I'm hoping they're wrong."

William shrugged, his irritation bubbling just beneath the surface. "Honestly, C.K., I don't give a damn. That dude can stay gone for all I care."

Coach studied him for a moment, narrowing his eyes. "Uh-oh."

"What? What's wrong?"

"That drink's already hitting you, isn't it? Lightweight."

"Nah, I'm good," William insisted, though the gym lights seemed brighter, the voices louder, and the floor unsteady beneath his feet.

Coach leaned in, lowering his voice. "Listen, don't do anything stupid. And if you do? You didn't get it from me." With that, he disappeared into the crowd, leaving William alone with his spiraling thoughts.

Needing to wash the taste out of his mouth, William headed for the punch bowl, downing two cups in quick succession. Isabella's face floated in his mind, framed by Devon's hands, and the image twisted in his chest like a knife.

By the time he stumbled into the bathroom, the warm buzz had morphed into a disorienting haze. Leaning over the sink, he splashed water on his face, but the cool droplets did little to clear his head. The porcelain beneath his weight creaked ominously, cracks spiderwebbing across the surface as his frustration boiled over. He staggered into a stall, slamming the door shut behind him.

The bathroom door swung open with a sharp creak, letting in a burst of muffled music and voices from the gym. Two boys stumbled inside, their laughter bouncing off the tiled walls.

"Hell yeah, dude—a lot!" the first boy exclaimed, his tone equal parts pride and mischief.

"What'd you do with the bottle?" the second asked, sidling up to a urinal. The splash of water against porcelain punctuated his words.

"It's right here, man." The first boy tugged at his shirt, revealing a faint bulge beneath it. "Tucked it in my pants."

The second boy snorted, shaking his head as he finished his business. "You idiot. Get rid of it before someone busts you with it. How much did you pour in, anyway?"

Standing before the mirror, the first boy leaned closer, scrutinizing his reflection. He pressed his fingers against his nose, squeezing a stubborn blackhead with exaggerated care. "I told you—*the whole bottle*. Dumped it earlier. What, you think I'd half-ass it?"

The second boy froze mid-step, his hand still dripping from the sink. "You dumped the *whole* bottle? In the punch?" His voice pitched higher, disbelief mingling with panic.

As the first boy chuckled and turned to reply, his eyes caught something in the mirror—a pair of shoes visible under the stall door behind him. His grin faltered, and his expression turned stone-cold serious. He pressed a finger to his lips, signaling his friend to silence, and pointed subtly toward the stall.

The second boy followed his gaze, his brows knitting in confusion before his face lit with alarm. He leaned closer, whispering, "You think it's the principal?"

"I don't know, man. I don't wanna find out. Just go—*now!*" The urgency in the first boy's voice broke their bravado.

They exchanged a look, then bolted for the door, the sound of their sneakers squeaking on the polished floor. As the door swung shut behind them, the bathroom fell eerily silent again, save for the faint hum of fluorescent lights and the distant bass from the gym.

Inside the stall, William's imagination ran wild. The image of Devon and Isabella resurfaced, more vivid and taunting. His fists clenched, knuckles whitening as he pounded the stall wall in frustration. Each impact left a dent, the thin metal giving way to his growing rage.

"If I'd just asked her—just *once*—she wouldn't be here with him," he muttered, the words choking in his throat. His fists struck the wall harder, the sound echoing through the room.

Chubby Corbin Mitchell, infamous for his awkward charm and nerdy reputation, waddled into the bathroom with purpose. His round face was flushed, and his thick glasses slid down his nose as he beelined toward a urinal. Without hesitation, he began unbuckling his belt and tugging down his pants, dropping them well below his hips—far lower than necessary.

Just as Corbin settled in, a deafening crash shattered the room's relative quiet. The stall door nearest him exploded outward, ripping off its hinges and slamming into the sink and mirror with enough force to send shards of glass skittering across the tile floor. The room seemed to shudder under the impact.

Startled, Corbin's mouth fell open, and his pants slipped all the way to his ankles. The sudden destruction cut his stream short, leaving him frozen in place. His round eyes, magnified comically by his glasses, darted toward the chaos. Slowly, he shuffled a step back, his hand still clutching himself as he peered around the edge of the stall.

"AAAAAAAAAAAAAAAGGGGGH!" William's roar of frustration tore through the room like a thunderclap, vibrating the remaining stall walls and reverberating in Corbin's chest. The sheer force of it startled a quick, involuntary spurt from him, staining the floor at his feet.

Panic seized Corbin. With an awkward, frantic motion, he yanked his pants up, nearly tripping in his haste to cover himself. His belt flapped wildly as he cinched it far too high, his cheeks burning crimson. Without daring to glance back, he bolted for the door, his sneakers squeaking against the tile as he escaped, leaving the wreckage—and William's simmering rage—behind.

PART THREE

Out in the gym, the DJ flipped the vibe with a smooth slow jam, dimming the lights to set the mood. The crowd shifted, the chaotic energy settling into something softer, more intimate. Boys shuffled nervously, stepping up to girls with hesitant smiles to ask for a dance. But Devon wasn't one to ask.

He grabbed Isabella's arm and tugged her toward the dance floor without a word.

"You know, you could've just asked?" she said, pulling slightly against his grip as they wove through the other couples.

"Why ask? That's stupid. You're my date," Devon replied, flashing her a cocky grin. "You're supposed to come with me. Besides, I know you want to."

Isabella sighed, a sharp, frustrated sound that didn't seem to faze him. As the music played, he pulled her closer, his hands sliding to her lower back. The warmth of his body pressed against hers felt suffocating. She tried to push him away subtly, creating even a little space between them, but his grip was firm. Too firm.

"Devon," she muttered, her voice low with warning. She reached for his hands, intent on peeling them off her waist. Her bare fingers grazed his skin.

The world tilted.

A flood of images and sensations hit her like a tidal wave. Blurred faces. Panicked screams. Cold laughter. Violent acts that weren't hers but felt too vivid, too real to ignore. Her eyes rolled upward as the onslaught took over, her body momentarily limp against Devon's.

"Hey, what's wrong—what the hell's wrong with you?" Devon asked, his voice rising with confusion as he shook her shoulders.

She snapped back to reality with a sharp intake of breath, her chest heaving like she'd just surfaced from deep water. Without a word, she shoved him hard, breaking free of his grip, and bolted off the dance floor. Laughter rippled through the nearby students who noticed, their mocking tones stinging in her ears.

"Hey! Where you going?" Devon shouted, his face flushed with embarrassment. He hesitated for only a moment before chasing after her.

Isabella's heels clicked frantically against the hallway tiles as she sprinted away, her pulse pounding in her ears. The dimly lit corridor stretched endlessly ahead, every shadow twisting into something menacing. She glanced over her shoulder, hoping she'd lost him, but instead, she collided with something solid and tumbled to the ground.

Devon stood over her, his expression a mix of confusion and irritation. "What the hell is wrong with you?" he demanded, extending a hand to help her up. "Why you acting crazy all of a sudden?"

She scrambled back on her hands and heels, pushing herself upright with a trembling effort. Her gaze darted around, looking for an escape.

"Don't come near me," she said, her voice sharp and trembling. "I don't want anything to do with you."

"All this 'cause I touched your hips?" Devon asked, throwing his arms out. "Did I do something else wrong? I thought we were enjoying the dance. Then you just cut out like my breath stank."

"Well, maybe that's part of it," she shot back, her voice shaking but defiant. "But it's not just that. Just... stay away from me. I'll find my way home."

Devon narrowed his eyes, stepping closer despite her words. "What else is there? That's nothing a damn stick of gum can't fix. You're scared of something else. I can see it all over your face." He smirked. "What's got you so shook, huh?"

Isabella's breath hitched, her anger and fear boiling over. "Not half as scared as the women you raped," she spat, her voice laced with disgust. "Is that what you had planned for me later?"

Devon froze, the air between them turning heavy. His smirk faltered, his bravado cracking. "Raped? What the hell are you talking about?" His voice was quieter now, but no less defensive. "Do I look like some damn rapist to you?"

Isabella's eyes burned with tears, her fists clenched tight at her sides. "I saw it, Devon. I saw *them*. Don't pretend. Just stay the hell away from me."

Her words hung between them like a sword, sharp and unyielding. For the first time, Devon didn't have a comeback. He just stared, his confident swagger stripped away, leaving behind a cold, unsettling silence.

Isabella's heart pounded in her chest as she stared at Devon, his false concern giving way to a sinister smirk. She cursed herself for leaving the dance floor, for stepping into this dark, empty hallway where no one could hear her over the bass thundering from the gym.

"You know," Devon sneered, his voice a low growl, "you kinda ruined the surprise. Right, fellas?"

Before Isabella could react, she felt hands grab her from behind. A muffled gasp escaped her as Chris and Marcel clamped down, one covering her mouth while the other locked her arms. Her heels scraped against the tiled floor as they dragged her backward, her struggles no match for their strength.

"Check the classrooms," Devon barked, rattling doorknobs with impatience.

Marcel grinned. "Yo, the music room's open, bro. Guess they forgot to lock it after setting up the speakers."

Her muffled pleas were ignored as the trio herded her inside, shutting the door with an ominous click. The air in the room was stale, the shadows heavy and oppressive. In a corner, hidden beneath the darkness, William stirred from his restless nap. The sharp clatter of maracas hitting the floor snapped him fully awake. Groggy but alert, he crept toward the door, intent on slipping out unnoticed.

A sharp scream cut through the silence, freezing him in place. "Get your hands off me!"

William's pulse quickened. That voice—it was Isabella. He turned, his gaze locking on the dim figures illuminated by faint light from the hallway window.

"Hold her legs! Don't let her kick me!" Devon ordered, his voice cracking under the pressure.

Isabella thrashed, her movements wild and frantic. Chris's grip slipped, and she screamed again, louder this time. William's fists clenched as the sound ricocheted through him, igniting something deep and primal.

"Shut her up, man!" Devon snapped. "Ain't nobody coming for you, girl, so you might as well chill."

As Devon reached for his tie, Isabella's scream was cut short by a sickening thud. Chris crumpled to the floor, eyes rolling back. Marcel turned, confused, only to be yanked backward into the shadows. A muffled struggle, a sharp gasp, and then silence.

"What the—Marcel?!" Devon's voice wavered as he spun around, dragging Isabella up as a human shield. His grip was clumsy, desperate. "Who's there? I swear I'll snap her neck!"

Isabella whimpered, her wide eyes scanning the darkness. Then, from the shadows, William stepped forward, his silhouette menacing and deliberate. Devon's breath hitched. He shoved Isabella aside, making a frantic dash for the door, but his foot caught on a chair. He hit the floor hard, groaning as he scrambled on all fours.

"Not so fast," William muttered, seizing Devon by the back of his belt and hauling him up like a ragdoll. Devon's bravado evaporated as he dangled in midair.

"Wait—hold up, man! It's not that serious! You—you want her? Take her!" Devon's voice cracked, his words spilling over themselves. "She's—she's not worth it!"

William's grip tightened. "Shut up, bitch! Ain't nobody coming for you, so you might as well chill and get this over with." William says, mocking Devon's previous comment to Isabella. With a calculated motion, he slammed his fist into Devon's abdomen, fracturing his spine with one blow. Devon's cry of pain was cut short by a gasp as he's slammed to the floor with tremendous force, reverberating through the room, his body crumpling into a heap.

The lights flicked on, revealing the chaos. A janitor stood in the doorway, eyes wide as he surveyed the scene. Without a word, he bolted down the hallway.

Isabella's knees buckled, but she forced herself to stand. "William?" she whispered, her voice trembling.

He turned, his face softening as he approached her. She reached for him, clinging to him as though he were the only solid thing in a crumbling world. "You have to go," she urged, her voice urgent. "They'll come back. You have to leave."

William hesitated, his eyes lingering on her tear-streaked face. Then, as if moved by instinct, he leaned in. Their lips met, brief but electric, a connection forged in the midst of chaos.

"Go," she whispered, her hands pushing him toward the door.

He nodded, peeking into the hallway before disappearing into the shadows. The door closed with a soft click, leaving Isabella alone with the groaning Devon. She crouched beside him, her lips curling into a grim smirk.

"You think you're tough?" she hissed, ripping open his shirt to reveal a patchwork of childish Band-Aids. With a flick of her wrist, she tore one off, taking tufts of hair with it. Devon howled in pain.

"Shut up," she spat, standing over him. "Ain't nobody coming for you."

PART FOUR

Panting heavily, his chest heaving from the sprint through the chilled night air, William slowed as he approached the familiar outline of his home at precisely 11:37 p.m. The sharp tug of his bow tie around his neck became unbearable, and with a frustrated yank, he tore it off, casting it to the ground like a shed skin. The driveway stretched before him, eerily quiet, the house itself shrouded in an unnatural darkness. Not a single light glowed—not even the steadfast porch light his mother always kept on like a beacon when he stayed out late. His brow furrowed. The car was parked in its usual spot; they had to be home.

"Momma?" he called hesitantly as he slipped through the kitchen door, his voice tentative in the unnerving silence.

The door refused to open fully, its edge colliding with a toppled kitchen chair. Pushing it aside, he stepped in, setting the chair upright with a mechanical motion, his eyes darting about the shadowed room.

"Shhh... please, don't wake your father," came Victoria's voice from the living room. It was soft but trembling, each word wrapped in a fragile uncertainty.

He hesitated, then made his way toward her, the stillness pressing in like a weight. "Why are you sitting in the dark, Momma? What's going on?"

His hand reached instinctively for the wall, brushing against the light switch.

"Don't," she murmured, sharper this time. "Leave the lights off, baby—my eyes... they're sensitive right now." Her silhouette, barely discernible, was seated stiffly in the center of the couch. The faint glow of a streetlamp filtered through the curtains, casting a dim halo around her. A glass of brandy glinted in her hand. "How was the dance? Did Bella like your suit? You look so handsome."

"It got... it got crazy," he muttered, shuffling closer. "You don't wanna hear about it."

He leaned in for the customary kiss on her cheek, but her voice stopped him mid-motion.

"Stay over there, baby. I'm not feeling too good tonight." Her tone was gentler now, almost pleading. "Why don't you sit on the loveseat and tell me about it? Just... sit over there."

He hesitated, the unease in her voice stirring a knot in his chest. Stepping toward the loveseat, his foot crunched against something on the floor—a plastic bag, its crumpled form catching the faint light.

"Momma... what's wrong?" he pressed, lowering himself onto the loveseat, his voice edged with concern. "Tell me."

Victoria drew in a trembling breath, her fingers tightening around the glass. "Son, I need to ask you something, and I need you to answer honestly, okay? Just... tell me the truth."

His confusion deepened. "Okay?"

She shifted, lifting a small box from the shadows beside her. Its edges were torn, its purpose unmistakable. "Did your finger hurt this morning?" Her words were slow, deliberate, heavy with unspoken meaning.

He glanced at his hand, frowning. "Yeah, it stung a little. I figured I just pinched it on something. Why?"

Her gaze dropped to the amber liquid in her glass. She took a sip, her shoulders rising with a sharp inhale before she spoke again. "Your father pricked your finger with this." She held up the box, her hand trembling slightly. "An instant DNA test."

The box tumbled onto the coffee table with a hollow thud as she whispered the words that shattered the air between them. "He ain't your father, baby."

William hesitated, the air thick with unspoken tension, before finally responding. "I don't care, Momma—I really don't. In my eyes, he was never my father, just a provider." His voice was calm, but it carried a brittle edge. He leaned back on the loveseat, his fingers creeping up the smooth, cool stem of the lamp beside him. Without warning, he pressed the switch.

The room was flooded with soft light. His mother recoiled instinctively, shielding her face with one hand while fumbling to set her glass down on the coffee table with the other. Her movements were hurried, but not quick enough to escape his notice.

William froze, his gaze locking on the truth she tried to conceal. Fury ignited within him, and he surged to his feet, closing the distance between them in a few swift strides. Grabbing her wrists, he pulled her hands away, revealing the battered canvas of her face. His own expression cracked, and his eyes brimmed with tears.

"Oh, Momma..."

His hand trembled as he cupped her chin, tilting her head gently upward. His anger simmered just beneath the surface as his eyes traced the injuries: the tender lump on her forehead, the grotesquely swollen right eye, the bloodied corner of her mouth. Finger-shaped bruises marred the sides of her neck like a grim necklace.

"He... he was angry," she stammered, her voice quivering as she struggled for composure. She drew in a shaky breath. "He thought I did something, but I didn't. So he... he..."

"Stop," William cut her off, his voice hard but laced with pain. "No, Momma. No. I can't let him do this to you anymore. Don't make excuses for him."

"William, wait!" she cried, her desperation tangible as she grabbed for his shirt. The fabric tore in her grip, but he didn't stop.

His steps faltered when his eyes fell on the plastic bag he had kicked earlier, now catching the light. Dirt smeared its surface and the floor around it. Something peeked out—green and familiar. He crouched, his breath catching as he pulled free his Incredible Hulk shoebox, its cartoon face staring back at him.

For a moment, he simply knelt there, heart hammering, his fingers tracing the edges of the box. A tear fell, splashing onto the printed Hulk, leaving a darkened smudge. Finally, with trembling hands, he opened it.

Empty.

The realization hit him like a physical blow. He rifled through the bag, checking each box, his hope disintegrating with every hollow container. They were all empty.

"Momma," he whispered, his voice low and taut, "where's my money?"

The shoebox crumpled in his grasp, its cardboard frame no match for the storm that roiled within him.

"Your money?" Victoria's voice cracked as she spoke, her face etched with worry. "Your father found it this morning in the backyard, when someone came to take that old rock. He told them he wanted to keep it now, said it was good luck." She paused, her breath hitching as realization dawned. "Oh my God, baby—no. Why didn't you tell me?"

William stared down at the crumpled shoebox in his hands, its once-proud form now a mangled remnant of hope. His voice trembled, barely contained. "Where is the money, Momma—please? That was *our* money. Our money to get away from him. I've been saving that since I was little. Where is it?"

Her lips parted, but the words faltered. "He... he..." she began, struggling to find her voice.

William's expression hardened, his nostrils flaring as the unspoken truth sank in. "He spent it? He spent *our* money?" His chest rose and fell rapidly, adrenaline coursing through his veins. His fists clenched so tightly that his knuckles cracked, the sound sharp in the tense silence.

"William, don't," she pleaded, her voice breaking as she reached toward him. "Don't do anything, okay? Baby?"

But he didn't answer, his gaze fixed on the ruined box in his lap, the crumpled cardboard emblematic of their shattered escape plan.

"What do you mean, don't do anything?" he snapped, his voice rising as anger seeped through the cracks of his composure. "Look at your face, Momma! Look what he did to you. And now he's spent our getaway money!"

Tears welled in her eyes, her voice soft yet resolute. "God will make him answer for what he's done. Just forgive him, as I do. Our day will come, William. Leave it in God's hands." She reached for his hand, her fingers trembling. "Please, baby, sit down next to me."

William didn't budge, the storm inside him growing fiercer.

"So you're saying I should forgive him?" he said bitterly. "That we should just sit here, take this, and wait for God to punish him? Is that what you're saying?"

"Yes," she whispered, her voice laced with desperation. "God will see us through this. Come on, sit down."

After a long moment, he relented, sinking into the cushion beside her. She embraced him, her arms trembling as they wrapped around his rigid frame. He didn't return her affection, his body unyielding, his mind elsewhere.

"Promise me you'll forgive him for what he's done. Promise me, baby," she sobbed, clinging to him as though her words alone could mend their fractured world.

William's silence stretched on, his thoughts a whirlwind of anger, doubt, and the weight of choices yet to be made. He thought of the years of torment his mother had endured, the stolen money, and their dashed hopes of freedom.

What if there is no God? he wondered, the thought both terrifying and galvanizing. *If God doesn't punish him, then what? I'll probably go to jail for what I did at the dance. I can't leave Momma here alone with him. I have to do something.*

"Promise me, I said!" she cried again, her tear-filled eyes searching his face.

Finally, William placed his hand over hers, his expression a blank mask. "I'll forgive him," he said flatly, the words devoid of conviction.

Victoria exhaled shakily, relief washing over her as if she had staved off disaster. She kissed his cheek and held him tightly once more before standing and retreating to the bathroom.

Left alone in the dim light of the living room, William sat motionless, his jaw tight and his mind racing. The words he had spoken felt hollow, a fragile shield against the storm that raged within him.

Will's snores reverberated through the room, a jagged symphony of indulgence and oblivion. His head lolled to the side, mouth slightly open, a faint smile playing on his lips as he murmured pet names to a woman who existed only in his dreams. The faint glow from the bedside lamp illuminated a small, sad stack of bills—a pitiful remnant of what had once been William's life savings.

The night was still, the kind of quiet that felt alive, pressing down on the house with an almost tangible weight. A single blade of grass floated lazily through the air, landing on Will's face, followed by a whisper of dirt that sprinkled across his closed eyes. Instinctively, he twitched, brushing the irritants away without waking.

Then, the floor creaked.

Another sprinkle of dirt drifted down, this time falling into his open mouth. Will gagged, coughing himself awake, blinking against the dim light as he wiped at his face. His disoriented gaze traveled upward—and froze.

Above him, suspended like some ancient curse, was the jagged edge of the boulder. The words *In God We Trust* were etched into its surface, looming with an unsettling clarity. William stood over him, his arms trembling as he balanced the massive stone above his head like a grotesque altar offering. His face was a mask of calm, but his eyes burned with something primal, something unrelenting.

"Now—now let's talk about this, boy," Will stammered, his voice cracking with fear. He held his arms out, palms up, as though he could catch the boulder or somehow shield himself from its crushing weight. "Whatever's goin' on in that head of yours, we can work it out. Just put that thing down, you hear me? Put it down!"

William's lips curled into a slow, unsettling smile as he stared down at his father through the narrow space between his outstretched arms. His voice was quiet, almost tender.

"Sssssshhhhhhhhh... I promised Momma."

Will's face contorted in confusion and desperation. "Promised her? Promised her *what?*"

"That I'd forgive you." William's smile widened, but there was no humor in it, only a cold detachment. "She told me to leave it in His hands. And look—how ironic." He nodded toward the inscription on the rock. "In God We Trust. So... I'm gonna leave this here. In God's hands."

The silence stretched taut as a wire. Then, with a simple motion, William released the boulder.

The crash shattered the stillness of the night, a thunderous cacophony that sent tremors through the house. The bed collapsed under the weight, splintering and groaning as dust and debris filled the room.

Victoria jolted upright from where she sat tending to her wounds, the sound reverberating through her chest like an ominous drumbeat. Heart pounding, she raced down the hallway, her bandaged hands fumbling to open the door.

Inside, the room was chaos. The bed was crushed to the floor, the boulder an unyielding monument to its destructive purpose. The window was wide open, sheer white curtains fluttering like ghostly sentinels in the cool night breeze.

"Will? *William!*" Victoria's voice broke as she screamed into the wreckage, her cries sharp and raw, cutting through the night like shards of glass.

Across the street, shadows danced between the trees. Partially obscured by darkness, William watched from the safety of the brush. The flashing red and blue lights of squad cars painted the scene in haunting strokes, their sirens wailing a discordant melody that mingled with his mother's anguished sobs.

He took a step back, his gaze fixed on the house for a moment longer. He could feel the weight of the moment pressing down on him—the irreversible line he'd crossed. The sirens weren't for this, not yet. They were coming for his earlier sins, for the violence he had unleashed at the dance.

But soon, they would know.

He turned, retreating into the shadows, the dense foliage swallowing him whole. The cries of his mother followed him, echoes of pain that burrowed deep into his chest. He clenched his fists, his breath ragged as he disappeared into the night, leaving the wreckage—and his humanity—behind.

The Sunday evening air hung heavy with the scent of roast chicken wafting from the kitchen, blending with the low hum of the television in the living room. Coach Kline reclined in his chair, his feet propped up as the local news played out before him. His brow furrowed, his hand absently gripping the remote.

The newscaster's voice carried a somber weight:

"Police are still on the lookout for a young man, William Strong Jr., who assaulted three boys at a homecoming dance on Friday, leaving one paralyzed. He is also wanted in connection with the murder of his father, William Strong Sr. Both incidents occurred the same night. Authorities are withholding specific details but urge extreme caution when approaching this individual. He is considered highly dangerous. If you have any information regarding his whereabouts, please contact law enforcement immediately. In other news..."

Coach Kline let out a low groan, his head falling back against the chair. He muttered to himself, "You should've never given him that damn drink, Kline. Look at what's happened now. That boy's life is ruined."

"You say something, babe?" his wife called from the kitchen, her voice warm and lightly teasing over the sound of clattering pots.

He straightened slightly. "No, sweetie, just watching the news. Is dinner almost ready?"

"For the second time in as many minutes, babe—yes, it's almost ready." She chuckled, her tone playful. "But Guss needs to go out. He's been whining at the back door this whole time. Can you handle it?"

"I'm on it," Coach replied, groaning as he pushed the recliner upright and rose to his feet with the deliberate movements of a man whose joints were feeling the years.

"Come on, Gussy. Let's go, boy!"

When he opened the screen door, Guss bounded out like a coiled spring, his excitement overtaking his usual manners. The dog shoved past him, bolting toward the shed with a singular focus.

"Guss, no!" Coach called, irritation creeping into his voice. "There's no time for catch, buddy. Do your business so we can get back inside and eat."

But Guss paid no mind. Instead, the dog sniffed frantically at the shed door, his tail wagging furiously. He pawed at the entrance, his whines escalating to barks.

"Guss, what's gotten into you?" Coach muttered, striding toward the shed. He reached for the dog's collar to pull him away, but his eyes caught on something—the lock, hanging askew, broken.

Frowning, he brushed his fingers over the jagged edges of the metal, then let it fall to the ground with a metallic clink.

The unease in his chest deepened as he pushed the door open slowly, its hinges creaking in protest.

Guss darted inside immediately, disappearing into the shadowy recesses at the back of the shed. Coach fumbled for the light switch, his pulse quickening as the bulb flickered to life.

There, crouched in the corner, was William. His suit from the dance was wrinkled and smudged with dirt. He sat cross-legged, his hands gently stroking Guss's fur as the dog licked his face with unrestrained affection.

"Sorry about the door, C.K.," William said softly, his voice weary but calm. He looked up, his eyes shadowed yet oddly serene. "I didn't know where else to go."

Coach let out a long, heavy sigh, the tension in his shoulders melting into something closer to resignation.

"Well," he said, rubbing the back of his neck, "to be honest, we were starting to wonder what was taking you so long to get here."

CHAPTER 14

Super Strong

Winter 2026. Eight Years Later

Late on a brisk Friday night, downtown Milwaukee thrummed with life. The streets, awash in a kaleidoscope of neon signs and holiday lights, were crowded with college students reveling in their freedom. Laughter and shouts echoed between the buildings, mingling with the faint jingle of a Salvation Army bell down the block. Winter's first whispers had arrived, but the air held a lingering mildness, an almost playful tease of the colder nights to come. Girls paraded in scant dresses, their coats long abandoned in favor of fashion, their heels clicking rhythmically on the damp pavement. A few on-foot police officers loitered in the distance, their watchful eyes scanning the intoxicated throng.

Amid the chaos, a tight-knit group of four college friends spilled out of a bar, their cheeks flushed with drink and the excitement of a long-awaited night of bar hopping. Winter break had come, and the time for exams and deadlines had given way to a festive escape.

"Shit, man, I'm out of cash. Gotta hit an ATM," Todd muttered, patting his pockets with exaggerated urgency. His voice carried over to Jason and their dates as they began moving toward the next destination.

Jason, walking backward with an easy confidence, smirked. "Forget it, dude. I got your drinks. Just pay me back later. Let's get moving or we're gonna be stuck in a line longer than the Nile."

Todd shook his head. "Nah, man, you know I hate owing people. I don't wanna feel like I'm your bitch buying me drinks and—"

"Excuse me?" One of the girls snapped, planting her hands on her hips, her eyebrows arching in disbelief.

"Oh crap, babe, I didn't mean—" Todd stammered, holding up his hands in surrender.

The girl silenced him with a sharp wave of her hand in his face, cutting his apology short. Jason burst into laughter, pulling his date closer as if shielding her from the growing tension.

"You're a real rock sometimes, bro," Jason teased, shaking his head. "Fine, meet us at the club. But you better hustle—your dumb ass isn't getting in if the line gets crazy."

Todd grinned, popping his collar with mock bravado. "Have you forgotten my cousin works there? If it's that serious, I'll just go in through the back. I've got connections, my dude." Without waiting for a reply, he jogged across the street, leaving his friends to laugh and carry on without him.

The glow of the ATM kiosk drew Todd like a beacon, but his confidence deflated as he saw the dreaded "Out of Order" sign glaring back at him. Muttering a curse under his breath, he turned to a disheveled stranger staggering past.

"Hey, man, you know where I can find another ATM?" Todd asked, trying to ignore the sour stench of alcohol and vomit wafting from the guy.

The stranger blinked slowly, his glassy eyes struggling to focus. "Yeah... uh, right behind you." His words slurred together as he lazily waved a hand in the general direction of the broken machine.

Todd cringed, raising a hand to his nose to block the odor. "Yeah, that one's busted. Got any other ideas?"

The man swayed, his arm looping in an unsteady arc as he pointed down a dim alley. "Try... State Street. Just cut through there. Save you... save you time. Trust me." He clumsily patted Todd's shoulder before stumbling off into the night.

Todd hesitated, glancing at the darkened alley the stranger had suggested. The thought of cutting through sent a small shiver down his spine, but the promise of cash—and a smooth reunion with his friends—urged him forward. With a resigned sigh, he stepped into the shadows, the lively sounds of the street fading behind him.

The alley stretched before Todd like a jagged wound, its poor lighting casting distorted shadows against the graffiti-covered walls. The air was heavy with the sour stench of rotting garbage, the occasional clink of a bottle rolling along the ground adding to the eerie quiet. Loose papers and plastic bags swirled around his feet, carried by sporadic gusts of wind.

"Just go. Don't be a coward, Todd," he muttered to himself, his voice trembling despite his attempt at bravado. To push the unease from his mind, he hummed the chorus of the last song he'd heard in the bar, the familiar tune offering a thin veneer of comfort.

Each step forward felt heavier than the last. His eyes darted to every dark recess, his breath quickening every time his imagination conjured something lurking in the shadows. He glanced behind him more than once, heart pounding until he reached the alley's end and spotted the glowing ATM sign. Relief surged through him momentarily, but his gaze snagged on the two men leaning against a 1977 black Oldsmobile Cutlass Supreme parked nearby. Their body language was casual yet watchful, their eyes fixed on him.

Todd swallowed hard, reasoning with himself. They're across the street. There are people around. Nothing's going to happen. Just get your cash and go.

At the machine, Todd fumbled with his card and punched in his PIN, his fingers clumsy with nerves. The soft whirring of the machine sounded agonizingly slow. He cast another glance over his shoulder. The men hadn't moved, but their presence felt like a weight pressing down on him.

"Come on, come on," he whispered, his voice cracking. "Give me my damn money."

Finally, the machine spat out his cash, and Todd snatched it up before bolting back the way he came. He moved faster now, his earlier buzz entirely replaced by a gnawing sense of unease. The sight of people walking on the main street ahead gave him a renewed sense of hope, a beacon of normalcy pulling him forward.

Then, the guttural rumble of an engine shattered the fragile calm.

Todd froze as the black Oldsmobile rolled into the mouth of the alley, its parking lights glowing like predatory eyes. His stomach plummeted. It was them.

Panic surged, and he turned on his heel, running back toward the opposite end of the alley. His path was immediately blocked by one of the men, who emerged from the shadows with deliberate menace. Todd's heart hammered in his chest as he pivoted again, sprinting toward the passenger side of the car, hoping to slip past.

The engine roared to life, the deep growl vibrating through the narrow space as the car lunged forward, cutting him off with an abrupt screech of tires. Todd stumbled back, nearly falling, as the vehicle came to a halt in front of him. The headlights switched to high beams, their piercing light rendering him momentarily blind.

A door slammed shut, and Todd shielded his eyes, squinting to make out the figure stepping into the light.

"What the fuck was that?" The driver's voice was sharp and laced with contempt. He slammed the door with a resounding thud and stalked toward Todd, his silhouette imposing. "Where the hell did you think you were going?"

Another figure emerged behind him, leaning casually against the hood of the car. "Aye, Cee," the man drawled, a smirk audible in his voice. "Where did this little shit think he was going?"

Todd's breath came in ragged gasps as the reality of his situation set in. Trapped. Isolated. He glanced around wildly, the familiar street now feeling a million miles away. The faces of his friends flashed in his mind, their laughter and carefree spirits a cruel contrast to the suffocating tension of this moment.

"I don't want any trouble," Todd stammered, his voice cracking as he raised his hands. "I just needed some cash."

The driver stopped a few feet away, tilting his head as if considering Todd's words. The pause stretched unbearably long, the silence broken only by the steady hum of the car's engine and the distant echoes of nightlife Todd now wished he hadn't strayed from.

"Trouble?" the man finally said, a mocking edge to his tone. "Oh, buddy, trouble finds you when you wander into places you don't belong."

Cee walks up behind Todd and pushes him.

The cold brick wall scraped against Todd's back as he stumbled, his breath hitching with panic. Cee's shove had left him cornered, desperation tightening his throat. "Come on, guys!" Todd pleaded, his words tumbling out in a rush. "I don't have much cash, but you can take it! Just—just be cool, alright? I've got forty bucks, maybe enough for a couple of hits or... whatever you guys need, right?"

The thugs exchanged a glance, their faces twisting into matching smirks. The tension hung heavy in the air, suffocating.

"Man, did you just call us crackheads?" Cee asked, his voice laced with mock offense. He waved a crumpled ATM receipt in Todd's face. "You really think we're that stupid? Says right here you pulled out three hundred bucks—and your balance? Let's just say you're doing a lot better than forty dollars."

Laughter echoed off the alley walls, a cruel chorus that made Todd's chest tighten. Before he could react, Nick slammed him against the wall, pinning him like a bug under glass. Todd flinched as Cee rummaged through his pockets, the invasive search amplifying his sense of helplessness.

"What's that PIN number, baby?" Cee demanded, his voice low and menacing.

Suddenly, *BANG!*

The sharp sound reverberated through the alley, cutting through the men's laughter. The headlights of the Oldsmobile flickered, casting erratic shadows that danced across the grimy walls. The thugs froze, their attention snapping to the source of the noise.

BANG!

This time, the impact shook the car, shoving it forward a few inches. The tires screeched as if protesting, sliding slightly to the side until the beams of light shifted and illuminated the scene. A tall figure stepped into the glow, his imposing silhouette commanding attention.

He was a giant of a man, standing at least six foot four, cloaked in a faded green military jacket. His hood obscured most of his face, save for the coarse black beard jutting out beneath it. In his hands, he clutched a modest paper bag. The man paid no mind to the thugs, walking past them with deliberate, unhurried steps.

Todd seized his chance. "Hey, bro! Help me out here!" he called, his voice a mix of hope and despair.

The man paused only slightly, his deep voice cutting through the tension like a blade. "Don't block the alley," he said, his tone calm yet laced with quiet authority. "You people act like you own them."

Nick's face twisted with anger as he took a step toward the stranger. "Hey, motherfucker, what'd you do to my car?" His hand dipped into his coat, producing a gleaming box cutter.

The stranger kept walking.

Nick sneered, quickening his pace to catch up. "What's in the bag, old man?" He swiped at it with the blade, slicing the paper open. Vegetables and cuts of meat spilled onto the grimy ground, rolling through shards of glass and filth.

The man stopped, staring down at the ruined contents of his dinner. For a moment, he said nothing, his stillness more unsettling than anger.

"Oops," Nick taunted, grinning back at Cee. "Looks like I made a mess."

Behind them, Todd tried to crawl away, using the distraction to his advantage. His effort was short-lived. Cee noticed the movement, landing two quick punches to Todd's gut. He crumpled to his knees, gasping for air. The cigars he'd carried fell from his jacket, forgotten beside him.

But Cee had already turned his attention back to the stranger, ready to back up his friend. He froze mid-step, though, as the hooded man loomed before him, his face still obscured, his presence utterly commanding.

Cee's breath caught in his throat as an eerie stillness settled over the alley. Then, faintly, he heard it—a cry. Nick's voice, high-pitched and panicked. But it wasn't coming from the ground or the shadows. It wasn't coming from the street or the car.

It was coming from above.

Cee's gaze darted upward. His face paled as he saw Nick dangling above him, suspended like a broken marionette, his knife clattering to the ground below.

The hooded man stepped forward, his shadow enveloping Cee completely. For the first time, the thug felt the cold, sharp bite of fear. He opened his mouth to speak, but the words wouldn't come.

Nick dangled precariously above the alley, his legs flailing in a desperate bid for balance. Each frantic movement caused the cable's bracket to groan and creak, the metal threatening to give way at any moment. The sound echoed against the walls, amplifying the tension that thickened the air like a storm about to break.

"Holy shit! How'd you get up there?" Cee shouted, his voice laced with both shock and fear. His hand darted toward his coat pocket, seeking the cold reassurance of his gun.

Before he could draw, the stranger moved with unnerving precision. In an instant, he had Cee by the back of the head, forcing his arm upward until the barrel of the gun was angled directly beneath his chin.

"Come—Come on, man," Cee stammered, his tough demeanor crumbling under the stranger's iron grip. "You gonna kill me over some vegetables? I got money! You can eat good tonight, real good! Just don't shoot—please. I got a wife and kids. A dog, too! Man, it's hard out here!" His voice cracked, tears streaming down his face as he clung to the hope that words might save him.

The stranger's grip tightened, his voice a low, steady rumble. "Shut up."

"Okay, okay! Whatever you say!" Cee babbled, his free hand inching toward his pocket, fingers brushing against the handle of his knife. "Just don't shoot, alright? What—what would Jesus do?"

At that, the stranger paused, his head tilting slightly as though contemplating the question. "Jesus, huh?" he said at last, his voice quiet but razor-sharp. "So, you're looking for forgiveness?"

The hammer of the gun clicked as the stranger applied pressure, an ominous sound that sent a jolt of terror through Cee.

"Too bad," the stranger muttered as he twisted Cee's wrist. A sickening crack followed, and Cee's scream was swallowed by the muffled roar of distant street noise. He crumpled to the ground, clutching his shattered wrist, his sobs barely audible over the din.

The empty gun fell beside him, and the stranger nudged it away with his boot. "You're lucky your boy didn't load this," he said, his tone ice-cold. "Looks like he saved your life, even if he didn't mean to."

Cee whimpered, cradling his broken wrist, but the stranger wasn't finished. With a swift, deliberate motion, he brought his heel down on Cee's face. The thug's jaw dislocated with a gruesome pop, leaving him slumped and silent on the filthy ground.

Todd watched from where he had collapsed against a dumpster, his breath shallow and ragged. Pain radiated through his body, but it was the sight of the stranger that froze him in place. The man moved with the unrelenting certainty of a predator, every step deliberate and unhurried.

As the man approached, the faint light from a distant street-lamp framed him in shadow, making him appear larger than life. Todd pressed himself further into the cold steel of the dumpster, his heart hammering in his chest.

"Th—thanks, bro," Todd stammered, his voice barely above a whisper. "What's your name?"

The stranger said nothing, instead kneeling beside him. Todd flinched as the man's hand moved toward him, only to realize with relief that he was reaching for the cigars that had fallen to the ground. The man plucked the pack from the dirt and lit one with a match, the flickering flame illuminating his face for the first time.

It was William Strong, now a man hardened by years Todd couldn't begin to imagine.

William took a slow draw from the cigar, exhaling a plume of smoke that hung in the air between them. His eyes locked with Todd's, and for a moment, the silence spoke louder than any words could. Then, he stood, his shadow once again consuming Todd.

"Let me give you some advice," William said, his voice calm but weighted with authority. "Stay out of the alleys."

With that, he turned and walked into the darkness, his figure disappearing as if the night had swallowed him whole.

"You have my word, bro!" Todd called after him, his voice trembling with both relief and awe.

Above them, the cable's groaning reached its crescendo. Nick, having finally managed to swing his legs over, let out a breath of triumph—too soon. The bracket gave way with a metallic snap, sending him careening through the air. His body slammed against the brick wall with a sickening thud before crumpling into a puddle below, his unconscious form lying still as water rippled outward from the impact.

Todd stared at the scene, the weight of the night crashing down on him. This was no alley he would ever walk again.

The evening cast a soft golden glow over the city streets as an older woman paused in front of a clothing store window, her gaze fixated on the elegant dress displayed behind the glass. She smiled faintly, lost in a daydream of how it might drape on her frame, a small indulgence in the quiet of her day.

Nearby, a young man shuffled along the sidewalk, his head down, his baseball cap pulled low to obscure his face. His fingers were buried deep in his pockets, his every movement calculated as he glanced toward his target, then scanned the street for any law enforcement or wannabe heroes. Satisfied that the coast was clear, his pace quickened.

The woman, still caught up in her reverie, adjusted her purse on her shoulder, taking a small step back to admire the dress from a different angle. The sudden shove against her back stole the air from her lungs, her body jolting as she was forced against the window. She barely registered the weight of her purse being yanked from her shoulder as the young man darted down a nearby alley.

Dazed and breathless, she turned, her hands trembling as she tried to find her voice.

"Umph!"

Before she could cry out, the thief reappeared, staggering backward out of the alley and collapsing onto the sidewalk. His cap tumbled to the ground as he scrambled to sit up, his face pale and his wide eyes fixed on the dark entrance from which he'd emerged.

The soft roll of two tomatoes and an orange spilled from the shadows onto the pavement. The faint, guttural groan that echoed from the alley seemed almost inhuman, a sound of profound displeasure.

The woman's shock gave way to anger as her voice rang out. "He stole my purse—someone grab him!" Her words were sharp and commanding, and she stepped toward the thief, one of her high heels in hand, poised to strike.

The young man didn't move, his chest heaving as he stared back at the alley, paralyzed. His terror only deepened when something unseen gripped his ankles, dragging him back into the darkness with the purse still slung over his shoulder. His muffled yelp disappeared as quickly as he did.

A pair of construction workers nearby ran to the woman's side, one kneeling slightly to check her over. "Ma'am, are you okay?"

"No, some lowlife stole my purse!" she snapped, her voice firm but tinged with residual shock. She pointed toward the alley, her hand shaking. "He went in there."

The workers exchanged a glance before cautiously approaching the alley. One of them pulled a flashlight from his toolbelt, its beam slicing through the shadows as he aimed it down the passage. Before they could take another step, the purse came hurtling from the alley like a missile, striking the flashlight from the man's grip and sending him sprawling.

"Ah, hell!" he cried out, clutching his arm. "Al, I think it's broken!"

The woman darted forward, snatching up the flashlight with practiced efficiency. Its beam illuminated the thief, now slumped against the alley wall, unconscious. His mouth was stuffed with a dirty apple, a grotesque parody of a roasted pig. The scene was so surreal that it momentarily halted her movement, her breath catching as her gaze lingered on the absurd sight.

Then, something flickered at the edge of her vision—a shadow, larger and darker than the dim alley should have allowed. She whipped the flashlight toward it, but it vanished as though it had never been there.

She exhaled, her voice trembling but resolute. "Thank you," she said softly, retrieving her belongings and clutching them tightly against her chest. With one last wary glance toward the alley, she hurried back toward the light and life of the busy street.

CHAPTER 15

Dumpster Baby

Later that evening, Coach busied himself in the bathroom while Jada tidied up after their late-night meal. Familiar with her husband's predictable routines, she switched on the television and tuned into the ten o'clock news.

"Want a beer, babe?" she called, standing near the screen, her voice carrying easily over the quiet hum of the house.

"Yeah, sweetie, thanks!" he shouted back, the sound slightly muffled.

Before she could make it to the fridge, the television's flickering images caught her attention. Her eyes narrowed as she focused on the news segment unfolding before her.

"Hurry and come out here, hun," she called, urgency threading her voice. "You're going to want to see this."

The toilet flushed, a loud mechanical groan temporarily drowning out the broadcast. As Coach opened the bathroom door, Jada reached for the remote, turning up the volume just in time to hear an elderly woman mid-sentence, her voice quavering with a mix of indignation and relief.

"...out of nowhere. He knocked me to the ground, and the *bleep* took my purse! Thank God that nice man in the alley stopped him. I don't know what I'd have done if I lost my precious picture of Pepper. She was such a beautiful dog... see?" The woman held up a photograph to the camera. It revealed a sorrowful, nearly hairless Chinese-crested dog adorned in a Green Bay Packers sweater, its mismatched features a bizarre contrast to the moment's gravity.

The newscaster's polished voice cut in: "Again, we're live downtown, where reports of a mysterious figure intervening in criminal activity are growing. Victims and even the appre-hended perpetrators describe encounters with this unknown individual. Some here are already calling him... a hero."

Coach's chuckle rumbled low in his throat as he grabbed a towel to dry his hands. "A *hero*? Oh, good God," he muttered, shaking his head.

"They interviewed a guy earlier," Jada said, handing him a cold can of beer. "He swears this 'mystery man' saved him from some gang members trying to rob him. Said the guy pushed the back of their car sideways *with his hands*. They think he's just some drunk college kid, but..."

Coach raised an eyebrow, his expression part disbelief, part amusement. As he cracked open the can, his gaze wandered to the backyard. The faint glow beneath the shed door caught his attention. He stared for a moment before muttering, "Hero, huh?"

His thoughts were broken by the thudding of paws against the floor. Guss, their eager dog, paced restlessly by the door, his tail wagging furiously. "Alright, Buddy, let's go," Coach said, opening the door. The dog darted outside, heading straight for the shed, sniffing intently at its base.

Coach followed at a leisurely pace, knocking on the shed door with a playful rhythm. "Shave and a Haircut—Two Bits." He leaned casually against the frame as the door creaked open. "Sup, hero?" he greeted, his tone dripping with sarcasm.

William, seated at a cluttered desk, turned to face him. His hands instinctively reached for Guss, scratching behind the dog's ears as the overjoyed animal licked his fingers with fervent devotion.

"Hero?" William echoed, arching an eyebrow. "What's on your mind, C.K.? You've got that look."

Coach smirked, taking a swig of his beer. "What look?"

"The one you get when you're either winning or hiding something. Spill it."

"All I know is the news is buzzing about some 'big guy' in the alleys putting criminals in the hospital. They're calling him a hero. Any idea who that might be? Maybe someone who could *push a car* with their bare hands?"

William let out a low chuckle, his smile crooked. "Seriously? The news?"

Coach's expression darkened. "Shit's not funny, man. You're just getting heat off your back for that cold case, and now you're pulling stunts like this? You're gonna get yourself caught—or worse. Lay low for a while, alright? Jada made some chow. Come eat."

William turned back to his desk, his gaze drifting to the collage of faded newspaper clippings tacked to the wall. At its center, a weathered photo of a young girl and another of him as a boy with his mother stared back at him, haunting reminders of his past. "You know I can't stop," he muttered. "I'm too close."

Coach sighed, running a hand over his face. "You've been chasing ghosts for years, man. Let it go. You think finding her will fix anything? If you really care about her, you'll leave her be."

William stood, towering over Coach as he pulled his hood up. "I'm out," he said, patting his jacket pocket to check for his cigars and lighter. As he headed for the door, he tossed over his shoulder, "Don't wait up, Mom. Oh, and trim your nose hairs—looks like a trapeze act going on there."

Coach instinctively wiped his nose, checking his hand. "What the hell, man? Did you not hear anything I just said?" But William didn't answer. He stepped out, the door slamming shut behind him.

Frustrated, Coach hurled his half-empty beer can at the door, the loud clatter startling Guss from his spot on the floor.

As the months slipped by, William's exploits grew increasingly ferocious, his interventions in the city's underbelly spiraling into brutal encounters. Criminals left in his wake found themselves in hospital beds, nursing injuries far beyond the scope of their crimes. His brand of justice was swift and merciless, meting out punishments that teetered on the edge of savagery. Rumors of the shadowy protector spread like wildfire, and now, victims of the city's grime and vice sought solace in the darkened alleys, desperate for the whispered promise of his protection to be true.

The community became a battleground of opinion. Many celebrated him as a grim savior, crediting the sudden plummet in crime rates to his relentless presence. Others, however, denounced his actions, branding him no better than the thugs he hunted, a monster in the guise of a hero.

It was inevitable that the authorities would eventually uncover his identity. A careless act—a car shoved aside by raw strength—left fingerprints as a calling card. Those prints matched an old case, a ghost from his past: the boy William Strong, whose childhood bedroom had once been meticulously combed for evidence. The connection was undeniable, and the name they had long since archived now carried a new, ominous weight.

Then came the letter.

Delivered anonymously, it arrived at the Milwaukee precinct with chilling precision, its message succinct but laced with sinister intent:

"I'm sure this William Strong is causing you a great deal of trouble; not only for your local authorities but for organized crime as well. I also know that there are other parties interested in his capture for scientific reasons. Now, because I take a slight personal interest in this, I won't charge my usual fee. Instead, I will deliver Mr. Strong to the highest bidder once I have ac-

quired him. If you agree to these terms, you need only reply with no text to the following email: YouWantemIGotem@ctc.com."

The detectives read the note in grim silence, the weight of its implications sinking in. Somewhere, someone was not only aware of William's abilities but intended to make him a commodity, a prize to be auctioned to the highest and most dangerous bidder. The stakes had risen, and the line between hunter and hunted blurred further with each passing moment.

Wednesday, 12:57 AM

A dimly lit bar near the downtown area buzzed with the low hum of patrons nursing their last drinks. The television, perched above the bar, played a pre-recorded segment of the nightly news.

(Prerecorded) Newscaster: "In other news, authorities have officially identified the so-called back alley boogieman as William Strong. Approximately eight years ago, we covered a high school incident where a young Strong assaulted a classmate, leaving him paralyzed from the waist down. Later, he was implicated in the death of his own father. While police remain tight-lipped on the details of these events, they urge extreme caution. If you spot Strong, contact authorities immediately. Tips leading to his capture may result in a hefty reward."

The grainy image of William's high school yearbook photo filled the screen, his eyes shadowed by the grainy quality of the shot, lending the picture an eerie, almost spectral quality.

"Leave the son-of-a-bitch alone, for Christ's sake!" came the slurred bark of a white-haired man, his face flushed from hours of drinking. He glared at the television, his hand gripping his beer glass as if steadying himself. "Shit, he's the only reason I can walk these streets this late without worrying about getting my ass jumped."

The bartender, a wiry man with sleeves rolled to his elbows, set down his rag with a sigh. "Alright, Vick, time to call it a night. Last call, everyone!" he announced, his voice cutting through the ambient murmur. "Anything else, or you good?"

"Nah, I'm good," Vick replied, sliding off his stool with a slight stumble. "You have a good one, brotha. I'll see you tomorrow!"

Across the room, a massive figure stirred in the shadows. A hulking man who had been seated quietly in the corner rose, his attention divided between the news and Vick's loud proclamations. Standing at least six foot five and weighing well over three hundred pounds, his presence was impossible to ignore. His thick frame suggested the power of a lifter, with broad shoulders and heavily muscled arms, though his round belly might fool a casual observer into calling him fat.

His heavy footsteps echoed as he approached the bar, leaving behind the creaking wooden chair he had dwarfed. From his massive hand, he unfurled a crumpled twenty-dollar bill, damp with the condensation of too many clenched moments, and tossed it onto the counter.

"Keep the change," he grunted, not bothering to make eye contact as he headed for the door, his pace steady and deliberate.

The bartender picked up the damp bill between thumb and forefinger, wrinkling his nose. "Gee, thanks a lot, man," he muttered under his breath, holding it like it was biohazardous. "Considering your tab was exactly twenty *fucking* dollars."

The man didn't turn back, his bulk disappearing into the cool night air. Vick, already outside, lit a cigarette and ambled toward the curb, oblivious to the sound of heavy footsteps closing the distance behind him.

Vick stumbled unevenly down the street, the sharp bite of vodka and cranberries still lingering on his tongue. His gait wavered as he fumbled with his watch, squinting to make out the time. 1:10 a.m. He muttered a curse under his breath and glanced up the street, catching sight of the tail end of the Number Eighty bus parked around the corner. It was a layover stop—typically idle until the driver was ready to move—but he knew his window was narrow.

Smoke erupted from the bus's exhaust pipe, a gray plume curling into the icy air as the engine roared to life. The driver, it seemed, was ready to leave.

"Son of a—!" Vick groaned, straightening his posture and breaking into a half-sprint, his arms flailing in a desperate bid to catch the driver's attention.

"Wait—damn it! Hey!!" he shouted, his voice straining against the cold night.

The bus lurched forward, picking up speed despite his protests. Fueled by frustration, Vick snatched up a discarded beer bottle from the curb and hurled it with surprising accuracy.

The bottle struck the rear of the bus with a dull thud, but the vehicle didn't so much as slow down.

"You no-good, bald-headed jackrabbit!" he bellowed, shaking a fist at the retreating taillights.

Defeated, he pulled out his phone, flipping it open and scrolling through his sparse list of contacts. Each name felt more useless than the last; no one would venture into this part of town at this ungodly hour to rescue him. Sighing heavily, he shoved the phone back into his pocket and resigned himself to the long, frigid trek home.

He rifled through his jacket and jeans, searching for cash, but his fingers found only lint and an old gum wrapper. A taxi was out of the question.

"Great," he muttered bitterly, zipping his coat tighter against the cutting wind. "Not getting home until 2:30, maybe 3:00 if I'm lucky."

The cold gnawed at his skin as he walked, each breath forming ghostly clouds that drifted behind him. To save time, he veered into a side street, then down a narrow alleyway. The shadows closed in around him, but his vodka-soaked bravado dulled any lingering sense of caution.

The air grew heavier, the silence pressing in, when a faint sound reached his ears.

"Pssst—"

It came from a darkened corner to his left. He slowed, his breath catching as his eyes strained to pierce the gloom.

"Hey—who's there? Somebody there?" he called, his voice rising as he stopped in his tracks.

The sound came again.

"Pssst—"

This time it was behind him, near the mouth of the alley he had just entered. Whipping around, he spun too fast, nearly losing his balance. "Don't mess with me!" he barked, thrusting his hand into his jacket pocket to feign a weapon. "I'm strapped!"

The silence pressed in for a long moment before the sound came once more.

"Pssst—"

This time it was ahead of him, from another darkened corner of the alley. His pulse quickened, and without a second thought, he bolted forward, desperate to escape whatever—or whoever—was toying with him.

But before he could clear the alley, a massive dumpster hurtled out of the shadows and slammed into the brick wall ahead of him. The collision rang out, metallic and deafening, the sound reverberating through the narrow space.

"Shit!" Vick yelped, stumbling backward in shock. His foot caught on a jagged piece of raised concrete, sending him sprawling to the ground. Scrambling to his feet, his heart hammered in his chest as his wide eyes darted around, searching for the source of the voice—or the force that had moved the dumpster.

The alley remained eerily empty. No one stepped into the faint halo of light cast by the single flickering streetlamp.

Breathless and panicked, Vick stood frozen, the icy air stinging his lungs as he struggled to determine whether he was being hunted—or haunted.

Vick staggered to his feet, brushing dirt from his coat with trembling hands. "Jesus Christ, this just ain't my night!" he muttered, his voice carrying a hollow mix of frustration and fear.

"And it ain't about to get any better!" a voice snapped back, sharp and sudden.

From the shadows, a man stepped forward, his figure blending with the night except for the gleam of his eyes and the jagged silhouette of a two-by-four gripped tightly in his hand. The weapon swung high, slicing the air with a menacing whistle as Vick instinctively dropped to the ground. The board passed just inches above his head, and he scrambled backward on all fours, his breath coming in ragged gasps.

The attacker loomed over him, the tension in his body coiled like a predator ready to pounce. "Wait—wait—wait!" Vick stammered, throwing up his hands in a desperate plea. "What you want, man? I ain't got shit but a dollar and ten cents for the bus!" His pockets emptied as he scattered the loose coins on the ground, their metallic clinking the only sound breaking the tense silence.

The man didn't even glance at the meager offering. "Oh no, my man," he said with an unsettling calm. "I don't need nothing from outta your pockets. What I need—needs to come out of your mouth."

Vick barely had time to process the words before the man lifted the board again. He flinched, trying to shield himself, but the splintered wood came down with a dull thud against his hand. A sharp crack rang out, followed by a searing pain that shot through his arm.

"Aaaaagh! Goddamn—aaaaagh!" Vick's cries echoed down the alley, raw and primal. He curled into himself, a futile attempt to shield his vulnerable body.

The man's strikes didn't relent. The board crashed into his ribs, forcing the air from his lungs and leaving a sharp, hollow ache in its wake. Vick coughed, crimson drops spattering the pavement as he gasped for breath.

The attacker paused, stepping back and scanning the alley, his movements jerky, like a marionette pulled by unseen strings. His gaze darted from shadow to shadow, a predator seeking his true prey.

Vick, still hunched and cradling his broken hand, spat blood onto the ground. "You gonna kill me, motha-fucka?" he rasped, his voice hoarse. "You must not be from around here." He coughed again, the effort doubling him over. "Messing around in these alleys? You don't know what you're calling for."

The man ignored him, his eyes fixed on the dark recesses of the alley. "Come on out!" he bellowed, brandishing the board like a torch to ward off the unseen. "I know you're here!"

Only silence answered him.

Frustration tightened the man's grip as he turned his fury back on Vick. The board struck again, and Vick cried out, collapsing onto the cold pavement. Even through the haze of pain, realization dawned. His voice trembled as he pushed himself upright, his words laced with bitter clarity. "I'm bait, huh?" He winced, teeth clenched against the sharp edge of his broken ribs. "You're calling the devil himself, boy, and you sure as hell don't want him to answer."

The attacker's patience frayed further, his voice rising in frustration. "Shut up! The only thing I want out of your mouth is screaming."

He raised the board again, its shadow stretching long in the faint light, when suddenly, the streetlamp above them shattered with a deafening *pop*.

The alley plunged into darkness. Sparks danced briefly from the broken bulb, casting fleeting, jagged flashes of light across the scene before fading into nothing. The hum of electricity ebbed into silence, leaving only the distant echo of their breathing and the oppressive weight of the night.

The attacker froze, his bravado wavering as the shadows around him seemed to press closer. The air grew still, heavy with unspoken menace. For the first time, it was unclear who was the hunter and who was the prey.

"Now you gonna get it," Vick rasped, a grim satisfaction lacing his tone despite the pain radiating through his battered body.

The man with the two-by-four froze for a moment, his heavy breathing audible even over the muffled city sounds. The oppressive darkness pressed in around him, and his fear was almost palpable. Desperation crept into his movements as he began swinging the board wildly, each arc slicing through empty air. His grunts and frustrated mutterings grew louder, their sharp edges betraying his growing panic.

High above, a figure crouched on the rooftop, observing the scene through night-vision goggles. The glowing green view revealed the hired assailant's erratic movements, the wild swings connecting with nothing but the shadows. The watcher zoomed in, catching every twitch and tremor of the man's increasingly frantic efforts. This was the same man who had been paid to orchestrate the evening's chaos, even down to ensuring Vick missed his bus.

The quiet flutter of pigeons taking flight drew the observer's attention to the rooftop across the alley. The goggles scanned the area, but nothing appeared out of place. Still, an unease settled over him, and his focus shifted back to the scene below.

"You're gonna need something better than that stick," Vick taunted through gritted teeth, his voice a mix of pain and defiance. "I feel like we're not alone anymore. You scared, ain'tcha? Breathing all hard and shit. I bet you look stupid right now."

His laugh came out ragged, but there was a sharp edge to it. "I wish I could see your face clearer. Better yet, I wish I could see when—"

Before Vick could finish, the man let out a sudden, strangled gasp. The wooden board fell to the ground with a hollow clatter that echoed unnervingly in the narrow alley.

A flicker of light sputtered from the broken streetlamp, illuminating the scene in brief, stuttering flashes. In one stark instant, Vick's eyes widened as he saw the violent man who had been tormenting him suspended above the ground, his throat caught in the iron grip of a much larger figure.

"Sweet Jesus!" Vick exclaimed, his voice trembling as he collapsed to his knees, his battered body unable to hold him upright any longer.

The towering figure of William Strong loomed over the alley, his arm extended effortlessly upward, holding the smaller man like a puppet dangling from a string. The attacker clawed at Strong's wrist with desperate hands, his feet kicking futilely at the air.

Strong's expression was unreadable, his dark eyes locked onto his prey. He could end this man with a flick of his wrist, snuffing out his life as easily as one might crush a paper cup. But that wasn't his way—not anymore. Punishment had become a ritual for him, a grim pastime he savored. Each gasp, each panicked thrash, was a small triumph. This man had called for him, taunted him, challenged him. Now, Strong would make him regret it.

The attacker's foot struck Strong's midsection in a desperate attempt to free himself. It was like kicking a steel beam; Strong didn't even flinch. Panic consumed the smaller man as his need for air grew dire. His gasps turned to choking sputters, his movements grew weaker, his struggles slowing to faint, twitching spasms.

Just as his eyes began to flutter shut and his body sagged, Strong released him. The man hit the ground face-first, coughing violently as he sucked in air. His breath was ragged, each gulp of oxygen mixed with dirt from the alley floor.

Above him, Strong stood still, his presence an immovable weight pressing down on the scene. The heavy thud of his boots echoed as he took a step forward, then another, until he was standing directly over the man's prone body.

The attacker didn't move. His strength was gone, drained by fear and lack of air. The only sound was his wheezing breath, underscored by the steady, ominous rhythm of Strong's footsteps.

Vick, watching from where he knelt, felt a strange mix of relief and terror. The man who had been his tormentor was now reduced to nothing more than a broken figure on the ground—but the one who had saved him was something else entirely.

The air grew colder, and the silence heavier, as Vick realized that in this alley, mercy wasn't guaranteed.

"This was definitely not worth the money," the hired man muttered between strained breaths, his voice rasping as the weight of Strong's Timberland boot pressed into his back. Each labored inhale felt like dragging air through a straw, and the pressure forced it all out again in shallow, wheezing gasps.

Strong tilted his head slightly, his voice low and deliberate. "Say something?" He shifted his weight, and the man beneath him groaned as his spine gave a sickening series of pops, echoing like distant firecrackers in the still night.

"Umph! ... yeah, I said you need to lay off the protein shakes, bitch!" The man's words were defiant, but his tone betrayed the tremor of regret as soon as they left his lips.

Strong stilled, his eyes narrowing as he processed what the man had said about money. His gaze darted upward, scanning the rooftop edges silhouetted against the cloudy sky. He swept the shadows behind him before glancing at Vick, who now leaned heavily against the alley entrance, watching like a battered spectator too drained to interfere.

"Where's your partner?" Strong asked, his voice quieter now, colder. He reached down, grasping the man's hand gently, almost as if offering reassurance.

The man scoffed, his bravado rekindled for a moment. "You wanna hold hands now? Fuck you!"

Strong's grip tightened, and the hired man flinched. "Not too smart, are you?" Strong said softly. With a sudden, crushing motion, he shattered the man's hand, the sound of bone and cartilage snapping like a handful of dry twigs. The man howled, writhing in pain, but still refused to speak.

"Stubborn," Strong muttered, his eyes sharp as he watched the man's frantic glances dart toward a nearby rooftop. His lips curled into a grim smile. "Your buddy must've paid you extra to keep your mouth shut. But the eyes... the eyes never lie."

Strong released him, the man collapsing in a heap, clutching his mangled hand. Without a word, Strong began moving toward the building, his strides slow and deliberate, his gaze locked upward on the shadowy outline at the roof's edge. As he drew closer, the shape began to solidify—motion, faint but unmistakable, caught his eye.

Behind him, Vick regained a measure of strength, his fear and pain now twisted into vindictive energy. He limped toward the downed attacker, his battered frame buoyed by the chance to unleash his frustration. Each step was punctuated by a vicious kick.

"Look—at—you—now—you—stupid—motha—fucka!" Vick growled, each word landing with a dull thud against the man's ribs. He ended with one final, satisfying kick before stepping back, breathing heavily, and wiping blood from his mouth with the back of his hand.

Strong stopped at the base of the building, his neck craning as he stared upward. For a moment, he was still, as if listening to the silence itself. Then, a flicker of light reflected from above—a subtle movement, barely noticeable but enough. "Got you," he murmured under his breath.

With a sudden burst of strength, he leaped upward, his powerful frame soaring almost two stories high before his hands found purchase on a window ledge. For a moment, he dangled there, the weight of his massive body straining against the structure. He glanced around, assessing his next move, and swung toward a nearby drainpipe.

The moment his hand gripped the pipe, it tore free from the brick wall with a shriek of ripping metal. Strong plummeted backward, landing with a thunderous crash in the dumpster below.

Vick froze mid-kick, staring in stunned silence as paper and debris erupted from the dumpster like a burst of fireworks. The broken drainpipe clattered down beside it, the noise reverberating through the alley.

"What the hell..." Vick muttered, shaking his head in disbelief. "Somebody definitely needs to go to superhero school."

In the dumpster, Strong lay still for a moment, staring up at the dimly lit sky. His chest heaved as he caught his breath, frustration curling through him. He replayed the moment in his mind, imagining how ridiculous he must have looked—a near-mythic figure brought low by a flimsy drainpipe.

Above, the rooftop was still. Whoever had been there was either laughing silently at his misstep or had used the commotion as the perfect opportunity to escape. Strong closed his eyes briefly, the cold, crumpled metal beneath him a bitter reminder that even he wasn't invincible.

The night's silence resumed, heavy and unbroken, as if the city itself had paused to watch what might happen next.

CHAPTER 16

Have A Nice Day

It was a crisp, blustery night, the air carrying the sharp bite of recent rain. The droplets had ceased their relentless assault, leaving the world outside glistening and dark, like polished obsidian under the dim glow of distant streetlights. Inside, Victoria sat alone, her late-night ritual in full swing. On her plate rested a few slices of apple and a smear of peanut butter—her modest, predictable comfort before the lull of sleep overtook her.

The oversized recliner creaked softly as she rocked back and forth, her eyes fixed on the television's shifting glow. Yet her mind wandered far beyond the flickering screen, returning again and again to that night—*the* night. The night that took her husband, her son, and the dream they had all shared. One cruel moment had unraveled the tapestry of her life, leaving her clutching at threads she no longer recognized.

After the accident, the dream house they had poured themselves into was no longer hers to keep. She had retreated to the familiarity of their old apartment building, though even that felt alien now. The new unit was smaller, more cramped, and its dimness seemed to seep into her soul. The television, casting sporadic flashes across the room from the violent scene of the film she half-watched, was her only source of light. Each flicker painted shadows on the walls, fleeting shapes that seemed alive in the restless night.

Then the wind began to howl. It squeezed through a gap in the window with a sharp, ghostly whistle, disrupting the fragile peace. Victoria sighed, pushing herself upright and shuffling to the offending window. She reached out, her fingertips brushing the cold glass. A fine film of condensation blurred her view, and she pulled her sleeve over her hand, swiping the pane clear.

Her breath caught. Across the street, atop the neighboring building, stood a figure. A man's silhouette teetered at the edge, motionless for a moment before stepping back, dissolving into the darkness beyond her view. Her heart raced, her pulse hammering in her ears as a familiar ache rose in her chest.

"William?" she whispered, her voice trembling, barely audible over the gusting wind. Tears pooled in her eyes, blurring the world all over again.

With thoughts of his mother pulling at his heart, William trudged toward the side door of Coach Kline's home—his home now, though it never truly felt like it. The large shed out back, with its unassuming walls and quiet seclusion, was where he found solace. It was his sanctuary, a place where the world could not pry. But tonight, he needed the comfort of a warm shower before retreating to his hidden corner of the world.

The door gave way with a gentle push, its latch yielding without resistance. Darkness greeted him, deep and consuming, a pitch-black void that seemed to stretch endlessly. He stepped inside, the air heavier within, carrying a faint, earthy musk. His boots scuffed lightly against the floor, the only sound in a house that felt unnervingly still.

Ahead, a faint glow seeped into the hallway, spilling from the half-open door of the bathroom. The light was pale and diffused, carving out a fragile sliver of illumination on the opposite wall. It stood in stark contrast to the rest of the home, which lay shrouded in shadow, as if the darkness were alive, pressing against the edges of the light.

As he twisted the hot water knob, the old pipes rattled to life, their metallic clatter growing frantic before fading into calm. The rising steam clouded the room as the water poured down, scorching away the grime of his day. His filthy clothes lay discarded in a heap, remnants of his long, grueling hours of walking, climbing, and sweating. He sighed, leaning his forehead against the shower tiles, his hands braced against the wall.

The warm stream cascaded over his head, soaking his coarse, matted hair and washing down his face in rivulets that mingled with his tears. The memory of his mother's despair—her isolation, her heartbreak—stabbed at his chest. He yearned to hold her, to tell her that everything would be alright. But how could he? The weight of guilt pressed heavier than the water on his shoulders. He was the reason her world had crumbled. How could he face her now?

The mist thickened, blurring every surface until the bathroom mirrors reflected only ghostly smudges. William shut off the water and stepped out blindly, soap stinging his eyes. His groping hand missed the towel, and as his foot slipped on the slick floor, chaos erupted. His arms flailed, yanking the shower curtain from its rings and tearing the soap dish clean out of the wall. He landed hard, the racket reverberating through the silent house.

Breathless, he sat among the wreckage, muttering under his breath. "Alright, Will... get ready for this shit." He tossed the broken soap dish aside and dried his stinging eyes, waiting for the inevitable stomping footsteps of Coach Kline. Any moment now, the lecture would begin.

But the house remained eerily quiet. The only sound was the dripping of water from the shredded curtain. William's gaze wandered to the fogged mirror. He frowned, noticing faint scribbles taking shape in the mist. Soon the subsiding steam revealed a crude, oversized smiley face with the words *Have a Nice Day* scrawled beneath it. He huffed a humorless laugh. "Yeah, just a little too late for that," he muttered, smearing the cheery message into oblivion.

After tugging on a fresh set of clothes, his boots loosely tied, William left the bathroom. The hallway's darkness seemed thicker now, the weight of the shadows pressing in as his boots clunked against the floor. When he reached the kitchen, his first step on the tile elicited a sharp crunch. He froze, the sound jarring in the silence. Another step, another crunch. He squinted downward, unable to make out the source.

Flipping the light switch, his stomach turned. The kitchen was a battlefield—glass shards, shattered plates, and scattered silverware littered the floor. A jagged hole gaped in the window above the sink, and muddy paw prints trailed across every surface. His pulse quickened as his eyes traced the path of destruction, the prints leading toward the darkened living room.

Heart pounding, William approached the room, his boots grinding against the debris. Dropping his dirty clothes to the floor, he crept forward, each step amplifying the dread pooling in his chest. He froze as the trail ended in a corner shrouded in shadow.

There, lying on his back with his legs splayed, was Coach Kline. The rest of his body lay obscured in darkness, but the ominous stillness of his form sent a chill surging down William's spine. The house, once silent, now seemed to buzz with an electric, suffocating tension.

William knelt slowly, his breath hitching as his hand rested on his knee. The oppressive darkness that shrouded the rest of the room seemed alive, pulsing with tension. From its depths came a low, guttural growl, resonant and primal, echoing like a warning. Two reflective green eyes appeared, catching the dim light, glinting like malevolent stars. It was Guss. His sharp, white fangs were bared, the growl rumbling from deep within his chest.

Fixing his eyes on the dog, William's mind raced. The pieces began to fall into place—he was certain Guss was the cause of Coach Kline's death. Keeping his gaze locked on the animal, he moved with deliberate slowness, his hand inching toward a fallen lamp nearby. His fingers found the switch, his other hand brushing against the cold metal of a knife buried in the debris.

Guss rose from the ground, his sinewy frame shifting as he stood on all fours. He took a slow, deliberate step into the light, his head low, ears flattened, and lips quivering as his tongue darted out to lick his teeth. The growl deepened, vibrating in the still air.

"Guss, it's me, buddy," William whispered, his voice steady but pleading. "I don't want to hurt you. Calm down!"

But the dog didn't waver. Instead, Guss took another step, positioning himself protectively over Coach Kline's lifeless body, his stance as menacing as a wolf guarding its kill.

William stood slowly, gripping the lamp and knife tightly, every muscle coiled and ready. Guss stared at him for another agonizing moment, then, without a sound, melted back into the shadows.

William's heart thundered in his chest as he flicked the lamp switch. Light flooded the room, revealing a calmer Guss now standing over Coach Kline's head. The growling had ceased, replaced by soft, mournful whimpers as the dog licked his master's lifeless face. Guss nudged the man's head with his nose, and it lolled to one side, lifeless and heavy.

The knife slipped from William's grasp, clattering onto the floor. He placed the lamp down carefully and crawled toward the motionless body. "No, no, no..." he muttered under his breath, his hands trembling as he cradled Coach Kline's head in his lap. His fingers sought a pulse at the man's neck, but there was nothing—no life, no hope. His friend was gone.

Tears blurred William's vision as he looked up at the ceiling, memories flooding his mind. Coach Kline had been more than a friend; he had been a lifeline, a constant in a world that seemed to shift beneath William's feet. And now, because of him—because of his mistakes—this lifeline had been severed.

He scanned the chaos around him, the shards of glass and overturned furniture telling a story he couldn't yet piece together. His eyes fell on a photograph near his feet—a picture of Coach Kline and Jada. Gently laying the man's head on the floor, William rose to his feet and began searching the room, his movements frantic. Guss, meanwhile, curled up beside the body, nuzzling his master's chin with quiet devotion.

William dashed to the back room and flicked on the light, the brightness stinging his eyes. He searched every corner of the bathroom, his hands brushing aside towels and toiletries, but found nothing. He hurried back to the living room, his pulse racing as he peered out the back door. The patio light illuminated the yard, casting stark shadows, but there were no signs of anything unusual.

He moved to the front window, his heart sinking as he saw Coach Kline's car still parked in the driveway. The pieces didn't add up.

"Gussy, where's Jada?" he asked, his voice tight with desperation.

The dog raised his head slightly, letting out a soft whimper before lowering it again, his grief palpable.

William's eyes darted toward the kitchen. Through the back window, the shed was visible, standing stoically against the night. His stomach tightened as he noticed the door swinging wide open, the wind catching it and pushing it back and forth. Whatever had happened here, the shed now held a dark and looming significance.

Approaching the shed, William moved cautiously, his eyes darting over the moonlit surroundings, searching for anything amiss. The crisp night air was tinged with the acrid scent of kerosene, sharp and unmistakable. As he reached the doorway, the smell grew stronger, and his stomach tightened with unease. The darkness inside was absolute, swallowing the faint glow from the distant house. With a sharp tug, he pulled the dangling cord overhead. The single bulb flickered to life, casting harsh, wavering light over the small space.

His heart sank. The heater lay toppled, its reservoir of oil spilled across the floor, pooling beneath his bed like a dark stain of misfortune. He stepped cautiously, his boots squelching in the slick puddle, and his eyes darted around the shed, searching for the two items he cherished most—the only photographs he had left of his mother and his lost love. But they were gone.

Desperation clawed at him as he dragged the heavy desk away from the wall, his broad fingers scrabbling in the dust and debris for some trace of his treasures. He found nothing—only dead bugs, scraps of paper, and the stale remnants of neglect. Kneeling there, he felt the weight of his loss pressing down, his fingers trembling as sadness gave way to a deep, searing anger.

It was too much. Everything he had clung to had been stripped away, leaving him adrift in a sea of sorrow and rage. His mother, Coach Kline, Jada, Isabella—each name was a wound, a reminder of what he no longer had. He stood abruptly, fists clenching as his vision blurred with red-hot fury. Gripping the metal leg of his desk, he lifted it with a guttural roar and smashed it to the floor. The sound of metal on metal reverberated in the confined space, as though the shed itself mourned with him.

His chest heaved, his breath ragged as he covered his face and screamed. The sound tore through the night, vibrating the shed's thin walls until they rattled and sent a ripple that cracked the windows in the distant kitchen. The noise startled Guss, who came bounding toward him, barking anxiously.

William barely registered the dog's presence, his heartbeat thundering in his ears as he stumbled outside. Blind with rage, he slammed into the sturdy oak tree just beyond the shed. Without thinking, he unleashed his fury on the trunk, fists pounding against it with such ferocity that bark and wood splintered, flying in every direction. Each strike seemed to shake the ground beneath him, an unrelenting storm of his bottled grief and anger.

Finally, he paused, arms wrapped around the tree in a crushing embrace, pulling with all his might. The groan of roots snapping and the soft shift of earth beneath his boots signaled the tree's impending collapse. His rage blinded him to everything else until he caught sight of movement—a wagging tail protruding from a nearby bush.

His grip loosened, his breathing slowing as he turned toward Guss. The dog whimpered and barked softly, his tail swishing nervously. Something gleamed in the dirt beside his hind legs. William blinked, his vision clearing as he stepped closer. Nestled in the soil were three glittering gems, the colors unmistakable—Jada's favorite hues, set in a bracelet Coach Kline had given her years ago. Still attached to her wrist.

William's stomach churned as his gaze followed the bracelet to its owner. His heart twisted, but there was no time to grieve. In the distance, the telltale flash of red and blue lights painted the horizon, and the low rumble of approaching engines shattered the night's fragile silence. Two, maybe three cars were heading straight for the house.

His mind raced. He knew what this meant. The police must have been called, and with his fugitive status, they'd assume he was to blame for everything here. There was no time to reflect, no time for farewells.

Hurriedly, he threw whatever he could salvage into his backpack—the laminated symbol from Coach Kline's old playbook among the few keepsakes he grabbed. Slinging the bag over his shoulder, he stood in the doorway of the shed. His hand trembled as he struck a match. The flame flickered, casting a brief, golden glow against his face before he tossed it into the oil-soaked floor.

The fire roared to life, consuming the shed and everything it held in seconds. William stood there, unmoving, watching the flames lick higher and higher, illuminating the night sky. Guss stood at his side, tail low, eyes wide, a silent companion in the face of destruction.

Without a word, William turned his back on the inferno and strode into the shadows with Guss at his side, the flames reflecting in the dog's eyes as the remnants of his past crumbled behind them.

CHAPTER 17

Man's Best Friend

Months had slipped by, and Milwaukee seemed quieter, almost too quiet. The tall, black phantom of the alley hadn't been seen or mentioned in recent memory, but its legend remained. Whispers among the streetwise kept fear alive. Criminals avoided the alleys like cursed ground, choosing longer, well-lit routes over the risk of venturing into shadowy pathways. Strangers to the city, oblivious to the tales, didn't share the same caution.

It was around 9:00 p.m. when two young men passed an alley entrance. The streetlights buzzed faintly, their glow dim and inconsistent. One of the boys smirked and shoved the other toward the yawning darkness of the alley.

"Yo, watch out, man. He gonna snatch your ass!" he teased, laughing hard.

The other stumbled, his sneakers scuffing against the sidewalk as he grabbed his friend's sleeve. His wide eyes darted toward the shadows like he half-believed the stories. Realizing he wasn't in danger, he swung back with playful punches, muttering curses as they moved on, their laughter fading into the distance.

Minutes later, a man in a puffy green jacket and a black beanie approached the same alley. He didn't hesitate, stepping into the shadows with the easy confidence of someone too familiar with dark places. As he entered, he pulled out his phone, the screen's glow briefly cutting through the black. He stopped near a loading dock, sitting heavily on a concrete step, phone pressed to his ear.

"Yo," he said when the line connected. "Yeah, I'm here. Been here. Where you at?" His voice echoed faintly off the alley walls. "Told you nine o'clock, man. Don't screw around. Just get here. This place is creepy as hell."

He sighed, tossing the phone beside him and pulling out a pack of cigarettes. Slapping the pack against his palm, he paused when something darted in his peripheral vision—a flicker of movement near the far corner of the building. His breath caught, and he turned sharply, only to see a page of newspaper drift lazily into the light. He exhaled a nervous laugh and shook his head.

"Damn wind," he muttered, sliding a cigarette between his lips and fumbling with a lighter.

Click. Click. Sparks lit his face briefly as he struggled to get a flame. The brief flashes revealed grime-covered walls, graffiti scrawled like ancient warnings, and shadows that seemed deeper than they should've been. He kept flicking, cursing under his breath.

"I can't believe I'm in motha-fuckin' Milwaukee waitin' on this fool," he muttered, shaking his head. The lighter flared once more, the flame catching at last, but his hand froze mid-motion.

For a split second, the flickering light exposed a shape in the corner. A hulking outline, crouched low, with eyes that glimmered faintly green. His cigarette dangled from his lips, forgotten as the lighter dropped from his hand and clattered to the concrete.

"What the—"

Before he could finish, a low growl rumbled through the alley, vibrating in his chest. He stumbled back, his foot catching on the edge of the step. The green eyes moved closer, slow and deliberate, their glow unwavering.

Paralyzed, the man's breath came in short, shallow gasps. He fumbled for his phone, but it was too late. The shadows seemed alive, creeping forward, swallowing the dim light as his world narrowed to the sound of the growl and the chilling realization that he was no longer alone.

Above him, a rhythmic thumping began to echo through the quiet of the alley, distant at first but steadily growing louder. The man's attention wavered from the glowing green eyes that had transfixed him, drawn instead to the sound overhead. He tilted his head back just in time to see a figure—a man—vaulting effortlessly from one building to another. The gap between the structures was at least twenty-five feet, an impossible leap for any ordinary person.

"Hooooly shit!" he exclaimed, his voice trembling with a mixture of awe and terror. His gaze snapped back to where the dog had been moments before—only to find it gone, as if it had dissolved into the shadows.

"Later for this shit!" he muttered, stumbling backward in a frantic retreat. His heels caught on the uneven pavement, and he landed hard on the ground just as he backed out of the alley. A small crowd of bystanders turned to the commotion, their laughter breaking the tension of the moment like a needle to a balloon. They pointed, jeering at the disheveled out-of-towner sprawled on the sidewalk.

Scrambling to his feet, he brushed himself off, muttering curses under his breath as he flipped them off. With a last glare at the alley, he melted into the night, leaving the darkness behind him to claim its secrets.

Four stories above, William Strong perched on the edge of a building like a gargoyle carved from shadow and resolve. He held a greasy brown paper bag in one hand, its contents wafting savory aromas into the chilly night air. From this vantage point, the city stretched before him in its usual murky splendor—lights scattered like dying embers in the dark. But William's focus wasn't on the city tonight; it was on a single illuminated window below, where his mother's silhouette had always been a comforting constant.

Settling in, he opened the bag and pulled out two generous pieces of roasted goose, their skins crisp and glistening. He bit into one, savoring the rich, smoky flavor, but his quiet meal was interrupted by a soft whimper behind him. Turning, he saw Guss. He had a knack for finding him no matter how high or far he went.

William chuckled, tossing the second piece of goose to the eager animal. "Not sure how you keep up, Guss—especially way up here. But hey, keep it up, buddy."

The dog devoured the meat in a matter of seconds, licking his chops as if it had been nothing more than a crumb. William leaned back, his eyes returning to the familiar glow of his mother's window. The room was as it had always been: dim and framed by the soft flicker of her ancient floor-model television. But tonight, something was off. The light in the living room didn't flicker like usual; it remained steady, unwavering.

Even stranger was the absence of movement. His mother was always there—either puttering in the kitchen or nestled in her chair, watching the screen with a quiet intensity. But tonight, the room felt static, as though the life had been drained from it.

A prickle of unease climbed his spine. Rising to his feet, he shifted to a better vantage point, pulling a pair of battered binoculars from the deep pocket of his Marine Corps field jacket. The lenses were old, one cracked and spider-webbed, but they worked well enough if he squinted and used only the right side.

As he raised the binoculars, something slipped from his pocket and fluttered to the ledge—a card, weathered and creased. William paused, bending to pick it up. It was the old bookmark C.K. had used in his playbook all those years ago, the faint outline of its symbol still visible despite the wear.

A faint smile tugged at his lips as he turned the card over in his hands. Memories of their first meeting, of the significance behind that symbol, flickered in his mind like the faint glow of a distant star. He tucked the card back into his pocket with care, then turned his attention once more to his mother's window, dread tightening its grip on his chest.

Through the cracked lens, he focused on the television screen. It wasn't showing the usual static-laden sitcoms or soap operas. Instead, the screen was a stark white, its center marked by a blurry yellow shape that defied definition.

The night's chill seemed to deepen as William stared, unease turning into a cold knot in his stomach. Something was wrong. Very wrong.

William adjusted the cracked lens of his binoculars, focusing intently on the apartment below. He scanned the dim interior, his view shifting until the television came into sharp relief. A yellow smiley face filled the screen, its cheery grin mocking him with the words beneath: **"Have a Nice Day."**

The binoculars slipped from his hands, clattering to the rooftop as his chest tightened with fury. Without hesitation, he launched himself off the building's edge with a force that shattered the ledge beneath his boots. The concrete cracked, raining small chunks and debris onto the startled pedestrians below. Gasps and curses followed as William soared through the air, crashing through his mother's apartment window in an eruption of glass and blinds.

The impact sent tremors through the building, dislodging plaster from the ceiling of the apartment below. Downstairs, the gluttonous neighbor stared wide-eyed as white dust sprinkled into his dinner plate.

"Son of a bitch!" the man bellowed, spitting half-chewed food from his greasy lips. His meaty hand slammed the table, knocking over his tray in a fit of rage. Rising with a grunt, he stormed toward his door, muttering curses under his breath.

Meanwhile, William stood in the wreckage of his mother's living room, his heart pounding as he surveyed the scene. The air reeked of burnt food and neglect. He called out, his voice tight and urgent.

"Momma?"

The kitchen offered no comfort—just a skillet of charred meat left abandoned on the stove. A neatly placed plate and fork sat beside it, a quiet testament to a meal interrupted. His throat tightened as he fought back the rising tide of panic, his mind racing through possibilities, none of them good.

The mocking smiley face on the television screen seemed to taunt him, its message loaded with malice. William searched the small, cluttered apartment from corner to corner, hoping for any sign of her. But there was nothing—no struggle, no notes, no answers.

He stood frozen in the living room, ignoring the frantic barking and whimpers of Guss from across the street. The television's glow reflected off his face, the *pause* symbol in the corner daring him to press play. His hand hovered over the button, trembling. Each time he reached out, fear pulled him back.

"Quiet, Guss!" he barked toward the window, more to silence his own nerves than the dog. With a deep breath, he forced his finger down on the button.

The screen flickered, and a video began. The camera was shaky, its operator breathing heavily. The lens hovered over the carpet as the person moved through the apartment, capturing the familiar bathroom, the living room, the faint sound of their footsteps reverberating through the speakers. Then the camera stopped, tilting upward in agonizing slowness.

William's breath hitched as his mother came into view, bound to a dining room chair, her face pale and terrified. She struggled against her restraints, muffled cries escaping through the duct tape over her mouth.

"Mmmmph!"

The camera zoomed in on her face, the image fading to black without a single word from her captor.

"Fuck!" William shouted, his fists clenching as he turned toward the television. He raised his hand, ready to smash the DVD player into pieces, when the screen blinked to life again. This time, a riddle appeared in stark white letters:

In your present state you seem to not care.

You think everyone's against you and feel life isn't fair.

You can bank on the fact that you'll show your true rage.

When you make a grandstand, where I've set the stage.

Solve this riddle and you may find what you've been looking for.

Tick-Tock

The mocking smiley face reappeared, its cheery expression twisting into a sinister grin.

William rewound the DVD, jotting the riddle down on a scrap of paper, his mind already churning through possibilities. The sound of angry pounding on the door jolted him from his thoughts.

"Get out here, you son of a bitch! You ruined my meal!" The neighbor's voice thundered through the apartment. "Open this goddamn door, or I'll put my foot so far up your ass you'll taste my boot!"

When no response came, the neighbor's voice grew louder. "Come on, you chicken shit!" The pounding turned to kicks, the doorframe rattling with each strike.

Inside, William ignored the commotion, his focus razor-sharp on the riddle. But the neighbor wasn't about to back down. He took several steps back, bracing himself to charge.

Before he could launch forward, the old floor-model television exploded through the door from the other side, its massive bulk slamming him into the wall across the hall. The air left his lungs in a single, strangled grunt before he slumped to the floor, unconscious.

The hallway fell silent except for the hum of the shattered TV. Neighbors peeked cautiously from their doors, exchanging wide-eyed glances. Two men stepped forward, heaving the heavy set off the motionless man. Another, emboldened by curiosity, approached the wrecked doorway and peered inside.

All he saw was an empty room, the broken window spilling moonlight onto shards of glass and tattered blinds.

Months ago, William had claimed his refuge in the skeleton of an abandoned steel mill near downtown. The cavernous building, with its rusting beams and shattered windows, seemed forgotten by time—a fitting sanctuary for someone who had slipped between the cracks of the city. At the mill's entrance, he had piled heavy, immovable debris: slabs of twisted metal, broken machinery, and old crates—his fortress against wandering intruders. The only viable way into his hidden domain was through a jagged factory window on the third floor, where a panel of glass had been broken out long ago.

His living space was spartan but methodically arranged. A queen-sized mattress, covered in mismatched brown sheets salvaged from some forgotten corner of the city, was tucked neatly into one corner. The glow of flickering candles bathed the area in warm, uneven light, mingling with the cold blue hue of an ultraviolet lamp suspended over a row of potted vegetables. A map stretched across one wall, its surface punctuated by thumbtacks—red to mark encounters, yellow to outline safe travel routes that snaked like veins through the city's alleyways. This was William's world: part survival, part strategy, and wholly his own.

As the sun dipped lower, spilling hues of amber and violet across the lakefront, William and Guss lingered in the shadows beneath a cluster of trees. The air was thick with the scent of damp grass and the distant tang of the lake. A flock of geese had settled in the open expanse of grass ahead, their soft honks blending with the faint rustle of leaves in the evening breeze.

This was their haven, a temporary escape from the chaos of the city—a place where the noise faded, and time seemed to slow. William knelt in the shade, pulling a folded piece of paper from his pocket. The riddle, scribbled hastily in his own hand, stared back at him, its words coiled with taunting mystery. He read it again, lips pressed into a hard line, then refolded it with a sigh and tucked it back into the depths of his jacket.

Guss crouched beside him, his muscular frame tense and his eyes locked on the geese. He was patient but eager, a hunter waiting for the signal.

William smirked and reached down to scratch the scruff of the dog's neck. "We're in luck today, boy," he murmured. His tone was low, deliberate. "But this time... don't go for the skinny one."

He waited for the last group of evening walkers to pass by, their laughter fading into the distance. The moment the path was clear, William rubbed his fingers together with a sharp, snapping sound. Guss's ears perked immediately, his focus unbroken. William made a quick swipe across his throat with two fingers—a silent signal as clear as words.

Guss sprang into action, his lean body moving like a shadow across the grassy expanse. The geese startled, their panicked honks rising into the stillness of dusk as the dog cut through their ranks with calculated precision.

In the fading light, William leaned against the tree, his expression unreadable, as if weighing the riddle's words against the simplicity of the hunt unfolding before him.

CHAPTER 18

Ain't Fair

The riddle echoed in William's mind, relentless and taunting, refusing to let him rest. Sleep would not come—not until he unraveled its cryptic meaning. At the foot of the bed, Guss watched him intently, his head resting on a pillow. The moment their eyes met, Guss straightened, ears perked, ready for whatever his master might say.

"I don't get it, Guss. I mean, I *get* the words, but I'm supposed to figure something out... something that'll lead me to Momma."

He sighed, pulling the crumpled paper from his pocket. Flattening it against his thigh, he scanned the riddle again, mouthing the words as if they might change with each reading. Frustration bubbling to the surface, he barked at himself, "Damn it, Will—get it together!"

Determined, he grabbed a pen and began circling the words that leapt out at him—*State, Fair, Bank, Grandstand.* A pattern teased at the edges of his thoughts. He froze, then smacked his palm against his forehead. "A map! I need a map!"

Stuffing the paper back into his pocket, he moved quickly, his decision made. He climbed out the open window, the cool night air rushing against his face. Behind him, Guss hopped off the bed and trotted toward the cluttered maze of their makeshift fortress of large scrap steel, slipping through a hidden path only he knew.

The night hung heavy and quiet, the world cloaked in the eerie stillness of 1:00 a.m. Near the entrance to the abandoned state fairgrounds, a homeless man had staked his temporary claim on a crumbling curb. His voice, hoarse and gravelly, wove a disjointed sermon into the air, a hymn to no audience but himself. A battered Bible, its cover peeling with age, was clutched in his trembling hands, and a nearly empty bottle of peppermint schnapps lay nearby, its contents his only solace from the cold.

The man rocked back and forth, his gaunt frame swaying like a frail reed in the wind. His long, ghostly hair tangled in the breeze, whipping across his weathered face. Some strands clung to his cracked lips, but he paid them no mind, the oily tang of hair mingling with the sharp burn of schnapps on his tongue. He paused only to take a deep pull from the bottle, tilting his head back and letting the liquid trickle down his throat. His chapped lips smacked once before he resumed his ceaseless murmuring, the verses spilling out as if they might stitch together the broken pieces of his soul.

From the shadows, William and Guss emerged, silent and deliberate as they approached the fairground entrance. They moved as if the man were invisible, their focus unbroken by his whispered prayers. But the man saw them—*felt* them. He froze mid-rock, his bloodshot eyes narrowing as he called out in a rasping voice, "God is watching you, son. God is watching."

His warning hung in the air, unanswered, as William and Guss continued past him, their figures slipping deeper into the darkness. Rising to his feet, the old man's voice climbed to a shout, raw with desperation. "All your sins can be forgiven! It's not too late! It's not too late!"

Above his head, a hidden camera swiveled to life, its mechanical eye locking onto William and Guss. Silently, it tracked their movements, switching between angles, observing, recording. The faint hum of its servos was lost in the wind.

The man, spent and unheeded, slumped back to the curb. His warning grew softer, like a mantra meant more for himself than for anyone else. "God is watching you. He's watching." Rocking forward once more, he slipped back into his muttered verses, a lone prophet lost to the night.

The high-pitched squeak of a warehouse dolly echoed through the dim hallway, its sound amplified by the vast emptiness of the building. Strapped tightly to the dolly was a metal chair, and in it sat Victoria, bound with layers of duct tape that pinned her arms to the chair's cold frame. Her breaths were quick and shallow, rasping through her nose, her chest heaving as tears streamed down her face, soaking the tape wrapped cruelly over her mouth and around her head. The tears mixed with the sweat on her cheeks, carving streaks of raw desperation into her expression.

The dolly came to a sudden halt, slamming the front legs of the chair hard against the concrete floor with a jarring thud. Victoria winced, the impact rattling through her body. Her captor stepped in front of her, his face obscured by the harsh glare of the single bulb overhead. The light cast his features into shadow, making him appear more like a silhouette than a man.

"Go ahead," he said, his voice low and gravelly. "Scream if you want to. Ain't nobody here gonna hear you." With a quick, brutal motion, he ripped the duct tape from her mouth.

Victoria gasped, her lungs greedily pulling in air as her lips trembled.

The man held up a bottle of water, tilting it back and forth in his hand as though considering something. "Now, here's the deal. You can sip on this and wait quietly for the show, or I can seal your mouth back up, and you can keep breathing through that snotty nose of yours. Up to you. Oh, and don't hold your breath waiting for that dumb-ass son of yours to come rescue you."

"Water," she croaked, her voice shaky and dry.

He tipped the bottle to her lips, pouring too quickly for her to drink. Water spilled down her chin, soaking her neck and dribbling onto her lap. He didn't stop until the bottle was empty, tossing it carelessly to the floor where it clattered and rolled away. Victoria coughed, gasping, then wiped her mouth against her shoulder as best she could.

"What do you want with my son?" she demanded, her voice trembling but resolute. "What is this about? We ain't done nothin' to you!"

Her captor sneered, kicking the empty bottle across the floor with a hollow rattle. "You don't get to ask questions," he said, his tone cold and final. "Let's just say you're a piece of the puzzle I need to finish. Sit tight—I've got company to bring in."

Without another word, he disappeared through the door, leaving her alone in the cavernous space. The moment the door clicked shut, Victoria began twisting her wrists, the tape biting into her skin as she strained against it. She shifted her weight, trying to rock the chair back and forth, but the heavy metal cart beneath her refused to budge. Her body, weak from fear and exhaustion, betrayed her, leaving her trapped.

Minutes later, the door groaned open again. Her captor returned, pulling another dolly behind him. Strapped to it was another chair, identical to hers. Slumped forward in the seat was a figure, their face obscured by a black pillowcase. The stranger's head lolled lifelessly, their body motionless.

"Who's that?" Victoria demanded, her voice rising in panic. "What kind of crap are you pulling?"

Her captor didn't answer. He parked the second dolly four feet away from her, then walked to the far wall and flipped off the light switch. The room plunged into pitch-black silence, broken only by the fading echo of his retreating footsteps.

"Hey..." Victoria whispered into the void, her voice small and uncertain. "Hey... can you hear me?"

Summoning what strength she had, she began inching her chair toward the other, using her weight to push against the floor. The metal legs scraped loudly against the concrete, each sound grating and amplified in the oppressive silence. Her progress was agonizingly slow, but determination drove her forward.

Then, one of the chair's legs caught in a small divot in the floor. Before she could brace herself, the chair toppled over, slamming her body to the ground. The impact drove the air from her lungs, her face striking the unforgiving concrete with a sickening crack. Darkness enveloped her entirely—not from the room, but from unconsciousness.

The words on the faded map seemed to taunt him, their clarity offering no solace: *"You are here."* An arrow pointed to the Gate 7 Entrance, but beyond that, the tangled maze of locations and landmarks only deepened William's frustration. He studied the map under the flickering glow of a nearby streetlamp, his brow furrowed as he murmured the clues to himself.

"You can bank on that... Bank on that? Grandstand?" The words rolled through his mind, their meaning just out of reach. His finger hovered over the map, tracing the names: *Bank Mutual Amphitheater... Milwaukee Mile Speedway Grandstand Seating.*

A sudden clatter jarred him from his thoughts. The sharp sound of a trashcan tipping over echoed through the quiet fairgrounds. William spun around, his heart pounding, only to see Guss sitting guiltily beside the fallen can. The dog's paw pressed down on a crumpled burger wrapper, his head tilted in an exaggerated display of innocence.

"Guss," William hissed, his voice low but sharp. "You're supposed to be watching my back, not digging through garbage."

Guss gave a low growl, his eyes darting from William to the wrapper. Then, with deliberate defiance, he snatched it up in his teeth and tore it apart.

"Guss, *leave it!*" William barked, his frustration mounting. But the dog ignored him, too engrossed in his scavenging.

With a sigh, William rubbed his fingers together, the subtle sound enough to catch Guss's attention. Once the dog's amber eyes locked on him, William raised two fingers in a peace sign and pointed them at his own eyes. Guss sat up straighter, his ears twitching. William then extended his index finger toward a patch of dense bushes nearby—a silent command.

Guss exhaled audibly, almost as if he were sighing, before dropping the shredded wrapper. He leapt into the brush, his dark coat vanishing into the thicket, leaving only a faint rustle behind. Satisfied, William turned back to the map.

His finger landed on *Bank Mutual Amphitheater.* He tapped it once before sliding it to *Milwaukee Mile Speedway Grandstand Seating.* The two locations felt like pieces of a larger puzzle, their significance gnawing at the edges of his mind.

"This has to mean something," he muttered under his breath, his eyes narrowing. The faint sound of wind rattling an old metal sign punctuated the silence, as if the night itself was waiting for him to make his next move.

CHAPTER 19

Victoria's Secret

The cool night air whispered against Victoria's face, stirring her from the heavy fog of unconsciousness. Her eyelids fluttered open, her vision swimming with faint outlines and hazy shapes. She blinked, trying to clear the blurriness, her tongue sticking to the dry, cotton-like interior of her mouth. Slowly, awareness crept in, and with it, a grim realization: her surroundings had changed.

She was no longer inside. The harsh scent of concrete and rusted metal mingled with the crisp breeze. Overhead, steel beams stretched across the night sky like the skeleton of a forgotten giant. Behind her, the structure rose higher, lined with rows of empty stadium seats that loomed like silent witnesses to her plight.

Directly in front of her, across a cracked and weathered pathway, stood a cluster of small buildings, their darkened windows blank and unwelcoming. She craned her neck slightly, her eyes catching a glint of movement above—a small camera mounted on one of the beams, its lens pointed directly at her. Beneath it, a tiny six-inch screen flickered faintly, its purpose unclear but foreboding.

Her throat burned as she summoned her voice. "Heeeeeeelp!" she cried, the sound raw and desperate, shattering the stillness. "Help!"

The echo of her plea barely faded before heavy footsteps thudded against the ground, growing louder with every beat. Panic clawed at her chest as the sharp rip of duct tape cut through the air like a warning. Before she could yell again, the sticky tape was pressed brutally across her mouth, wound tightly around her head, sealing her cries into silence.

"Oh no, young lady," her captor sneered, his voice low and mocking as he leaned close. "You're not gonna spoil the surprise. Won't be long now before dumb-dumb figures out my riddle. When he gets here, you'll have your time to talk. Trust me."

His words hung in the air, chilling and final, as he straightened and turned away. Victoria's muffled breaths came in frantic bursts as she twisted her wrists, the bindings cutting into her skin. She watched helplessly as the man disappeared into the shadows, his figure dissolving into the eerie, stadium-like expanse, leaving her trapped and waiting for whatever dark plan he had in store.

Standing before the shadowy expanse of the amphitheater, William exhaled a slow plume of smoke from the dark cigar clenched between his teeth. The faint aroma mingled with the cool night air before he flicked the spent stub away, watching as it tumbled into the dirt, leaving a faint ember in its wake.

"Stage, Grandstand... it's got to be here," he muttered, his voice low and edged with determination.

His eyes swept the scene, scanning for any sign of movement. The space was eerily still, save for dry leaves skittering across the ground in the breeze. Rows of empty picnic tables stood in silent disarray, their surfaces weathered and scarred. At the far end of the stage, a massive white screen loomed like a pale monolith against the darkness.

Unease prickled at the edges of his thoughts. He needed something—*anything*—to confirm he was in the right place. Tightening his grip on the map folded in his hand, he began walking through the metal benches toward the stage. His boots clinked softly against the gravel with every step. Five paces in, the stillness shattered.

The screen at the back of the stage suddenly flared to life, flooding the area with harsh white light. William froze, shielding his eyes as flickering news clips played across the screen. Each snippet showed people being interviewed, their faces etched with fear or curiosity, recounting tales of his supposed sightings. The montage lasted barely twenty seconds before the images faded. In their place, a garish yellow smiley face appeared, its grin impossibly wide and mocking.

William stood motionless, his heart pounding as he waited for what would come next.

A voice crackled through the amphitheater's speakers, deep and cold, its tone curling through the air like smoke. "You like the dark?" it asked, almost conversationally. "You hide in it—from the police, from society, from responsibility. But most of all... you hide from yourself."

William's fists clenched, his voice thundering through the empty space. "*Where's my mother?!*"

The voice chuckled, low and hollow, before continuing, its words sharp as knives. "You hid in the dark when you were young, too. When your father beat your mother, you cowered in the shadows. All that strength you had in your little body, and you did... nothing."

William's jaw tightened as the voice paused, letting the words sink in.

"Oh, I know plenty about you, William Strong. Let's just say I've done my research. Learned a thing or two from personal experience."

"Personal experience?" William demanded, stepping closer to the stage, his movements tense and deliberate. "Who are you? Why are you hiding? *What did you do with my mother?!*"

The voice softened, almost playful now. "All the answers you need—and more than you want—will come soon, old friend."

Suddenly, a sharp, electric jolt ripped through William's body. His muscles locked, seizing him in place, before gravity took over. He fell sideways, crashing into a metal bench with a deafening crunch, crumpling it like foil. Pain lanced through his ribs as he lay helpless on the ground.

Out of the darkness, the old man from the fairground entrance emerged, standing over him with a Taser gun in hand.

Two wires snaked from the weapon to William's lower back, where the prongs remained embedded.

"I warned you, young man," the old man said, his voice calm, almost pitying. "God is watching you."

William struggled to push himself up, his body trembling, but the old man pulled the trigger again. A second dose of electricity surged through him, sending him collapsing back to the earth.

As William's body spasmed and his vision blurred, he felt a sharp pinch at the nape of his neck. His head lolled to the side just as his gaze caught a figure stepping into view—a woman clad in an all-black bodysuit, her face obscured by a grotesque smiley mask.

She leaned over him, withdrawing a syringe from his neck with deliberate precision. "Sleep tight, Strong man," she said, her voice lilting and mockingly sweet. She wiggled her gloved fingers in a playful goodbye as William's vision dissolved into darkness, her distorted smile burned into his fading consciousness.

A rush of icy water cascaded over William, yanking him violently from unconsciousness. He gasped, sputtering as the freezing liquid soaked his skin, sharp as needles against his exposed body. The chill was unrelenting, made worse by the brisk autumn wind biting at his damp flesh. His breath came in ragged gulps, and as clarity returned, he realized his predicament.

His arms and legs were strapped down with tightly woven metal bindings that dug into his skin. Stripped to his boxers, he was splayed against an upright metal table, every inch of his body vulnerable to the elements. In front of him loomed the massive stage screen, its glow pulsating in the darkness. The once-cheerful smiley face on the screen now twisted and contorted, alternating between a benign grin and a sinister leer. The grotesque image sent a jolt of dread through him—it was eerily similar to the symbol he'd seen at his mother's apartment.

"There are a lot of people looking for you," the voice boomed through the speakers, smooth but menacing. "And a lot of money to be made. But first... I have to have my fun."

The screen flickered, and William's heart sank as an image of his mother appeared. She was still bound and gagged, her wide, tearful eyes brimming with fear. The sight ignited a surge of adrenaline in him. He twisted and strained against his bonds, his muscles trembling with the effort. But his strength had been sapped, either by the drugs injected into him or the lingering effects of the earlier electric shocks.

His struggle was cut short as another jolt of electricity coursed through his body. His muscles locked, pain searing through every nerve. The smell of damp skin and faintly singed hair filled the air. When the current finally ceased, he sagged against the table, steam rising from his chilled, wet body as laughter erupted around him.

"Yeah, I wouldn't try that too much," the voice taunted with cruel amusement. "Unless, of course, you enjoy that kind of thing."

To his left, William caught sight of the old man standing smugly near a control switch, his leathery face split into a wide grin as he chuckled. The sight fueled William's anger, overriding the lingering pain.

"You better pray I don't get free," William growled, his voice strained but steady. His glare burned into the old man, defiant despite his predicament.

The voice on the speakers cut in again, dripping with mockery. "Oh, what's the plan, Strong? You gonna take us down like those thugs in the alley? Maybe dazzle us with some of that legendary strength?" A pause, then a cruel laugh. "Those binds are made of reinforced tungsten, my friend. You couldn't cut through them with the Jaws of Life. And the table? Compliments of my buddies at EvoTech. You're not going anywhere."

The voice softened, oozing satisfaction. "Besides, with old pops there giving you a jolt every five to ten minutes, you'll stay nice and docile until it's time to deliver you."

William's lip curled in contempt. "Since you're so confident, why don't you step out here and show your face? Or are you afraid?" His words were a gamble, laced with enough disdain to provoke a reaction.

Almost immediately, a blinding spotlight snapped on, bathing him in harsh white light. The sudden brightness seared his retinas, forcing his eyes shut against the sting. The voice chuckled, now amplified to an almost theatrical cadence.

"Oh, William, you're in for quite the show tonight. I've worked *very* hard to make this moment perfect. So, as the host of tonight's little talk show, I suppose it's only fair I introduce myself."

A metallic clang echoed from the stage as a door creaked open. Heavy, deliberate footsteps followed, reverberating through the amphitheater. A large man emerged from the shadows, his figure hulking and imposing. He stopped just short of the spotlight, remaining a silhouette on its edge.

"I've waited a long time for this, William Strong. A *very* long time." His voice was deep and measured, carrying the weight of something personal.

He stepped forward, his face now partially illuminated, his expression unreadable. "Take a good look at me," he said, his tone teetering between venom and satisfaction. "And you tell me... do you know who I am?"

Leaning into the harsh glare of the spotlight, the man tilted his head, revealing the left side of his face. William squinted, searching for recognition, but the features didn't spark any memories. A salt-and-pepper goatee framed a round, fleshy face, shadowed beneath a thick nose and dark chocolate skin. The man's eyes remained hidden behind dark sunglasses, further concealing his identity.

Slowly, the man rotated his head, removing the glasses with deliberate flair. What William saw sent his mind crashing back to his childhood. Images flickered in his head: the metallic clang of lockers, the sting of dodgeballs, and the unmistakable mark of an old injury.

"Buddha?" William muttered, disbelief cutting through his voice.

"Got-damn," the man said, a grin spreading across his face. "You *do* remember me. Been a long time, huh? What've you been up to, man?" The sarcasm in his voice dripped like venom. "Back then, I went by Lamont, but that doesn't quite suit me anymore. Buddha's got a better ring to it. And that 'God is watching you' bit? Thought it up myself. Clever, right? Buddha's a god, and, well... I was watching you." He chuckled, then shook his head. "Never mind. So, what gave it away? Was it the lazy eye you gave me with that damn tetherball? Or this lovely smiling scar?" His fingers traced the disfigured line with mock affection. "Still itches, even after all these years."

With a sudden motion, Buddha's hand lashed out, backhanding William across the face. "That's for the eye," he snarled. Before William could recover, another slap came from the opposite hand, splitting his lip. "And *that's* for the scar!"

Blood pooled in William's mouth, the metallic tang sharp against his tongue. He licked it away before spitting at Buddha, a crimson spray staining the man's cheek. "If you weren't messing with me, you wouldn't have those scars," William growled. "That's on *you* for being a fucked-up kid. Let me loose, and I'll give you something even worse to remember me by."

Buddha wiped his face with a handkerchief, his expression darkening. He turned to the old man by the switch, nodding once. A moment later, electricity tore through William's body, forcing his back into an agonized arch as his scream echoed into the night.

"Stop it!" Victoria's voice cried from the screen, trembling with desperation. "Leave him alone! He did nothing wrong!"

The old man dialed down the voltage, and William collapsed against the table, unconscious once more.

Buddha turned toward the screen, his grin returning. "*Nothing wrong?*" he repeated mockingly. "Lady, you clearly don't know your son—or haven't been paying attention to the news. He's responsible for nearly a quarter of the ER's activity downtown. He's disrupted businesses, pissed off the wrong people—powerful people. People who've hired me to *handle* the situation. But hey, like mother, like son, right, Ms. Strong?"

Victoria hung her head, shame washing over her. Buddha's grin widened as he pointed to the water bucket at the old man's feet. "Wake him up."

The old man upended the bucket over William, drenching him with a torrent of freezing water. William sputtered and gagged, coughing violently as water shot up his nose and into his mouth. He tugged weakly at his restraints, his muscles trembling.

"No time for naps, old friend," Buddha said with a cold laugh, retreating into the shadows. "We've got a lot to discuss before the real fun begins."

William gasped for air, his voice raw. "I know you killed C.K. and Jada," he rasped. "How could you murder a helpless old man and his wife? What kind of coward does that?"

Buddha paused, his silhouette framed by the open door. "Kill them? Let's set the record straight, Strong—you did that. Your actions caused their deaths. Your hate, your selfishness. You interfered in things you didn't understand, and people paid the price. You might've thought you were helping, but it was all for you, wasn't it? You didn't care about the consequences—about the people who'd come looking for revenge. Collateral damage, brotha. That's on you."

The door slammed shut behind him, his words lingering like smoke. William turned his head, his vision swimming as his eyes locked on the screen where his mother's face remained, tear-streaked and heartbroken. He couldn't bring himself to meet her gaze.

With every labored breath, his mind raced, scanning his surroundings. The pang of betrayal and fear gnawed at him. Amid it all, one thought stood out like a blade in his chest: *Where was Guss?*

About a block away, Guss poked his head out of a rusty dumpster, his jaws clamped triumphantly around an old burrito. The stale, crumbling tortilla reeked of grease and mystery meat, but to Guss, it was a treasure. Settling on the pavement, he devoured the find, greasy wrapper and all, his tail wagging with satisfaction. Once finished, he leapt back into his stinky lair, rummaging for more hidden delights.

Back at the stadium, the speakers crackled to life, breaking the stillness. The faint rustle of paper echoed through the sound system, followed by Buddha's voice, its mocking edge amplified over the amphitheater.

"You might think I'm doing this for the money," he began. "And yeah, the payout for you is huge. But my satisfaction? That goes deeper than cash. When we were kids, *I* was the strong one. *I* was the kid everyone looked up to—or feared. Then you came along."

The sound of paper crinkling stopped as Buddha's tone shifted, his words slowing. "You ruined all of that. You left me with this scar—this constant reminder of what you did. The locker. My eye in the gym. Every time I looked in the mirror, it wasn't just the pain that stared back at me—it was the envy. I hated you for taking what I thought should've been mine."

He paused, letting the words hang in the air before chuckling softly. "Does this sound like I'm reading it? I wanted it to flow with more anger, but I'm not exactly a pro at speeches."

"Maybe because it's bullshit," William spat. "You were a hateful ass kid—a bully who couldn't handle getting what he deserved. What's this supposed to be, some sick revenge trip because you can't let go of your own mistakes?"

Buddha laughed, a deep, echoing sound. "Vengeful? Me? Oh, you want to talk about vengeance? Maybe you should ask your *mother* about that."

The screen flickered to Victoria's face, her eyes darting away from William's piercing gaze.

"What's he talking about, Momma?" William asked, his voice tinged with confusion and frustration.

Victoria hesitated, her voice trembling as she finally spoke. "I'm just... so happy you're alive, son. Why haven't you come to see me? Why did you do those terrible things to people? To your father?"

William's jaw tightened. "I did what I had to, Momma. Because *you* didn't. I stepped up. I took care of it like a man."

"Like a man?" Victoria's voice rose, thick with pain. "You *killed* your father, William! You crushed him and left me to pick up the pieces!"

"He wasn't my father!" William shouted, the words raw with anger. "He didn't love you, Momma—he *destroyed* you. He crushed who you were long before I did anything. That night, when he was beating you—" William's voice cracked. "You wouldn't get rid of him, so I had to."

Victoria's lips trembled as tears streamed down her face. "You think I wasn't handling it? I didn't need you to step in. He was still your father, whether you liked it or not. There's so much you didn't know about him, William."

A bitter laugh escaped William's lips. "Do I even know who my *real* father is?"

Victoria's expression darkened, her head snapping up toward the camera. "How *dare* you," she hissed, her voice trembling with fury. "How dare you speak to me like that—as if I'm some common street *hoe!* You have no idea what I went through for you, William Theodore Strong—no idea!"

There was a beat of silence, followed by Buddha's booming laugh. "Theodore?" he repeated, his tone dripping with incredulity. "Your middle name is *Theodore?*"

The laughter exploded, rich and manic, echoing over the amphitheater. The tension in the air paused, suspended as Buddha reveled in his mockery.

"Okay—okay," he wheezed, holding up his hand as if to apologize. "I'm sorry, I just... I needed that." He shook his head, still grinning. "Go on, please. Don't let me interrupt."

The tension in the air thickened as William's voice sliced through the silence. "Then who is he? If you know, tell me—I think I deserve to know."

Victoria's expression hardened, her face shadowed with anger and hurt. "You don't deserve to know *shit*, boy," she snapped, her voice trembling with frustration. "You run around hurting people because of the pain you've been through. You've ruined lives—disabled people permanently—acting like some damn superhero. What gives you the right to do what you've done? To judge who you've judged?" Her tone softened into a broken whisper, her eyes glistening with unshed tears. "You should learn to forgive, William. Let God take care of the rest."

Buddha's mocking laughter boomed over the speakers, shattering the fragile moment. "Oh, *Lord*! God? Really, Ms. Holy-Christian-From-Hell? That's rich. Real funny coming from *your* lips. Your momma's a hypocrite, boy!"

"What's he talking about?" William demanded, his eyes narrowing as they flicked to the screen. But Victoria wouldn't meet his gaze. Her head dipped, her shoulders slumping as if crushed by an unseen weight.

Silence fell, deep and suffocating. No one moved, no one spoke. In the stillness, William's fingers grazed the edge of a loose screw on the contraption holding him. Slowly, carefully, he began twisting it, his thumb and forefinger working with quiet precision.

On the screen, Victoria's composure crumbled. A single tear slid down her cheek, followed by another, until the floodgates opened. Her voice cracked as she began to speak.

"He just wouldn't leave me alone," she sobbed, her tears streaking her weary face. "He put his hands on me for years... and threatened me to keep me quiet. I moved out on my own when I was sixteen, thinking I'd finally escaped. But he told me—he *promised* me—that if I ever said anything, he'd make my mother pay for it."

Her eyes lifted to the camera, her pain raw and unguarded. "So I stayed quiet. I bottled it all up inside, praying—*begging*—that something would happen to his perverted ass. That one day, God would deal with him."

William's chest tightened, a mix of anger and confusion bubbling inside him. "What are you talking about, Momma?" he asked, his voice softer now, edged with uncertainty. "You never told me any of this."

"I wanted it to go away, baby," Victoria whispered, her voice barely audible. "I thought if I didn't talk about it, I could somehow forget. But I couldn't. I saw it every time I looked at his face. I felt it every time I heard the word..." She hesitated, the word catching in her throat before spilling out. "...'True.'"

William froze. His fingers stopped working the screw as realization dawned, chilling him to his core.

"Yes," Victoria said, her gaze steady now despite the tears cascading down her face. "He is your real father, William."

The revelation hung in the air like a bomb waiting to explode, its impact rippling through William as he stared blankly at the screen. The screw beneath his fingers turned uselessly in his grasp, forgotten in the wake of a truth he hadn't been prepared to hear.

CHAPTER 20

A Bitter Soul

Guss had gorged himself on a feast of stale leftovers scavenged from dumpsters, his belly nearly bursting with the spoils. But the familiar scent of his master lingered in the air, drawing him like a compass needle to true north. He galloped toward the stage, his ears perked and his gait steady, until the sight of the old man stepping out from the stage door halted him in his tracks. The man struck a match, the faint glow illuminating his face as he lit a cigarette, exhaling smoke into the brisk night.

Lowering his body to the ground, Guss slinked toward the right side of the stage, staying low and out of sight. He paused when he caught sight of William strapped to the upright table, his hands working methodically at a stubborn screw. A soft whimper escaped Guss's throat, barely audible but enough to catch William's attention.

William's head snapped in his direction, his whispered words harsh and sharp. "Where the hell have you been?"

Guss tilted his head, his amber eyes filled with dogged confusion, as if he were trying to decipher his master's tone.

William glanced over his shoulder to check the old man, who remained oblivious, his back still turned. Turning back to Guss, he frantically motioned with his fingers, pointing toward the old man before slashing his hand back and forth in exaggerated movements. Guss simply tilted his head further, his expression perplexed.

"Get him," William hissed, urgency in his voice. "Go—*go!*"

But Guss didn't budge. Instead, the dog flopped onto his belly, his tail wagging lazily. His tongue lolled out, and if William didn't know better, he could swear the dog was grinning.

Frustration boiled over. William slammed the back of his head against the metal table with a dull thud. "Unpredictable mutt!" he muttered under his breath.

Turning his attention back to the screws he'd managed to loosen, William began to strategize. Three small screws rested in his palm—not enough to free himself, but perhaps enough to turn the tide. Memories from his youth flickered through his mind: nights spent flicking BBs at dots on the wall, or knocking out alleyway lights with well-aimed pebbles. A thought struck him. *Maybe I could get one of these screws in the back of the old man's head.*

Before he could act, a sharp burst of feedback screeched through the speakers, making him wince. Buddha's voice followed, dripping with theatrics. "Things got a little too quiet, and I'm on a schedule here. How about we pick up where we left off, Mom and Son?"

William froze, his fingers curling around the screws. For now, his plan would have to wait. He concealed the small metal pieces in his fist.

On the screen, Victoria's voice emerged, tired and cracked. "I got nothing else to say."

Buddha chuckled, a deep, mocking sound. "Ohhhh, Ms. William," he drawled. "You and I both know better than that. If you don't tell him, I *will*."

Victoria's silence hung heavy, her gaze fixed on the ground. Her lips trembled, her tongue darting out to moisten them, but no words came.

"Go on," Buddha goaded. "School him on forgiveness again, like you did earlier. I mean, *really*, after what you told me when you thought I was the cops raiding your house, you should *not* be giving lectures on morality! You should've been there, boy. Your momma spilled the beans as soon as I kicked that door in."

"I couldn't take it anymore!" Victoria's voice broke the tension, rising with raw emotion. Tears streaked her face as she confessed. "The guilt... the more I tried to hide it, the more it built up inside me." She sucked in a shaky breath, her voice trembling as the words poured out. "I felt like he had to pay for what he'd done. But it wasn't happening fast enough."

Her voice cracked, and she hung her head, her shame laid bare for all to see. William stared at the screen, his mind racing, but he said nothing. The pieces of her story hung in the air, waiting for him to fit them together.

Victoria's mind drifted back to that fateful evening, the memory surfacing like a shadow she could never fully outrun. She had left the house after Tru's violent outburst against William, seeking refuge in her mother's home. Placing her bags on the living room floor, she tried to steady herself, to find a moment's peace. But her reprieve was short-lived.

Tru arrived uninvited, sauntering in as if he owned the place. He settled into the recliner, his gaze locking on her with the same predatory stare she remembered from her childhood. That sick feeling—cold and twisting—rose in her gut. Ignoring him, she focused on unpacking, spreading the sheet and blanket her mother had loaned her across the couch, preparing her temporary bed. She bent over to tuck the sheet into the cushions, her mind on anything but him.

"Mmmm-mm, still got it," Tru murmured, his voice low and slimy, meant for her ears alone.

Victoria froze, the words hitting her like a slap. She straightened, quickly pulling her top down over her hips, trying to shield herself from his vile attention. Her chest tightened, the air in the room growing heavy as memories of his sinister stares, his unwanted touches, flooded her mind.

"Momma, you got any pillows?" she called out, her voice trembling slightly. "This throw pillow's too small."

The silence that followed was deafening. She waited, her pulse quickening when no response came. Forcing herself to stay calm, she walked toward the back of the house, calling out again. "Momma?"

Still nothing. She stepped into her mother's bedroom and knocked gently on the bathroom door. When there was no reply, she pushed it open slightly.

Behind her, the sound of the bedroom door closing sent a chill down her spine.

"She gone," Tru said, his voice like poison, oozing through the space. "Ain't gonna be back for a good minute. Tonight's girls'

night out." He leaned against the doorframe, biting his bottom lip as his eyes roved over her. "Damn, girl, you done grew up."

Her breath hitched. Without a word, she slammed the bathroom door shut and backed into the tub beneath the small window, frantically searching for something—anything—to defend herself. The scissors on the sink were just out of reach, and she knew the flimsy door wouldn't hold him for long.

The crash came moments later. The door splintered as Tru kicked it open, pieces of the frame flying into the bathroom and landing in the tub with her. She pressed herself into the corner, her body trembling with fear as he approached, his intentions unmistakable.

Victoria's voice cracked as she stared at the camera, reliving the nightmare. "He told Momma I tried to kill myself. Said I ran into the bathroom, and he had to break the door to stop me. My busted lip? He told her it was from him trying to 'knock some sense' into me."

Her jaw tightened, anger flashing in her eyes. "And she believed him. She *believed him!* That bastard could do no wrong in her eyes. She loved him more than she ever loved me."

Her hands clenched into fists as she continued. "When I got home a week later, Will tried to take advantage of me too. But when he saw the bruises on my body, he stopped and asked me what had happened. I didn't tell him—I couldn't. I just cried. And what did he do? He decided I must've run off to be with another man. So, he hit me."

Her voice wavered but didn't break. "We didn't have sex for a long time after that. Almost a month and a half. I figured that little hoe he was messing with was keeping him satisfied, but I didn't care. I was done. I was planning to leave."

Her gaze drifted downward, her voice softening. "But then I found out I was pregnant with you, son. I had no job, no money, and nowhere to go. I couldn't go to Momma's—Tru was still there. I lied about how far along I was when I told him I was pregnant so he wouldn't hit me anymore. I needed the benefits. I needed a roof over my head. I needed a place to stay."

Her eyes returned to the camera, her expression a mix of shame and resignation. "I told him it was his... because I didn't have a choice."

Victoria's words lingered in the air like a storm cloud, heavy and charged. She paused, her gaze locked on William, hoping for something—*anything*. A flicker of understanding, a hint of forgiveness, even just an acknowledgment of her pain. But his face remained blank, his body unmoving. He refused to meet her eyes, leaning back against the cold surface of his restraints, his expression distant.

When he finally spoke, his voice was low and cold. "Are you telling me I'm the product of incest?"

Victoria flinched, the weight of his words cutting deep. "William, Tru was my stepfather," she explained, her voice trembling. "Your real grandfather left when he found out my mother was pregnant with me. He took off without a second thought, and she struggled for years as a single mother. When I found myself in the same situation, staring down the same hopeless path, I couldn't let it happen again. I thought I could make things better."

William's jaw tightened, his eyes still fixed on the ceiling. "So, staying with a man who beat you... that was your version of better?"

Her breath caught, and for a moment, she said nothing. Finally, she whispered, "At the time, yes. I had hope. I believed in the man he used to be. You think you're the only one with scars, William? You think you're the only one who's been broken?"

Her voice gained strength as she continued. "You don't know the anger I carried inside me—the fury for everything I endured at the hands of men like Tru. You don't know what it's like to feel trapped, powerless, and desperate. I thought I could endure it. I thought I could survive for you."

Victoria's gaze dropped as the memory of that fateful night resurfaced, vivid and unrelenting. Her voice softened, tinged with pain and guilt. "But sometimes, survival demands something darker."

It was a bitterly cold evening when Victoria left the store, her arms laden with groceries. The wind whipped at her coat, and her breath came in frosty clouds as she trudged home. Then she saw him—Tru—standing across the street outside a bar, the orange glow of his cigar illuminating his smug face. He stood with his shoulders hunched against the cold, puffing lazily, unaware of her presence.

Her heart raced as her eyes darted to the alley. Her mother's car sat unattended.

She watched as he flicked his cigar and began walking down the street, his pace slow, unbothered. Her stomach churned as she crossed the street, her feet crunching against the icy pavement. She felt detached, as if watching herself from afar. By the time she reached the alley, her decision had already been made.

She slipped into the backseat of the car, the shadows swallowing her whole. The cold air inside bit at her skin, but her focus was singular, unwavering. She clutched a knife she removed from her purse tightly in her trembling hand, her knuckles white. Her heart pounded in her ears as she crouched low, listening to Tru's footsteps approach.

The car door creaked open, and he slid into the driver's seat, one foot still on the pavement. He fiddled with the radio, his fingers smudging the knobs, his foot tapping lazily to the music. He fumbled in the armrest, scattering ash from his cigar in the process. Victoria's breathing slowed as adrenaline took hold. Time seemed to stretch, each second a lifetime.

Then he leaned back, savoring a long drag of his cigar, his eyes fluttering shut.

The moment arrived.

Suddenly feeling something was off, Tru's eyes shot open just as the knife flashed in the dim light, its cold steel catching his gaze in the rearview mirror. His eyes widened in realization, but it was too late. The blade plunged into his neck, silencing his gasp. Blood spurted across the dashboard as his body convulsed, the car shaking violently as he thrashed. A choking gurgle filled the air, wet and grotesque, before his movements slowed and then stopped altogether.

Victoria sat frozen, her breath ragged, the knife slipping from her grip and clattering onto the floor. Her hands were sticky with the warmth of his blood, her mind numb with disbelief. She stared at his lifeless body slumped against the seat, her reflection staring back at her in the rearview mirror, pale and wide-eyed.

Somehow, she moved. Her hands worked mechanically, lifting his leg into the car and wiping her prints from the door handle with his coat sleeve. She closed the door softly, her movements careful, deliberate. Then she stepped back, the cold air burning her lungs as she glanced around, ensuring no one had seen. Wrapping her coat tighter around her pregnant belly, she turned and walked away, her steps quickening as she disappeared into the night.

Back in the present, Victoria's voice cracked as she finished, her confession raw. "I thought I was protecting you. I thought I was doing what needed to be done. But now... now I don't know."

Her tear-filled eyes locked on William, waiting, but he said nothing. The silence between them was deafening, heavy with everything unspoken.

Victoria's voice trembled as she finished her confession, her gaze fixed somewhere far away, as though she could still see that fateful night unfolding before her. "I had thought about killing him for so many years, but I never had the guts to do it," she admitted, her words heavy with the weight of old wounds.

William remained silent, his eyes shut tight, as though closing them would shut out the world—or the bombshell his mother had just dropped. His breathing was measured, controlled, but beneath it, the turmoil churned.

Victoria continued, her tone shifting to a bitter imitation. "Will used to talk about it all the time. 'One day, Im-ma kill that bitch for what he did that night he put his hands on me—I ain't forgot nothing!' Always saying it, but never doing a damn thing, just talking shit like he always did." She let out a hollow laugh. "I used to hope he'd actually do it, you know? Then I could kill two birds with one stone. Tru would get what he deserved, and Will would be out of my life for good."

Buddha's laughter erupted from the speakers, a harsh, mocking sound that filled the room. "A natural-born killer—just like you, boy!" he crowed. "Guess the apple doesn't fall too far from the tree. You got that vengeful streak from your momma, didn't you? Poor dude, didn't even see it coming—taken out by a *pregnant chick* hiding in his back seat!" He laughed harder, the sound grating against the already tense atmosphere.

"I've never killed anyone," William growled, his voice taut with restrained fury. "The people I dealt with had it coming. That's not the same."

Buddha's chuckle softened into a sinister grin that could be heard in his voice. "Oh, it's only a matter of time, boy. Didn't you already murder your daddy? Or are you so good at this, you've even convinced yourself it didn't happen?"

Victoria's voice cut through their exchange like a blade. "That night haunted me for years," she said, her tone distant and haunted. "I thought about what would happen if they found the knife, the fingerprints I left behind. I was terrified. But when they arrested Will after my mother told them about his fight with Tru..." She let out a short, humorless laugh. "The night Will got his *ass beat.* They fingerprinted him, questioned him—but nothing matched. They didn't even consider me. I was small, pregnant. The idea that I could take down someone like Tru never crossed their minds."

William opened his eyes and stared at the ceiling, his jaw tightening. Victoria pressed on. "Will didn't even know I'd left the house that evening. He told them I was home watching TV or something. And because Tru had a record and so many enemies, the cops wrote it off as gang activity. The investigation went cold." She paused, her voice cracking. "And I just... kept going. For you."

William's head turned slightly toward the old man lingering near the back door. His voice, now laced with anger and exhaustion, cut through the heavy air. "So now what?" he snapped. "My mother's a killer. My real father was a monster. My life is a mess, and I'm hiding in alleys like a damn rat. Is this all just some sick game to piss me off, Buddha? Or do you actually have a point?"

Buddha's laughter returned, smooth and unsettling. "Oh, there's a point, Strong. It's about revenge, yeah—guess you could call me a hypocrite. But it's also about money. Gotta eat, right? I've got bills to pay, same as anybody. But enough about me." His tone sharpened. "Let's move on to *chapter two*, shall we? There are some folks who've been dying to see you."

The camera facing Victoria jolted as someone adjusted its angle. Then, stepping into view, the girl with the smiley face mask waved cheerfully before pointing the camera at the figure seated in the other chair. The black pillowcase over their head obscured their identity, but the masked woman tiptoed toward them in a mocking, exaggerated gesture, as though afraid of waking a sleeping child.

In one swift motion, she snatched the pillowcase away.

A cascade of dark brown hair tumbled down the mystery guest's back, catching the light. They blinked against the glare of the camera, their eyes adjusting to the harsh brightness. William's breath caught in his throat as he stared at the familiar face. The features had changed—but those emerald green eyes were unmistakable.

"Bella?" he whispered, disbelief thick in his voice.

"Surprise!" Buddha's sadistic shout boomed through the speakers, the feedback screeching like nails on a chalkboard.

CHAPTER 21

Reasons

"I knew you'd enjoy that one," Buddha said, his voice dripping with self-satisfaction. "What's it been—almost ten years?" He grinned, his shadowy figure looming on the edge of the spotlight.

William's eyes stayed locked on Bella, disbelief and anguish swirling in their depths. His voice cracked as he pleaded, "Why her? What has she done for you to drag her into this? This doesn't make any sense. You have me. Do whatever the hell you need to, but let them go!"

He yanked at the bindings around his wrists, his muscles straining. The tension in the screws holding the restraints wavered, unnoticed by Buddha, as William's strength—long sapped by shocks and exhaustion—began to creep back into his limbs.

Buddha chuckled, an unsettling sound that vibrated through the speakers. "Let me break it down for you, my man. Think of it as storytime. This is gonna sound like some crazy-ass science fiction movie to you, but trust me—it's all true. We're what I like to call *EvoBabies*—products of EvoTechnology. Well, all of us except you."

William's eyes narrowed, suspicion lacing his voice. "What the hell are you talking about?"

"Glad you asked." Buddha's grin widened, the sadistic delight evident in his tone. "EvoTech scientists developed a chemical they thought could create superhuman abilities. We—me, Bella, and others—were given that chemical at birth. Different delivery methods, of course. Bella got hers orally, I got mine injected into my arm, and one unlucky bastard inhaled it as a vapor."

"Let me guess," William said, his voice dripping with sarcasm. "That unlucky bastard was me?"

"Nope. I said *except* you," Buddha shot back, wagging a finger. "That 'unlucky bastard' was one of the scientists working on the project before we were born. He used an early version of the chemical on himself, trying to cure something he had—Myasthenia Gravis. Weak muscles, the exact opposite of what *you've* got going on. It killed him, but not before he passed it down to his son—the guy who's now president of EvoTech."

William's jaw tightened. "So, where do I come into this little EvoBaby fairy tale? You didn't mention me at all."

"Oh, I assure you, this ain't no fairy tale," Buddha sneered. "Your DNA is their golden ticket—a potential breakthrough for EvoTech and the cure for their president's disease. You've got something rare, my man. Myostatin deficiency. You were born with it. Your muscles don't know when to stop growing, but for him? He's stuck in a wheelchair, struggling to lift his own damn arm."

Buddha leaned closer, his tone turning venomous. "EvoTech wants you because you're the answer to their prayers, and I want you because, well, payback's a bitch. Plus, there's a payday in it for me."

As Buddha reveled in his twisted monologue, William's gaze flicked toward the old man by the door. The man stood with his back turned, the faint glow of his cigarette illuminating the outline of his hunched shoulders. William noted the lack of recent electric shocks; the man, too distracted by his smoke break, seemed oblivious to his prisoner's growing strength.

To buy more time, William pressed Buddha further. "So, let me get this straight. You're planning to haul me into EvoTech so they can cut me open? I get the part about your payday, but all this other shit you're doing—dragging Bella into it—feels a little personal."

Buddha smirked, his amusement evident. "Oh, it's personal, all right. But enough chatter, Strong. Let's move on to the next chapter. Time's ticking, and I've got people waiting to see you."

William barely registered Buddha's words. His focus shifted to the screws he'd managed to pry loose, their cold weight resting in his palm. He tilted his hand, angling one screw toward the unsuspecting old man. With a practiced flick of his thumb, the screw shot through the air, spinning in a deadly arc.

The metallic dart embedded itself into the wooden door-frame just above the old man's head, the sharp *pop* startling him. He spun around, his eyes scanning the room for the source of the sound. William lay motionless, his head tilted back, his expression disinterested, as if he hadn't moved at all.

Seeing no immediate threat, and entirely missing the screw lodged above him, the old man shrugged and returned to his cigarette, exhaling a plume of smoke into the dimly lit space.

William smirked faintly, his grip tightening on the remaining screws as he prepared for whatever came next.

"...I never liked you from day one," Buddha confided, his voice smooth yet dripping with lingering resentment.

William arched a brow. "Ugh, really?"

"Oh, I'm sure you knew that," Buddha continued. "But you never knew why. You were playing with *my girl* when I first met you—the only girl I've ever had a crush on to this day." He paused, savoring the words, letting them sink in. "I didn't know you, but everyone knew me. I was the strongest kid on the block. That is—until *you* came along and busted that metal locker to shit from the inside."

He stopped, replaying the past incident in his mind. "I won't lie, that was some amazing shit for a little kid to pull off. But it pissed me off. Made me jealous—and yeah, I still am in a way. You have the strength that should've been mine. The attention that should've been mine.

William shifted slightly, his grip tightening around the second screw in his hand. As Buddha continued his self-indulgent monologue, William calculated his next move. He tilted the screw, aiming lower this time. The back of the old man's head or spine—whichever he hit—it had to incapacitate him. If the man realized what he was up to, he'd flip that switch without hesitation, and William knew he couldn't survive another surge of electricity.

"You were just a hater!" William shot back, a grin spreading across his face. With a flick of his wrist, he launched the screw with more force than before, the tiny projectile slicing through the air with precision.

The impact was immediate—and unexpected.

"Aaaaaagh! Son-of-a—!" The old man's scream filled the air as he grabbed for his behind, where the screw had embedded itself squarely in the most humiliating spot imaginable. He dropped his cigarette in the commotion, the smoldering stick slipping inside his jacket. Panic overtook him as he slapped frantically at his coat, trying to dislodge the burning ember with one hand while yanking the screw from his backside with the other.

In his frenzy, he lost his balance and toppled backward off the steps, landing in a heap among the trash cans. A metallic clang echoed as the bins scattered, their contents spilling around him.

When he scrambled to his feet, his face was red with fury. He charged toward the doorway, his eyes blazing as they locked onto William, who was grinning from ear to ear.

"I'll give you something to smile about, you son-of-a—!" the old man roared, his hand reaching for the electrical switch.

William's grin faltered, and he closed his eyes, bracing for the inevitable pain. "What happened to 'God is watching you?'" he quipped, though the humor barely masked his dread.

Seconds passed. Then ten. Then fifteen.

Nothing.

Confused, William cracked one eye open and saw that the doorway was empty. He frowned, straining to hear the faint sounds beyond the room. Suddenly, a scuffle erupted outside, the old man's voice rising in a symphony of yells and curses. Amidst the shouting came another sound—a low, guttural growl, unmistakably belonging to Guss.

William shook his head, a mix of relief and exasperation crossing his face. "Stupid dog," he muttered under his breath. But his moment of reprieve was short-lived as his gaze dropped to the bindings still clamped around his wrists and ankles.

The cold, unyielding metal caught the faint glow of the room, and for the first time, William noticed the engraving on the bands: *"EvoTech."*

His brow furrowed as his eyes drifted to the surface of the structure beneath him. There, etched almost as an afterthought, were the faint words: *"Made in China."*

A dry laugh escaped his lips. "Of course," he muttered, his mind already racing toward a plan to free himself. Outside, the sounds of the struggle continued, Guss's growls growing louder, more ferocious. The distraction had bought him precious time, and he wasn't about to waste it.

CHAPTER 22

Redemption

PART ONE

William sat quietly, his mind racing beneath his calm facade as Buddha's voice droned on through the speakers. The taunts and threats didn't bother him—not anymore. His fingers flexed slightly, testing the strength that had returned. He knew he could snap the bindings if he wanted to, but recklessness wouldn't serve him now. His thoughts turned to his mother and Bella, their fates unknown and their locations hidden. If he broke free too soon, he might lose the chance to protect them.

He exhaled slowly, forcing himself to remain still. For now, he would play along, gathering information and waiting for the perfect moment. Maybe, just maybe, he could provoke Buddha enough to lure him out of his lair and close enough to take him down.

Interrupting Buddha's rambling, William's voice cut through the static of the speakers. "What's your take on all this? How much are they paying you?"

Buddha chuckled darkly. "That should be the least of your worries, boy. You ought to be thinking about the poking and prodding you're going to endure after I deliver you."

William smirked. "Do you really think you can hold me like this forever? It's only a matter of time before I get free of this thing."

The speakers crackled as Buddha laughed, a sound that grated on William's nerves. "You wouldn't get far. Maybe I should remind you what happens if you try. How about a little demo, just in case you're getting ideas? I think it's about time anyway."

William leaned back, his smirk widening. "If that's what gets you going, Princess, go ahead. Handle your business."

On the stage, the red light near the electrical switch blinked three times, paused, then blinked again. William's eyes followed the light's rhythm, his smile never wavering. He could see Buddha's little power game unfolding.

In a small, dimly lit security room, Buddha sat in front of a bank of monitors, his fingers jabbing at the control panel that triggered the red light. His brow furrowed as he stared at the screen showing William's unbothered face. There was no struggling, no signs of pain—just that infuriating grin.

"What are you doing, you old bastard?" Buddha muttered, his frustration mounting. He slammed his fist onto the desk, sending his chair skidding backward with a loud screech. Rising to his feet, he stormed out of the room, his mind racing with suspicion.

As he approached the back entrance of the stage, he froze at the sight of the old man's body sprawled near the steps, motionless. A wave of realization hit him like a punch to the gut. His eyes darted to the slightly ajar door leading to the stage.

"That damn dog," Buddha hissed under his breath. "How could I forget about that goddamn dog?!"

Cursing, he sprinted toward the door, his boots echoing off the cold ground. He shoved it open with a forceful kick, the door swinging wide as he burst into the room.

The moment Buddha crossed the threshold, he was greeted by William's fist, already mid-swing. The punch connected with a sickening crunch, snapping Buddha's head to the side. Before he could recover, William followed with a brutal uppercut that sent him sprawling backward, landing hard on the ground.

Standing a few feet away, William calmly stripped the last remnants of his restraints from his wrists, letting the metal bands clatter to the floor. The device that had once held him was now a crumpled heap of steel, folded and crushed by his strength.

"Like I said," William growled, stepping closer, "just a matter of time."

Reaching down, he grabbed Buddha by the front of his jacket and hauled him to his feet with ease. The menace in his voice was as sharp as a blade. "Now, let's have a little chat about where my mother and Bella are."

The stage groaned under the strain of the battle as Buddha's body crashed into the far wall, the wooden structure shuddering from the force of impact. Splinters rained down around him, and a dark chuckle escaped his lips as he braced himself against the cracked surface, his grin defiant despite the pain.

"Where do you have them?" William demanded, his voice low and steady, like the rumble of distant thunder. His footsteps were deliberate as he approached, every inch of his posture radiating control. "Tell me, and I might show you some mercy."

Buddha's grin widened, blood smearing his teeth. "Mercy?" he scoffed, his words laced with mockery.

William didn't wait. With a surge of strength, he grabbed Buddha's ankles and swung his body upward in a fluid, almost effortless motion, slamming him back into the wooden stage. The boards cracked and groaned beneath the impact, leaving Buddha sprawled in a jagged crater. His arms lay limp at his sides, momentarily stunned by the sheer force.

Before Buddha could recover, William straddled his chest, pinning his arms beneath his knees. His gaze burned into Buddha's, unrelenting. "*Where are they?*" he demanded again, his voice sharp enough to cut through the tension in the air.

"Close," Buddha wheezed, his lips curling into a defiant smirk. "Very close."

The smirk was met with a crushing blow to his face, then another. Each strike sank his head deeper into the fractured wood, splinters catching in the scalp of his bald head.

"Okay, okay—stop!" Buddha sputtered, his voice hoarse and desperate. "I'll show you."

William hesitated, his fists tightening as he studied Buddha's bloodied face. He stood slowly, towering over him, his breathing heavy. For a moment, he thought it was over.

But beneath him, Buddha's right hand clenched, and veins pulsed visibly along his arm, snaking down to his fist. His muscles swelled, the sinews twisting unnaturally as the transformation began. William, focused on the task at hand, failed to notice.

"Let's go, then," William said, turning away. "Show me."

Buddha's laughter rumbled behind him, low and menacing. "Okay. But first, I want my turn."

In a blur of motion, Buddha rose and charged, his enhanced fist connecting squarely with the center of William's back. The blow sent him hurtling through the rear wall of the stage, the wooden planks shattering around him like brittle glass. He tumbled across the paved road before coming to an abrupt stop at the feet of Isabella and his mother.

William groaned, shaking off the dizziness. He looked toward the stage, where Buddha now stood in the jagged hole he'd created, his massive arm raised in triumph. The sound of crackling bone and tearing flesh faded as his transformation completed, leaving his fist grotesquely larger, almost inhuman.

Buddha admired his new strength, clenching and unclenching his hand as he stepped forward. "All I've thought about for years was getting to you, Strong," he sneered. "The money? That's nothing. Some things are bigger than that. When I turn your mother in for murder, that'll be icing on the cake. As for Bella..." He paused, his grin twisting into something darker. "I have *other* plans for her. But this? This isn't about them. This is personal."

Before he could take another step, a blur of fur and muscle leapt over William. Guss collided with Buddha mid-stride, knocking him back into the stage. The two disappeared into the wreckage, their yelps, growls, and grunts echoing through the air as they tore through the debris.

"Get up, William—get up!" Isabella urged, her voice shaking as she scooted her chair across the concrete toward him.

William staggered to his feet, his focus shifting to the bindings around his mother and Isabella. With practiced ease, he broke the last of their ties. "Go. Get out of here!" he said, urgency thick in his voice. "Take Momma with you!"

"To where?" Isabella asked, grabbing his mother's hand.

He hesitated for only a moment, his mind racing. "The tree. The grandpa tree. You remember, don't you? The field trip."

A faint smile touched Isabella's lips, even in the chaos. "I remember."

Guss let out a loud, pained yelp, silencing their brief exchange. Isabella's hand flew to her mouth, her eyes wide with fear.

"Go!" William commanded, his voice firm.

Isabella hesitated, then kissed him—briefly, but with unmistakable emotion. "Be careful, William," she said softly.

He nodded, watching as the two disappeared into the distance before turning toward the hole in the stage. Cautiously, he approached, the sounds of the scuffle fading to an eerie quiet.

Peering inside, William saw the stage in ruins—props and debris scattered like the aftermath of a storm. The air was thick with dust, the faint smell of wood and metal mixing with something sharper. He climbed inside, his heart pounding as his eyes scanned the wreckage.

"Guss?" he called, his voice low but steady as he searched for his loyal companion. The silence that answered sent a chill through his chest.

The wreckage of the stage was like a graveyard of shattered dreams, the splintered wood and twisted metal strewn about in chaotic disarray. William sifted through it all, his movements fueled by desperation and dread. Each piece of debris he tossed aside felt heavier than the last, though his strength didn't falter.

His hands worked tirelessly, but his heart grew heavier with each second of silence.

Finally, he reached the last unturned piece: a painted wooden backdrop depicting a serene forest of apple trees. Its cheerful imagery stood in painful contrast to the devastation around it. With a trembling hand, William lifted it, and his heart sank like a stone in water.

Beneath it lay Guss, his once-vibrant form now still and lifeless. The sight hollowed William, leaving an ache so deep it seemed to consume him. He dropped to his knees, the weight of the moment pulling him down, and placed his hands gently on the dog's soft black fur.

"I'm sorry, boy," he whispered, his voice cracking as tears welled in his eyes. He stroked Guss's fur, the familiar texture now carrying the unbearable weight of guilt. "I caused all of this. All of it. I was so tied up in what I wanted, in my own damn pride, I didn't think about the consequences."

He paused, the words catching in his throat. His tears fell silently onto Guss's still form. "I ruined everything. I made Momma lonely and sad. I can't show my face in public. I lost Bella. I got C.K. and Jada killed. And now this." His voice broke entirely. "You were the only friend I had left, and I got you killed too."

William bowed his head, his hand resting lightly on Guss's chest. His breath came in shuddering gasps as he fought the storm of emotions building inside him. For the first time in his life, he felt completely and utterly lost.

He closed his eyes, his mind spinning with everything he'd denied for years. Talking to an unseen presence—something he had always dismissed as foolish—suddenly didn't seem so far-fetched. If anything, it felt like the only option left.

"God. Lord. Whoever, whatever you are…" His voice was barely a whisper now, trembling with raw emotion. "I'm tired. Tired of all of this shit. If you're out there, if you're real… show me how to make this right. Please. I can't do this alone."

He pressed slightly harder on Guss's chest, as if grounding himself in the moment, or perhaps hoping for a miracle. Silence enveloped the room, broken only by the faint creak of the ruined stage and the soft rasp of his own breathing.

It wasn't much. But it was a start.

PART TWO

William gently lays Guss on a dusty blanket he'd scavenged from the wreckage, his hands moving with care as he checks him once more.

"Touching," Buddha's gravelly voice cuts through the silence, venom laced in every syllable. He stands a few feet away, a dark silhouette in the muted light, his arms crossed with mocking ease. "During all of this, you've finally found God. How quaint. Sad, though, that it took the deaths of nearly everyone you've ever loved to bring you to this revelation. Oh, and by the way," he adds, his tone dripping with sadistic amusement, "you do know you're not leaving here alive, right? Guess your sudden union with the Almighty will be complete."

William straightens slowly, his back still turned to the looming figure. The air around him feels charged, as though the room itself holds its breath.

"Funny," he replies, his voice low and measured. "I was just thinking the same thing about you."

A flicker of uncertainty crosses Buddha's face, quickly replaced by a sneering grin. He takes a few steps back, his posture shifting to a more advantageous position. With exaggerated flair, he raises both hands, beckoning William forward with a cocky, double-handed "Bring it" gesture.

William moves deliberately, his steps carrying him to the center of the stage. His expression is cold, his eyes narrowed with an intensity that hasn't surfaced in years—not since the night he'd ended his stepfather's life. The rage simmering inside him feels almost like an old friend, yet beneath it lies a new clarity, a certainty in what must be done. His life has been a series of wrong turns, his reputation a millstone around his neck. If he is ever to find love again, to grasp happiness, this moment must be the turning point. And the obstacle standing in his way is Buddha—hulking, grinning, daring him to fight for his future.

Buddha's massive frame shifts into a boxer's stance, his meaty arm guarding his face while his twisted grin peeks through. William, by contrast, remains unguarded, his posture loose and unreadable. Without warning, he lunges low, aiming for Buddha's legs. His arms wrap around them with a vice-like grip, and with a guttural roar, he heaves Buddha off the ground and drives him backward, sending both of them hurtling off the stage. The impact is thunderous, shattering two metal benches in the front row beneath Buddha's bulk.

Without hesitation, William wrenches a bent bench free from its concrete moorings and swings it with savage determination. The heavy metal crashes against Buddha, who raises his grotesquely mutated arm to block the blows. The bench folds further with each strike, nearly wrapping around Buddha's forearm with every blow. Buddha snarls, his grin vanishing as he grabs the weapon mid-swing, yanking it away with a force that sends William stumbling. One swipe of Buddha's massive arm sends him sprawling across the broken ground.

William scrambles to his feet, barely steadying himself before Buddha is on him. In one swift motion, the hulking figure loops a muscled arm around William's neck, pulling him into a crushing Full Nelson. Buddha's rancid breath brushes against William's ear as he tightens his grip.

"I'm gonna do you a favor," Buddha growls, his voice a guttural snarl. "Rip this ugly head off your shoulders and mount it above my fireplace. Tell Coach Kline I said 'Hi', bitch."

The crushing pressure intensifies, darkness creeping into William's vision. But through the haze of oxygen-deprived confusion, he notices an opening. Buddha's grip is too high, his balance precarious. Summoning the last reserves of his strength, William bends at the waist, arching his back to lift the behemoth off his feet. With a guttural shout, he twists forward and drops, slamming Buddha's face into the unforgiving concrete with bone-jarring force.

The impact stuns them both, but William recovers first. Seizing the opportunity, he grabs Buddha's arm, forcing it into an improvised armbar he's seen on TV. It's not a practiced move, but desperation fuels him as he wrenches back, attempting to hyperextend the limb. Buddha roars in pain, his dazed state giving William a fleeting advantage.

But the brute's resilience is monstrous. Buddha curls his arm, lifting William into the air as though he weighs nothing. William fights to regain control, pulling with every ounce of strength he has, but a backhanded swipe from Buddha's massive hand sends him sprawling once more. His vision blurs as he hits the ground, pain radiating from the impact. Still, a flicker of determination burns in his chest. This fight is far from over.

"That's it?" Buddha's mocking voice reverberates through the space as he stands triumphantly at the feet of his fallen adversary. His grin stretches wide, a grotesque blend of triumph and disdain. "That's all the fight you've got? Coach would be so disappointed in you right now."

Without hesitation, Buddha grabs William by the ankles, his massive hands tightening like vices. With a bellow of exertion, he spins William in a brutal arc, the force sending the man careening through the air. William's head clips the sharp edge of the stage, the impact spinning him into a somersault before he crashes onto the platform's center with a sickening thud.

Buddha's chest heaves with satisfaction as he strides to the edge of the stage. "Pathetic," he sneers, slamming a colossal hand against the stage's edge. The wood creaks under the force as he propels himself into the air, his bulky frame arching gracefully despite its size. He lands with a thunderous crash at William's feet, the vibration rattling through the platform.

"Get up!" Buddha roars, his voice echoing like a war drum. "You've never had a real opponent to test your skills, huh? Sad! You're outmatched here!"

William stirs, his movements sluggish but deliberate as he pushes himself to his feet. His face is a mask of frustration and determination, his fists clenching so tightly that his knuckles whiten. Fueled by anger, he lunges forward, swinging a wild right hook aimed for Buddha's jaw.

Buddha anticipates the strike with ease, his weaker arm snapping up to block the blow. In one fluid motion, he counters with his other arm, delivering a devastating open-palm strike to William's chest. The force sends William hurtling backward, his body skidding across the stage like a ragdoll.

"I think I'll call that the Buddha's Palm!" Buddha crows, swaggering toward his downed opponent. He kneels beside William, rocking playfully on his enormous fist, his grin more venomous than ever.

"Let me ask you something," Buddha begins, his voice adopting a mockingly casual tone. "So, Coach was kinda like your dad, huh? You two were close, right? Did a little digging on him. Man, he was one badass Marine back in the day—decorations, training, the whole nine yards." He leans in closer, his breath hot and acrid. "But he didn't show you a damn thing, did he? Isn't that what fathers are supposed to do? Pass down their skills to their boys so they can defend themselves in times like these? You'd think he'd have taught his only 'son' a thing or two, but here you are."

William remains silent, his body still but his mind far from idle. As Buddha rocks back and forth, his hulking frame swaying from knuckles to feet, William bides his time, each breath steadying him and replenishing his strength. Coach had been more than just a mentor—he'd passed down everything: the precision of hand-to-hand combat, the discipline of military tactics, even the loyalty embedded in training a companion like Guss. Buddha's mockery only sharpens William's focus.

"You know," Buddha continues, his tone dripping with cruel humor, "when I'm done with you, I think I'll pay Bella a visit. Damn, she's a fine ass woman! Did you even...? Nah, of course you didn't. It's been a while for me, though. Girls don't exactly flock to big guys like me. Guess it could be the lazy eye. Maybe?" He taps his grotesquely distorted eye with a finger and chuckles, a low, guttural sound that fills the air.

As Buddha's words sink in, a new sensation rises within William. It's not the blind, unbridled rage that had fueled him before. It's something deeper, more precise. Memories flood his mind—the warmth of Isabella's smile, the quiet strength of Coach's guidance, and the unyielding love his mother had shown him despite her own struggles. These fragments of his life, of the people who mattered, coalesce into a singular purpose.

His anger crystallizes, no longer chaotic but laser-focused. This isn't just about survival—it's about protecting what's left of the good in his life. Slowly, deliberately, William begins to rise, his gaze locked on Buddha. The predator towering over him doesn't see the shift, but something has changed. For the first time, William feels the weight of his purpose—and it steadies him.

William's heartbeat pounded like a war drum, its rhythm strong and steady as adrenaline surged through his veins, fueling his every movement. A newfound confidence spread across his face, sharp and resolute, as he felt his body awaken to a strength he hadn't known before. Muscles taut and ready, his mind clear and focused, he rose to his feet. Buddha, oblivious to this shift, stood posturing, unaware of the storm brewing before him.

"So, I guess this is round two?" Buddha sneered, the grin on his face as wide as it was mocking. "Dog's still got some fight in him, huh? Did I piss you off? What?"

He let out a booming laugh, returning to his boxer's stance. William's eyes narrowed as he scanned his opponent. Buddha's upper body was as formidable as ever, his defense tight, but William's gaze traveled downward, taking note of the slight unevenness in his footing. His legs—thick but imbalanced—betrayed his stance as weak and unstable.

William stepped back deliberately, his movements measured, drawing Buddha toward the center of the stage. Without a word, he reached up and pulled his hood over his head, shadowing his face. Only his scruffy beard remained visible. The simple gesture had a purpose: it blocked Buddha's gaze, allowing William to focus entirely on his rival's body—its shifts, its rhythm, its tells. Coach's voice echoed in his memory: *"A man's eyes can lie, but his body never will."*

Buddha's weight shifted subtly, his impatience growing. William saw it before it happened—the lean of his opponent's body as he prepared to strike. Buddha launched forward with a Superman punch, his massive fist carving through the air, but William sidestepped just in time.

The missed punch seemed to ignite Buddha's fury, and he unleashed a barrage of blows, one haymaker after another. William dodged each with precision, his movements fluid as water. The final punch came in hot, but this time William countered. Spinning swiftly, he delivered a crushing back-fist to Buddha's jaw.

The impact echoed like a gunshot, and the hulking man dropped to his knees.

"You like that?" William taunted, his voice steady and mocking. "That one's called 'Buddha's Fist.'"

The veins in Buddha's neck bulged as he clenched his fists, his massive knuckles cracking like thunder. He rose with a feral growl, swinging his fist down like a sledgehammer. William raised his forearms in a cross to block the strike, the force reverberating through his body. With a sharp movement, he twisted Buddha's forearm under his armpit and pressed upward, threatening to snap the giant limb. Buddha roared in pain, his free hand slamming into William's chest, driving him back toward the wall.

Locked in a furious struggle, their bodies collided with the wall's rough surface. Buddha's hand splintered through the wood, becoming lodged. William saw the opportunity and didn't hesitate. He unleashed a barrage of punches, each one landing with punishing precision, jerking Buddha's head back and forth like a speed bag.

Buddha managed to block a punch with his weaker arm, then lunged forward with a devastating headbutt. The impact staggered William, and Buddha seized the moment, twisting to free his trapped arm. He glanced at William, desperation flickering in his grotesque eye. But when he looked again, his rival was gone.

For a heartbeat, the stage was silent. Then, suddenly, Buddha felt a sharp grip on his trapped hand—on the other side of the wall.

"Let me help you with that," came William's voice, cold and cutting.

With a violent yank, William pulled Buddha's arm, slamming the brute's face against the wall. The sound of splintering wood and flesh colliding with it, filled the air as William continued pulling, until Buddha's massive form crashed through the wall and onto the pavement outside.

Before Buddha could react, William was on him. He grabbed the dazed man by the shoulders, lifting him effortlessly before slamming him into the building's exterior. The impact rattled the structure, dust and debris cascading around them. With relentless force, William drove his knee into Buddha's diaphragm, over and over, each strike a declaration of dominance and purpose.

The air around them was electric, charged with the ferocity of their battle. For William, this wasn't just a fight—it was a reckoning.

Buddha swung his massive arm in one desperate, final attempt to overpower his aggressor, but William anticipated the move. With precision, he caught the arm beneath his own, trapping it in an unyielding grip. Pressing Buddha against the wall, William drove his weight upward, forcing the tremendous arm into an unnatural angle. The grotesque sound of popping and snapping echoed in the air. He was soon overwhelmed by Buddha's guttural screams of agony. The limb gave way with a sickening crack.

As the shattered arm dropped lifelessly to Buddha's side, William seized the moment. He drove his right knee into Buddha's diaphragm once, then again, each blow landing with brutal precision. The impact crushed ribs, sending shockwaves of pain through Buddha's body and forcing blood to seep from his lips.

His enormous frame sagged, crumbling to the ground in a heap of defeat.

William stood over his broken foe, fists still clenched, ready to deliver the final blow. But then, out of the corner of his eye, he caught his own reflection in a jagged shard of mirror hanging precariously on the wall beside them. His hood had been knocked away in the struggle, revealing his face—twisted with rage, his eyes burning with a primal fury.

C.K.'s voice echoed in his memory, calm and resolute: *"Pain is inevitable, suffering is optional."* He'd never fully grasped the meaning of those words during their training, but now the lesson was clear. A bitter irony lingered in the realization—the quote was by the true Buddha.

William's gaze shifted back to his opponent, now slumped and broken. His chest rose and fell with ragged breaths, blood pooling at the corner of his mouth. Another voice echoed in William's mind, softer this time, tinged with warmth and wisdom: his mother's.

"The weak can never forgive, baby. Forgiveness is an attribute of the strong. I want you to remember that, okay? You are who you make yourself to be. Let no man's negative actions change who you are deep inside. Because when all else fails, that's all you have."

Her words reverberated in his soul, cutting through the haze of anger. William stepped back, lowering his fists, the storm inside him calming.

"I'm done here," he said, his voice firm yet weary. His eyes bore into Buddha's. "Don't follow me, and don't come near my family again. If you do, I promise you a painful ending." Without waiting for a response, William turned and began to walk away.

Behind him, Buddha coughed, cradling his mangled arm, now shrinking back to its original size. A twisted grin spread across his bloodied face. "Look, when I get better, I—" he began, his voice hoarse with pain.

William stopped mid-step and interrupted, his voice low and steady. "When you get better, you know where to find me. I won't be hiding. But somehow, I doubt you'll ever make it to that day."

Buddha let out a wet, rattling laugh, spitting blood onto the ground. "And why is that?" he croaked, his words barely audible.

William glanced over his shoulder, his eyes cold and unyielding. "Because last I checked, animals don't know anything about forgiveness."

He disappeared into the shadows, his figure swallowed by the night.

Buddha slumped back against the wall, wincing as chips of wood from the shattered opening above rained down onto his shoulder. He felt a wet drop land on his forehead and instinctively wiped it away, grimacing at the slimy texture. When he glanced up, his blood ran cold.

Above him, snarling through the jagged remains of the wall, was Guss. His bared fangs gleamed in the dim light, a growl rumbling deep in his throat. More saliva dripped from his maw, splattering onto Buddha's face.

Before Buddha could react, Guss lunged.

As William strode away, the sound of the attack—growls, snarls, and screams—echoed behind him. He reached into his pocket, pulling out a Brown and Smooth Cigar. He placed it between his bloodied lips and lit it, the small flame briefly illuminating his worn features before fading into the darkness.

Smoke curled around him as he walked, his silhouette vanishing into the night.

314

CHAPTER 23

Reunited

Miles away, in a stately home perched above the shimmering expanse of Lake Michigan, the faint buzz of an alarm clock shattered the early morning stillness. A middle-aged man stirred, his face lined with the weariness of years and burdens untold. His nurse, a brisk and efficient woman with a strong British accent, moved to silence the offending sound. She adjusted the pillows behind his back and handed him his morning dose of medication, her movements precise and practiced.

A cool breeze swept through the open balcony door, carrying with it the crisp scent of autumn. It sent a shiver through the man, prompting him to tug the fine cotton sheets up to his chest.

"Madeline—please. The doors," he said, his voice groggy but authoritative.

The nurse turned quickly, her brow furrowing. "I'm sorry, sir. The wind must've blown it open!" She crossed the room with swift determination and shut the doors against the morning chill. "Don't forget," she continued, smoothing her apron. "Your docta's comin' at 10:00 a.m. today. You may be president of EvoTech, but yah still need your medical care. No changin' the appointment this time, yah?"

He gave a faint grunt of acknowledgment, waving her off as she bustled out of the room. Once the door clicked shut, he moved with deliberate slowness, reaching for his glasses on the nightstand. Sliding them onto his face, he paused, peering over the rim and scanning the room. The silence had taken on a strange weight, as though the air itself held its breath.

"So," he said finally, his voice calm and measured, "I take it by your presence that our little mission has failed."

Reaching for the neatly folded newspaper on the nightstand, he didn't flinch as a shadow detached itself from the corner of the room. A girl in a smiley face mask stepped out from behind the door, her movements fluid and deliberate. She strode to the foot of the bed and tossed a twisted metal brace onto the pristine duvet, its cold weight landing with a dull thud near his feet.

"I worked really hard on this one," she said, her tone sharp with irritation. "But your little 'indestructible' toy that was supposed to hold him? It didn't."

She reached up and pulled the mask from her face, revealing Jada's sharp features and piercing gaze. Her frustration was evident in every line of her expression. "Next time you want to cut costs, fill me in," she demanded, her voice biting.

The man folded his newspaper slowly, his expression unreadable as he studied the brace and then turned his gaze to her. The room, once still and serene, now brimmed with an undercurrent of tension.

The sunlight filtered through the canopy of golden fall leaves, dappling the forest floor in a soft, warm glow. Victoria and Isabella sat beneath the towering trees, their breaths shallow with anticipation, their silent prayers carried on the crisp autumn breeze. Each passing moment stretched their nerves tighter as they waited, hoping their hero would return unharmed.

Victoria broke the silence with a laugh, her voice light despite the worry etched into her face. "Girl, when he was just a toddler," she began, her eyes glinting with the memory, "he reached through that playpen and grabbed that pit bull's tail. Pulled so hard the poor dog yelped and yelped. By the time William let go, that tail looked like the capital 'L.'"

Isabella chuckled, her laughter bright and unrestrained. The two women shared the moment, but as the sound faded, Victoria's smile faltered. She glanced over her shoulder, her unease growing heavier with every second of silence.

"Should we go back?" she asked, her voice trembling. "We should have never left him back there."

Isabella shook her head, her fingers idly peeling bark from a fallen branch. "He'll be okay, Ms. Strong," she said with quiet certainty. "You have no reason to worry."

Victoria's brow furrowed. "How would you know? That man was a monster. He could've hurt him. If William was okay, he'd be here by now."

Isabella turned her gaze to Victoria, her eyes calm, almost serene. "You just have to trust me. I have a way of seeing things," she said, her tone gentle but firm. "He'll be fine. God gives His hardest battles to His strongest soldiers."

A faint smile tugged at Victoria's lips, her resolve softening under Isabella's reassurance. She watched as the younger woman dropped her stick and sat cross-legged before her, arms outstretched and palms turned skyward. Isabella closed her eyes, her face serene, as if drawing strength from the earth itself.

Victoria blinked, puzzled. "What are you doing?" she muttered, thinking the girl had lost her mind.

The forest seemed to hold its breath, the quiet broken only by the rustling of leaves in the gentle wind. A single leaf drifted down, landing softly in Isabella's lap. Then another. And another. Within moments, the leaves began to rain down faster, spinning and fluttering in a golden cascade. Victoria glanced up, startled, as the branches above them quivered and swayed, releasing their vibrant burden.

Isabella giggled, standing to her feet as the leaves swirled around her like a choreographed dance. She twirled in the cascade, arms outstretched, her laughter ringing through the forest. For a fleeting moment, Isabella was that child on a field trip so long ago, when William stomped his feet at the base of the tree. The memory brought a bittersweet warmth to her chest.

A shadow fell across Victoria, large and unmistakably human. She froze, her breath catching in her throat, until a strong hand rested gently on her shoulder. She reached up, trembling, her fingers finding William's. Relief flooded her as she closed her eyes, a tear slipping down her cheek.

319

TO BE CONTINUED...

ABOUT THE AUTHOR

TERRENCE DAMON SPENCER is an Amazon bestselling author known for his gripping horror and mystery novels, crafting chilling tales that have captivated readers since 2007. A veteran of the U.S. Marine Corps, Terrence shares with his wife a deep fascination for exploring haunted locations—experiences that often find their way into his eerie narratives.

Terrence's journey as an author began gradually, after years of spontaneously entertaining his wife and children with vivid, imaginative stories during long family road trips. However, it wasn't until one unforgettable day at the movies—when a trailer mirrored one of his impromptu tales so closely that his family's jaws dropped in disbelief—that everything changed. In that pivotal moment, his wife finally dared him to write his first novel, setting him on a path he never expected.

Since then, Terrence Damon Spencer's novels—including fan favorites such as *Premises* and *Strong*—have gone on to grace the shelves of his local Barnes and Noble, where they continue to captivate readers with spine-tingling suspense and unforgettable characters. Beyond his writing desk, Terrence enjoys delving into supernatural mysteries and spending quality time with his loved ones. Together with his five adult children, two grandchildren, and their loyal Mastiff/Dane, Tank, he finds inspiration and comfort in their home nestled in Pueblo, Colorado.

www.ingramcontent.com/pod-product-compliance
Lightning Source LLC
Chambersburg PA
CBHW020737310726
48969CB00002B/299